TIMESWEPT

A LOVE THROUGH TIME

"I've had it with you," Libby cried. "Nothing I try to do for you ever works out. You won't talk to me, you won't let me help you, and because of some damned misunderstanding you won't even admit you care for me. I love you, John Faulk, you stubborn jackass. And it's your loss if you don't want that love."

For a long moment they stood, silently staring into each others eyes. Then he smiled.

"So you love me, do you?" His hard arms held her close, her arms pinned at her sides. She tipped her head back and glared at him but he only arched a golden eyebrow in question.

Libby hadn't meant to make that admission. Not sure what his words meant, or that secretive smile, she refused to repeat her confession.

"You don't deserve me," she chided, fighting the hot wave of awareness his nearness caused. "You're stubborn and muleheaded. I made a mistake once, I'll admit that. But you made a bigger one. Because you're throwing away the chance at something wonderful."

"Am I?" The smile disappeared. He rubbed her back tenderly, his fingers rippling over every curve and plane. "Show me how wonderful."

Other *Leisure* and *Love Spell* books
by Marti Jones:
DREAMWEAVER
TIME'S HEALING HEART

A Love Through Time

Marti Jones

Book Margins, Inc.

A BMI Edition

Published by special arrangement with Dorchester
Publishing Co., Inc.

Printed in the United States of America.

This book is dedicated to Liz, Gloria, Frances, Dolores, Hortense, Gerry, Sharon, and Sandra with much love and many thanks.

A Love Through Time

Chapter One

Three-fifteen. What an ungodly hour for the phone to ring.

Libby Pfifer batted the thick comforter away from her face, swatted the sheets aside, and groped for the bedside phone. Instead her hand slapped the on button of the alarm clock, sending it off in ear-piercing fits of buzzing. When several attempts to quiet the stubborn clock failed, she snatched it up and shoved it beneath the pile of pillows she'd been happily snoozing on moments ago.

Again she reached blindly for the phone and finally succeeded in grasping the receiver.

"This better be good," she grumbled in a sleep-roughened voice.

"Hey, Pix," a man's disgustingly cheerful

voice rang out. "Rise and shine."

"John? What the blazes are you doing, calling me at this hour of the morning?"

His answering chuckle did little to brighten her mood. "I've got good news, Pix," he said, the anticipation in his tone finally rousing her.

Libby struggled upright in the bed and brushed her wispy bangs out of her face.

"Actually," he added, solemnly, "it's good news and bad news."

Libby reached for the lamp on the bedside table and touched the base, activating the automatic switch. The glare blinded her momentarily. She squinted and shifted into a more comfortable position. The alarm clock decided to give up being difficult and she shook her head to clear the ringing in her ears.

"Libby, you there?"

"Yeah, yeah, what's up?"

"I'm standing on the dock and your ship just came in."

"It's three-fifteen in the a.m., John. Don't get witty on me."

He chuckled again and then sighed. "We've had some trouble out here. I got a call from one of the campers who couldn't sleep and was out taking a stroll. He said he saw the vandals—"

"Vandals!"

Libby came instantly awake. Fort Pickens National Park was a popular tourist attraction

10

and campground near her home on the Florida Panhandle, but more than that, it was living history. She swore under her breath and shoved her bangs back again, harder this time.

"What did they do this time?" she asked, almost afraid to hear the answer.

"It's bad, Pix," he answered.

Libby didn't even bother to take offense at his use of the irritating nickname. She'd tell him later how much she truly hated it when he referred to her as a pixie.

"They took a chain saw to Old Patriot."

Libby choked back a strangled gasp and hit the base of the lamp two more times to bring the light up to ultra bright.

"Is this a joke?" she hissed.

"Come on, Lib, give me some credit. I know how you love that old tree. I'd never joke about something like this."

Tears filled Libby's eyes and she shook her head, her tangled crop of black hair slapping against her cheeks.

"Oh, God, oh, John. How bad is it?"

"That's what I called you for. The press will be here at daybreak to cover the story, and the citizens are gonna be in an uproar. We need an expert, and we need one fast, so we'll be able to give them some answers."

"Omigod, you mean I'm it? I'm gonna have first go at the job?"

John chuckled one last time. "Only if you get

11

your butt out here before all the tree doctors in the whole South descend on us. This is big, Lib. Get the lead out."

The phone went dead in her hand, but Libby didn't notice. She'd already shoved aside the covers and was racing across the plush carpet to the bathroom.

After an all-time record-fast shower Libby dressed in black leggings, a thigh-length T-shirt, and hiking boots. She swiped her hair a few times with a brush, forgot about makeup, grabbed the oversized purse holding several small tools, and dashed out to her Jeep.

Her emotions ping-ponged between despair and gratification as she headed for the bridge to Santa Rosa Island. Anger boiled when she thought of someone trying to destroy the oldest and biggest live oak in the park. But she knew, beyond a doubt, that this would be the coup of her career if she could save the tree.

After getting her degree in horticulture, she'd found there wasn't a world of opportunities awaiting her. So she'd taken her unflagging optimism and a couple of hundred bucks and opened *The Tree Works*. She was classified, in her yellow pages ad, as a tree surgeon. But so far, she'd done nothing more exciting than remove some storm-damaged pines and diagnose a few cases of Japanese beetle.

It paid the rent, but could hardly be called a

challenge. But this—Old Patriot. That tree was loved by all the rangers and employees at the park. Folks from neighboring Gulf Breeze, and even Pensacola, thought of it as their own. It had been in hundreds of photos and on numerous postcards.

If that tree could talk, Libby thought, a sad smile tipping her lips, what a world of tales it could tell.

She slowed at the entrance to the park, peered into the empty guard booth, and passed through. It was five long miles to John's post. She caught herself exceeding the speed limit several times in her haste to reach him.

Finally, she spun her Jeep into a parking space and grabbed her bag. Before she'd even closed the door, a wedge of light illuminated the front porch of the wooden ranger station and John called out to her.

"Climb back in, Pix. We'll take your Jeep."

Libby slid back behind the wheel, tapping her fingers anxiously on the padded cover as she waited for John to jump in beside her.

"You know the way," he said, nodding his red head toward the main road. He flashed her a crooked grin that wrinkled his freckled nose and settled back in his seat.

"How bad is it?" she asked again, concern for the old oak taking precedence over her career goals now that the time had come to view the damage.

13

"Bad enough," he answered baldly. "I hope you can save it, but it'll take a miracle."

Tense silence seemed to crawl in and hitch a ride with them as they zigzagged down the dark, narrow road. The luminescent clock on the dash read four-twenty. The speedometer read sixty. Libby chewed her lip and thought back to all the times she'd shared lunch with John beneath the out-spread branches of Old Patriot.

John had been her best friend since high school, and they spent a lot of time together even now. She'd cried on his shoulder when a good-looking professor dumped her for a willowy blonde in her freshman year of college. And John had shed a few tears himself when his marriage broke up.

They frequently went out together when neither had a date, or if a special movie was playing that they both wanted to see. Recently they'd gone to an animated movie heralding the dangers of destroying the rain forest. John teased Libby that she looked and sounded a lot like the main character in the film, a pixie who preached ecology. And so he'd started calling her pixie, or pix for short.

"Here we are," he said, a fresh note of anxiety in his voice. Libby glanced over, saw the tight lines on his usually jolly face, and felt her first real shiver of fear. What if she couldn't do the job? What if she did the old tree more harm

14

than good? What if she failed? It always came down to that, she thought. Failed relationships, failed opportunities. Failure. Her greatest fear.

Libby brushed her doubts aside. She'd overcome all her old insecurities, and she refused to let them resurface now.

"Come on, Pix," he said, swinging his door open. He dragged her heavy bag across the seat and draped it over his shoulder, affecting a silly pose which succeeded in lightening her mood.

"Cut that out, you goof," she admonished, taking her bag from him.

They trekked over the sandy ground at the tip of the island, crossed several of the newer, iron-and-concrete batteries, and then shuffled through the underbrush to the old tree. The warm spring breeze carried a hint of salty mist, and Libby smelled the familiar scent of brine.

Libby's heart plummeted as John turned his flashlight on the tree. Tears welled swiftly and burned her eyes. She stared in horror at the grand old oak.

A string of off-color words raced to the tip of her tongue and she had to bite them back. Such wanton destruction made her want to kick something, or somebody. Whoever had damaged the tree had intended to kill it. Why they hadn't just chain-sawed right through the middle and severed the massive trunk, she didn't know. She supposed, to their warped minds, this random chopping seemed more vicious.

"Damn," John whispered beside her. "I didn't get a good look at it earlier because I was scrambling to get to the phone. I didn't realize how bad it was. Looks like you might have to cut it down."

Libby whipped around to face him, the glow from his flashlight catching the flash of fury in her apple-green eyes.

"Don't write this old-timer off so quick, John. I haven't." She dug into her bag and drew out a tape measure. "Give me a leg up."

John's eyes widened in surprise, but he'd seen Libby scamper up taller trees than this. He bent forward, making a cup with his hands. Libby slid her laced boot into his palms and lunged for the fork in the trunk. She caught hold, pulled herself up, and settled her fanny in the wedge.

"I'm gonna take some measurements, see how deep these gashes are. We'll go from there."

A high, scratching noise split the silence of the early morning, and John reached for the two-way radio on his belt. He spoke into it, waited for the reply, then turned the radio off again and replaced it on his belt.

"Looks like a busy night," he called up to Libby.

"What is it?"

"Some tourist hit a raccoon back on the main road. Poor critter's hurt pretty bad. I need to check it out."

"Go ahead," Libby called down, reaching for the flashlight.

"You sure?"

"Yeah. I'm going to be a while here. Just take the Jeep and pick me up when you're through."

She slipped the flashlight between her knees and angled it up into the heavy branches.

"Are you going to be all right up there until I get back? I might be a while."

Libby cut him a disgusted look and quirked one of her raven eyebrows. "I do this for a living, you know. Now go. I can't stand the thought of that creature lying there in pain."

"I'll probably have to call wildlife rescue and take the raccoon to the station for pickup."

"Go, go," she said, waving her hand. "And bring back coffee."

"Deal," John said, already jogging across the familiar terrain toward the Jeep. The moon hung high in the sky, and he trotted away at a good pace.

Libby immediately turned her attention back to the angry, open slashes on the tree. The worst one crisscrossed the inner side of the trunk's left fork and was about seven inches wide and at least twelve inches deep. It resembled a pie wedge cut out of the rich blond wood. The bark chips littered the area where she sat and the ground around the trunk.

Anger and dismay roiled in her. She measured and surveyed every wound in the area nearest her, then stood to reach the higher ones. Whoever had done this had gone to some trouble to make a thorough job of it.

"Creeps," she said, rubbing her fingers gingerly over the cuts. The careless ravagement of the tree filled Libby with a rage beyond compare. This tree, this old-timer, had seen a lot of years. It had weathered hurricanes and droughts. It had withstood the attack levied at the fort during the Civil War. All to fall prey to a cheap, two-bit vandal.

"Well, Libby's here now, Old Patriot," she whispered, reaching around the tree to measure a long cut. Her foot hit a chunk of wood loosened by the vandalism and the wedge fell away. Libby grabbed for the flashlight, lost her grip on the skinned trunk, and felt herself falling through air.

She hit the ground with a dull thud, her bottom bruised and her head striking against a root. Blue, wavering lights flickered before her eyes. She blinked rapidly, watching odd swirls of color dance and career before fading away.

"That's what you call getting your lights knocked out," she said disdainfully, checking herself for any serious injury. Her palms were scraped and raw, and one pant leg was torn, but otherwise she seemed in one piece.

Thank goodness. She had no idea how long John might be gone, and she didn't relish the idea of lying hurt and humiliated on the cool, hard ground.

She slipped her hands along the grass and roots around her, searching for the flashlight. The moon still shone brightly, but darkness cloaked the area under the tree's branches. Apparently the fall had extinguished the beam, since she couldn't see so much as a flicker.

"Terrific," she grumbled. Drawing her legs beneath her, she slowly rose to her feet.

Shaking her head, she smoothed out her bobbed curls and dusted off the seat of her pants. She'd have to step out from the trunk into the moonlight to examine her now-throbbing body better.

She'd taken only two small steps when she saw the shadows along the line of brush in the distance move. Libby froze. Fort Pickens boasted a full range of wildlife, including fox, raccoon, and squirrel. And although she wouldn't have minded meeting any of those critters while alone at the farthermost point of the island, she would not like to encounter one of the many skunks in residence.

The shadows moved again. Libby swallowed hard. That was no four-legged animal. The tall, hulking shapes inching closer to her were of the two-legged variety. Thinking John had returned, she enjoyed a brief flash of relief. Then her fear returned tenfold. John had driven away in her Jeep. If he'd come within a mile of her out here in the stillness of night, she'd have heard the engine.

Maybe they hadn't seen her. Maybe they were just tourists out for an early-morning walk. Maybe they were the vandals, come back to finish the job. That thought started her knees shaking.

She backed against the tree, every news report and rumor she'd heard about murderers and rapists speeding through her mind. Even here in the park there'd been a murder just last year and several reports of Satanic cults holding rituals. She gulped, feeling strangely like a future statistic.

The shadows separated from the underbrush and formed themselves into the distinctive shapes of men. Lots of men. She scanned the group, at least fifteen in all, and knew her chances of escape were nonexistent.

"Come on, John," she whispered shakily, pressing closer to the tree. "Ride in like the cavalry and rescue me." She held her breath and listened, but didn't hear any sound of her Jeep.

The night grew quiet. No birds twittered, though this was a natural bird sanctuary. No crickets chirped. Even the sound of the lapping waves, less than fifty yards to her left, seemed to disappear. The Gulf, the wildlife, the very air, seemed to hold its breath, anticipating.

She just stood there like a deer caught in

headlights. Even if escape was impossible, she had to try. But her legs, paralyzed with terror, refused to move.

The men spread out, fanned the perimeter of the tree, and effectively cut off any chance of escape. She wanted to curse, but her mouth had been swabbed dry with fear. Every beat of her heart reverberated in the sore places she'd sustained in the fall. Legs, palms, elbows—everything thumped out her panic, faster and faster.

The circle of strangers closed, stepping toward her as though in slow motion. She swung her head around, trying to keep each in her sight.

But they made no threatening moves. They merely came within the circle of the tree's branches and stopped.

For a long moment no one moved. She eyed each one, wondering if she'd be able to give an accurate description later, if she ever got the opportunity. In return, they stared boldly back at her.

She could see now that all the men were Indians. Full-blooded, or close to it, unless she missed her guess. But what in the world were they doing out here at this time of the morning? And, more important, what did they want with her?

She began to make out features, details. The stark black hair, the olive skin painted purple with a yellow stripe across the nose. Each one was so like the others, yet different. All wore hats, but there the clothing similarities ended. Some wore light-colored pants, some dark. Some had shirts on, some were bare-chested. She stared, her eyes widening. One even wore what looked like a breechclout.

"Omigod," she whispered, panic rioting within her. What kind of lunatics were these men?

After a lengthy perusal, during which no one moved, one of the men stepped forward. Instinctively, Libby tried to step back, but her shoulder blades pressed flat against the tree.

"What do you want?" Libby asked, glad to hear her voice sound strong and authoritative.

The man remained silent. He took another step toward her, and she could see him clearer now. The moon reflected off the paint on his nose. Somehow, she thought he looked familiar. Of course, that was impossible.

"Usen right," he mumbled. Libby, taken by surprise, jumped. Her shoulder hit the rough bark of the trunk, and she winced.

"Usen?" she said, wanting nothing more than to run screaming from the area. "Who is Usen?"

The man pointed into the sky and then pointed to Libby.

"The Great Good Spirit say tonight bring magic."

He waved his hand in an elaborate arc, like a circus ringmaster, and the other Indians grunted as if on cue.

"This Usen," she said, clearing her throat nervously. "You said he's a good spirit?"

"Great Good Spirit," he bellowed. She flinched and drew back.

All right, Libby thought. Don't insult the man's spirit again, for that certainly had a bad effect on his disposition. But the word spirit brought her to the conclusion that she had stumbled on some cult members, and her fear rose again.

"And who," she squeaked, dismayed to hear that her calm tones had deserted her, "are you?"

The man in the lead stepped closer to her, his body now only a few feet away, and thumped his chest.

A string of garbled, guttural sounds emanated from his throat. Libby frowned. Surely that wasn't a language, she thought. Her eyes scanned the other men. Obviously they'd understood their leader.

Libby shook her head in confusion. The man thumped his chest again.

"Medicine man," he grunted. "Geronimo."

In a flash, Libby remembered where she'd seen the man before. Of course, old yellowed photographs couldn't begin to compare to the flesh-and-blood man before her. But she knew without a doubt that the man was telling the truth. He was Geronimo! Or rather, someone painted and dressed to look like Geronimo, the Chiricahua Apache medicine man who'd been brought to Fort Pickens as a captive in the last century.

"This is great. John didn't tell me they were doing a reenactment. You guys look terrific," she said, finally letting her breath out in a whoosh. Surprised looks plastered the faces of the men around her.

"So you're supposed to be Geronimo. And these guys must be your band of braves. Still, you're out kind of early, aren't you?"

The leader frowned at her and grunted something to the others. They all nodded silently.

Again he spoke to the others, and again Libby wondered if the language he spoke was truly Apache. She'd never heard it before, but supposed it could be. It sounded like so many grunts and groans to her.

"I lost my flashlight when I fell out of the tree . . ." She started forward. The men stepped quickly back, startling her. "Do you have a light?" she asked, wondering why they now seemed wary of her.

The leader grunted angrily, and the men resumed their positions. He turned to them and muttered something, looking displeased. Their expressions smoothed out, hiding all traces of apprehension.

"Guess not," she mumbled to herself. "I'll just go on to the ranger station and see if John's there."

"Ranger?" the man said, frowning again. His cold eyes narrowed, his flat face lined with a scowl.

"Yeah. I'm sure John's there by now. He'll have another light I can use."

A hum of excitement swept over the band. The man's face eased somewhat. "You know Captain John?"

"Captain John?" she said, laughing nervously. "Well, I didn't know he was a captain, but yes, I'm a friend of his."

Another murmur of excitement rippled through the group. The leader took on an air of animation, his black eyes less fierce than before. They'd certainly gotten a good candidate to play the part of Geronimo, Libby thought.

"Captain John gone," Geronimo said, stepping up to Libby. He reached out and touched her arm, startling her, and the others murmured in the background.

Maybe they thought she was hurt? "I'm fine," she assured them. "But I can't do any more right now without another light. I'll have to wait for John at the station. He shouldn't be too long."

Geronimo began to nod and poke at her arm. Libby bristled at the action and, feeling less

25

threatened now that she knew they were only playing a part, swatted his hand away. She was sore, more than a little angry with herself for falling in the first place, and in no mood to put up with some fresh guy pretending to be the big chief. Or medicine man, in this case.

The leader barked something to the other men, reminding Libby of her precarious position. Her fear returned, but she fought it down. They were only hired actors, she told herself, having a little fun by frightening her. She refused to let them know they'd succeeded.

Trying to appear in control, she took a step away. If only they'd let her pass, she thought. As long as no one tried any fast moves, she'd make good her escape. Less than half a mile spread between her and the group of buildings housing the museum and gift shop. The actual remains of the fort lay just beyond that. The ranger station was farther away, but surely someone would be on duty at the visitor center. Already the sun peeked over the horizon. It would be daylight soon.

She tipped her head up and took another step. Almost there. Just let me get past the blockade, and I'll run like a rabbit, she thought. Just then a hand closed over her elbow, and Libby cried out. She whirled around, and the hand jerked away. Geronimo, or the man portraying Geronimo, grunted out what could only be an order.

Libby had had enough. She was a fighter, not a quitter. "I don't understand what you're saying," she told him fiercely. "And I think you're carrying this part a bit far. Now let me go, or I'll tell John what you did and you'll lose your jobs. All of you."

"Captain John," the man repeated.

"Yes, Captain John," she said. "Captain John is the senior ranger out here, so I'm sure he was the one who hired you. Now are you going to let me go, or am I going to have to get mean?"

She knew she looked ridiculous. All five-feet-four of her bristling and rigid as she faced down the stout man. She trembled with anger, her fists clenched, her curls twitching. But she didn't care. She'd always been tough and determined—she'd had to be—and she wasn't about to be cowed by this bully.

"Come," the man said. Then he walked off, leaving her to follow or run away. She considered turning around and cutting out like the dickens, but they were headed in the direction she needed to go. Behind her the Gulf lapped at the shore. Since they didn't appear dangerous now, she decided she'd just follow behind at a safe distance. After all, the old wooden structures were . . .

Gone. Libby stopped, blinked, and squinted into the fading darkness. She turned on her heel in a complete circle. What the devil had happened here? Where was the battery she and John had passed on their way to the tree? Where was the pier?

The men continued to walk on, unaware that she'd stopped dead in her tracks. A sharp breath lodged in her chest, the pain quickly spreading out until she clasped a hand to her breast. Old Patriot! What had happened to the old-timer? she thought crazily. He wasn't . . . old.

He wasn't big or massive any more. He stood tall, but not as tall as he had a half hour earlier. His branches were mere twigs compared to what they had been. She leaned closer, and all the air rushed out of her lungs so fast that she felt light-headed. No cuts scarred the tree. Not one!

She'd have thought she had the wrong tree except for one thing. Old Patriot was the only oak tree standing on this section of the park. This area boasted only small scrub brush and a few palmettos.

"Guys," she called softly, stepping backward in the direction the Indians had gone. She stumbled on a clump of brush and twirled around. The Indians were shadows on the horizon as she hurried to catch up with them. "Wait up, guys," she called again, louder this time.

Geronimo stopped and turned toward her, and she wondered which was worse—going with him, or staying in the inexplicably altered area of the park.

"You know," Libby said, falling into step with the band of actors. "Something weird is going on here."

Chapter Two

"Omigod," Libby whispered, turning a complete circle. "Omigod."

Her breath lodged painfully in her throat; her stomach flipped, then flopped. She clasped a hand over her mouth and another over her stomach.

The Indians kept walking, paying no mind to her ashen face or trembling legs. But Libby didn't follow this time. She stood at the entrance to the fort, stunned and staggered by what she saw. Gone were the signs of disrepair, the crumbling bricks and heavy lime deposits. In their place were cannons, relics which had long since been removed from the present-day fort.

"What's going on here?" she said. "How can this be?"

Libby knew better than to think, even for a

moment, that all of these changes involved a reenactment. The park lacked the money for this kind of detail—John's biggest complaint since taking over as senior ranger. But then how . . . ?

Another oddity caught Libby's eye, and her world tilted on its axis. The northwest corner of the fort, the section blown sky-high on June 20, 1899, was intact!

"Come."

The leader of the Indians spoke directly behind Libby. She jumped and turned, closely inspecting his face in the dawning light.

The flat features, the cold eyes, chilled her. A bizarre thought entered her head. She tried to push it aside, telling herself she was crazy even to think such a thing. But it returned full-blown, and she caught her breath.

"You really are Geronimo!" she gasped.

He nodded briskly and took her arm. This time Libby didn't even consider telling him to remove it. Dumbly, she followed him as he led her back into the dark interior of the fort.

He lit a lamp, and a chill feathered along her spine. No electricity. No bulbs and wires strung along the ceiling. It almost came as no surprise after the shock she'd already sustained.

"It can't be," she mumbled, drawing a confused look from the old Indian. "It isn't possible."

But Libby knew this was no dream. She'd

visited this section of the fort a hundred times or more, and this was *not* the fort of her time. There could be no mistaking the massive changes she saw with her own eyes.

Geronimo motioned for her to stay on the parade ground while he went into the officers' quarters on the south side of the fort. No door blocked the interior of the room from her sight, however, and she saw the gleaming white plaster walls and marble fireplace mantels. She swayed with the added blow.

Only a moment passed before Geronimo came out, followed by an Indian woman, tousled-haired and groggy with sleep. He pointed at Libby, muttered more unintelligible words, and returned to the quarters, leaving Libby and the woman alone.

Hand signals accompanied another round of gutteral speech, instructing Libby to follow. Back into the long hall they went, past the pyramids of cannonballs and mine chambers.

Libby's mouth felt parched, her tongue too large. She tried to swallow. The pain in her throat protested the movement, and she realized that she had no saliva.

John could not have repaired the fort in so short a time. The brick on the damaged area perfectly matched the old, handmade brick of the original section, and the cannons and cannonballs she'd seen were solid iron.

Did that mean these were real Indians—not

actors here for a reenactment?

As she followed the Indian woman back out onto the parade ground, lighter now with the quickening dawn, she stopped a moment to reorient herself and met still another shock. Men, dressed in the old-fashioned uniforms of the Federal Army, ambled around the wide expanse of grass and lounged on the huge guns ornamenting the ramparts.

The Indians seemed to have free rein, coming and going around the interior and exterior without meeting any resistance, but the soldiers dotted the fort grounds at regular intervals. They spotted her immediately, and their faces showed their disbelief.

After several interminable seconds, one finally stepped toward her. He stopped, stared in stunned silence at her leggings and T-shirt, and then closed the distance between them in several long, albeit cautious, steps.

Libby found that her mouth had not yet regained enough moisture to speak, and when she tried, only a choked sound emerged, much to her disgrace.

"Ma'am," the young soldier said, removing his hat almost as an afterthought. "What are you doing here? Who are you? Where did you come from? What happened to your clothes?"

Libby's lips formed the words, but she couldn't manage a single sound. Her frustration at the debilitating fear must have shown on her face because the young man took another tentative step.

"Are you hurt? Can you speak?"

Like a blessing from heaven, her mouth filled with saliva and she began spouting everything she'd longed to say for the last few minutes.

"I'm lost, or confused, or something. Can you help me? Can you tell me where the ranger station is? Do you know John?" She grabbed his arm and in desperation cried out, "What's going on around here?"

The man jumped back, his eyes wide with shock, and she thought he meant to bolt. She tightened her grip and clung to his arm until she felt him relax.

"Ma'am, who are you?" the soldier repeated.

All right, Libby thought, that made sense. One question at a time. And, after all, he did ask his first.

"My name's Libby Pfifer."

He nodded as though pleased by her simple answer. "How did you get here?"

Libby shook her head. "I don't know." Which was more or less the truth, she thought.

Her admission seemed to calm him a good deal, and he grasped her hand. "Are you hurt?"

"I don't think so, but I'm confused."

He frowned at her again, considered her words, and nodded. "I think you'd best come with me, ma'am, whilst I send someone for Captain Faulk."

Again, Libby allowed herself to be led to the officers' quarters, this time the ones on the north side of the fort. Her escort showed her to one of the archways and she preceded him inside. A fire burned in the fireplace, dispelling the damp chill blown in off the Gulf. A cot sat against one wall, a cane-backed chair beside it. A washbasin and pitcher of water caught her eye.

He saw her look and motioned her to the chair while he poured some of the water into a tin cup. Libby accepted it gratefully, drank deeply, and nearly gagged. It tasted brackish. Too late she remembered that the men at Fort Pickens had never found fresh water the whole time the fort was in use. Instead, they caught rain water in copper drain pipes which ran from the curved roofs over the cannon casements to a cistern.

She also recalled that the foul water had caused several epidemics of typhoid and yellow fever. With a grimace, she set the cup aside and scrubbed the back of her hand across her mouth.

The soldier shifted on the balls of his feet and cleared his throat nervously. "You can make yourself comfortable until the cap'n gets here," he told her. "He'll know just what to do."

He turned quickly before she could answer, then looked back over his shoulder. "Can I get you something to eat, or anything?"

The mere idea of food sent her stomach somersaulting again and she shook her head, wincing. She doubted she'd be able to eat a thing until this nightmare was over. The young man ducked his head and shot through the archway as though his heels were on fire.

Libby eased back in the chair and tried to sort out the baffling thoughts tumbling through her aching head.

She might look like a fragile flower, but she'd always prided herself on being as tough as nails. She hadn't handled the morning's developments well, she admitted, but then who would have? After all, she'd fallen from a tree, been overtaken by a pack of Indians, misplaced Old Patriot, and apparently gotten herself lost. In a big way.

But, calm and rational now, she could handle this situation. Of course, she had to figure out just what the situation was first.

Just the facts, ma'am. The old phrase, left over from a popular detective drama of her childhood, leapt to mind and Libby almost smiled at the image.

Fact one, she *was* at Fort Pickens, just not the Fort Pickens she knew.

But how could that be? She didn't want to have to think about that question yet.

Fact two, she wasn't likely to find John, or even the ranger station here, so she was on her own. That thought brought on more than a little apprehension, so she filed it away also.

36

Fact three, she had to get out of here. But how? That one was easier.

The answer to this whole mystery must lie with the tree. She'd heard legends of the Druids who'd worshipped trees. Could Old Patriot be more than an ordinary oak? It seemed likely, since it had managed to survive so long in an area sparsely populated by little more than pines.

If the tree was the key, then she had to get back to the tree and find out what was going on. Easy enough.

With a plan to sustain her, she leapt out of the chair and crossed to the archway. Suddenly another soldier stepped in front of the doorway and blocked her path.

"Excuse me," Libby said, stepping to the side. The man, an older one this time, stepped in front of her again. Libby frowned.

"Pardon me," she said determinedly, trying to step around him. He anticipated her move and cut her off again.

"What's the deal here, stoneface? Let me pass."

"I'm sorry ma'am, but I have orders to keep you in the Captain's quarters until he arrives."

"Keep me. Keep me? What the hell are you talking about? You can't keep me here. I'm not a prisoner. I want to talk to whoever's in charge."

"Word's already been sent to Captain Faulk,

ma'am. He'll be here before you know it."

"I already know you're ticking me off," Libby said, straightening to her full, albeit minimal, height.

"Yes'm," the man mumbled, clearly baffled by her words and actions. His sharp gaze raked over her body and then immediately snapped back to her face. A bright flush crept along his neck and he tipped his head back, stretching the veins in his neck almost to bursting with the effort not to let his gaze fall below her chin.

"How long until this Faulk gets here?" Libby snapped, knowing it was no use trying to get around the guard. She'd wait for the man in charge, but then she intended to give him a large piece of her mind. Holding her against her will! The very idea.

"It won't be more'n a few hours, ma'am," he assured her. "Can I get you something in the meantime?"

"A few hours? You must be kidding."

The man scratched his head and met her eyes with a bewildered expression. "No, ma'am, I ain't joshing you. Why would I want to do that?"

"Why indeed," Libby mumbled, turning back into the small room. Temporarily defeated, she sank onto the cot and sat cross-legged, contemplating this newest development. Did they think her dangerous? Deranged maybe? She pursed her lips and tipped her head. Not that the idea didn't have some merit. She was beginning to wonder the same thing herself.

Perhaps when this Captain Faulk arrived, he'd be able to shine some light on what had happened. In the meantime, there was nothing for her to do but wait. She leaned back against the cool plaster and decided to rest her eyes for a moment.

Libby awakened, a thought jolting her from the light sleep she'd fallen into. Why hadn't she thought of this sooner? she wondered. Geronimo had said he knew John. Hadn't he? Libby tried to recall exactly what words had passed between her and the Indian, but the whole morning's events seemed more like a dream now than they had before. However, one look at the room confirmed that she was still in the odd surroundings.

If Geronimo knew John, then she couldn't have done anything as bizarre as traveled through time, a notion which had sprung to mind when she'd first seen the fort. She nearly laughed aloud at her own foolishness. Imagine her, sensible Libby Pfifer, even considering such a thing.

She leapt from the cot and stumbled, her legs tingling with the sudden circulation of blood. She stretched and gave them a moment to come to life. Adjusting her T-shirt over her bottom to cover as much of her leggings as possible, she went to the doorway and peered out. Sure enough, her sentry jumped to life and stepped in front of her.

"I thought you'd still be here," she said tartly. "Any word from the head honcho yet?"

"Ma'am?" he choked out.

Libby rolled her eyes. "My name is Libby," she told him, speaking slowly as if to a child. "You're making me feel old with all this ma'am stuff."

"Yes, ma'am," he mumbled, flushing scarlet again.

Libby shook her head. "Never mind. I asked if you'd heard anything from the man in charge. Captain . . . whoever."

"Faulk, ma'am. And no, ma'am, we haven't. But it's a good little skip across the bay and back. He might'a been busy when the message arrived."

"Do you think I could take a look around? Stretch my legs?"

Astonishment skidded across his face, and he paled before another flush swept his cheeks.

"No—no, ma'am," he sputtered. "There ain't no way I can let you go walking around. Not dressed like that. Not here."

"Why not?"

He swallowed hard, as though he'd choke on his own Adam's apple, and shifted his feet. "Them's savages out there," he said, aghast.

"Savages?"

"Yes, ma'am. And you ain't even supposed to be here. The island's been closed to tours since the Indians' womenfolk arrived. How'd you get here anyway?"

Libby thought it better if she didn't say anything more until she figured out what exactly was going on. She shook her head and turned back to the officers' quarters. She whipped around, caught the soldier looking at her bottom, and frowned.

"Tell me," she said, stepping closer to him, a scowl darkening her face. "What is the date today?"

It was a hunch, and she felt stupid for even asking the question, but she needed the reassurance of hearing she hadn't lost her mind completely.

"Ma'am?" he said, his face ridged with confusion.

"The date today. You do know what day it is, don't you?" she snapped.

"Yes'm, I know the day. Do you?" His tone challenged, as though she might know something he didn't, something he should be truly interested in hearing.

Libby drew back in surprise and frowned. "Of course I do," she lied.

"What is it?"

He looked eager to hear her answer, and Libby tapped her foot in irritation. "I asked

41

you first," she said, pleased with her quick thinking.

He pursed his lips as he considered that, and finally nodded. "It's the last day of May, ma'am."

Libby almost groaned aloud in frustration, but she knew she had to ask one more question. And she knew it would make her look like a fool or a lunatic. With a grimace, she blurted, "May of what year?"

The soldier stepped back, jerked a little in dismay, and eyed her with trepidation. "What year?"

"Yes," she asked, "what year?"

Her tone dared him to say anything insulting, and her bright green eyes flashed a warning. He seemed to catch both and swallowed.

"Why, eighteen eighty-seven, of course," he stated, then added, almost as an afterthought, "ma'am."

Libby braced herself to keep from swaying. *You will not run screaming like a madwoman*, she told herself firmly.

"Do you . . ." Her voice shook and she closed her eyes, struggling for calm. "Do you have any proof of that?"

He blinked, frowned, and scratched his head. "Proof? What kind of proof?"

"Anything," Libby whispered, licking her dry lips and praying he was having a good laugh at her expense. He glanced around, as though looking for assistance, then his face brightened.

"Yes'm," he crowed, patting his hands over his chest and thighs. "I've got this here"— he patted some more, frowned, patted, then smiled broadly—"letter," he said, whipping a crumpled piece of paper from his front pocket. He held it out to Libby with a flourish. She eyed it warily.

She couldn't make her fingers reach out and take the letter. She stared at it as though it might bite her.

Seeing her reaction, the man hastened to assure her that he had the proof she'd asked for. Libby wondered suddenly why he seemed so eager to convince her of what he said. Could this be part of a plot? she thought crazily. An elaborate prank designed by John to fool her?

He opened the letter and shook out the folds. "You see," he said, holding it out to her. "It's a letter from my wife, Beth. It's dated a month ago, but she says it should arrive by my birthday and she offers me felicitations. Here, look at it. She's wrote right there, *your birthday, the thirtieth day of May.* That was yesterday."

Libby reached out a shaking hand to accept the letter. The paper was dry and coarse, the scrawl on it feathery and light. She quickly scanned the first two lines and immediately noticed the formal tone. *My dearest beloved husband, Richard.* So, his name was Richard.

Libby glanced at him; his perpetual flush had returned. She realized she'd embarrassed him by reading his letter, so she ignored the actual text, letting her eyes go to the date in the upper right corner.

Stark panic tightened her stomach. Her heart missed a beat, then raced wildly out of control. She clasped a trembling hand to her chest and felt the erratic pounding against her sweat-covered palm.

She gasped for air, realized she'd crushed the letter in her hand, and reached out to return it to Richard. Their eyes met. His were filled with concern and apprehension.

"Are you all right, ma'am?" he asked, accepting his missive and quickly stuffing it back into his pocket.

"I—I have to go," Libby said, her voice sounding hollow and faint to her ears. "I have to . . ."

She stumbled forward. In his shock, Richard hesitated. Libby took advantage of his delay to brush past him.

"I have to go," she said, more fiercely this time.

"You can't do that—" he began. But Libby didn't hear the rest of his words. She broke into a run.

Across the parade ground she darted, ignoring the shouts from Richard and the other men. She pumped her legs, though they longed to collapse beneath her. *The tree,* she thought frantically. *I must reach the tree.*

She shot past a group of soldiers standing by a cook pot drinking coffee. They looked up at Richard's shout of warning and took up the chase. Libby raced on.

The doors of the fort appeared, and she breathed a sigh of relief, but didn't slow down. The sallyport, doors which hadn't been on the fort the last time she'd visited John here, were blessedly open.

Beyond the doors lay freedom. Beyond the door was Old Patriot, and her way back home. She clutched her side where a stitch had developed and dashed through the brick archway. Her footsteps echoed on the uneven bricks beneath her boots, and she splashed through a small puddle of water on the floor.

She chanced a quick glance behind her as she reached the fort's exit. Relief washed over her. Her headstart, combined with their surprise, gave her the advantage and the soldiers, about five in all, fell behind. She was going to make it. She was almost free.

She flew past the opened doors and through the opening on the other end of the archway, and ran smack into a hard, solid barrier. She grasped for a hold to steady herself, crying out in surprise.

Hard hands descended on her shoulders. Strong fingers held her upright in a steely grip.

The morning sun blinded her as it streamed through the entrance to the fort, and she squinted in an effort to see the rock-hard object she'd crashed into. She blinked, stunned.

"What in the name of Sam's cat do you think you are doing, madam?" a cold, sharp voice asked.

Libby squinted again, tried to shade her eyes, and realized that she was paralyzed by the man's hold on her.

"Who . . . who . . ." she gasped out the word but was too winded from her sprint across the fort's grounds to finish the question.

"My question exactly," the voice said. "Who? Who the hell are you?"

Chapter Three

"And where do you think you're going, little lady?" Libby's captor added derisively. He pushed her back and let his eyes rake boldly over her body. Down over her breasts his gaze traveled, to her waist, hips and finally her legs, clad only in the tightly fitted leggings. He scowled blackly.

"If, indeed, that's what you are."

"What?" Libby muttered, confused and deeply disturbed by his heated perusal.

"A lady. Judging by the way you are clad, I might have been a bit hasty in attaching that title to you."

Libby bristled and jerked her shoulders out of his grasp. The other soldiers skidded to a halt behind her.

"Captain Faulk, she got away. I tried—"

The man facing her waved them all back to the fort without a word. They mumbled, muttered under their breaths, and turned shamefaced back toward their posts.

"I resent your implication," Libby told him as soon as the others were out of hearing.

"You misunderstand me, madam. I wasn't implying anything. I was stating a fact. No one is allowed on this island at the moment except the Apache, their families, and my men. And prostitutes, however attractive, are never allowed here to ply their trade."

Libby's mouth fell open, ready to hurl curses at the man, but she was so taken aback by his accusation that she found herself in a position she'd never before encountered. She was speechless.

"Now," he said, taking advantage of her silence. "You have exactly one minute to convince me to have you escorted back to the mainland and not to the guardhouse."

"You bastard!" Libby cried, shaking with suppressed rage.

"That may be," he said, tipping his head in what might have been an apology. "But this island and its inhabitants are my responsibility and you are trespassing."

Libby's wounded pride refused to acknowledge his gesture and she glared at him. "I'm no whore."

Appreciative eyes caressed her legs once more. "Be that as it may, I still await your explanation as to your purpose for being here. And, for that matter, *how* you came to be here."

"That's none of your business," she snapped, smoothing her T-shirt back into place.

"I have been patient up to this point, but do not mistake my intentions. If you cannot convince me otherwise, I will be forced to hold you in the guardhouse on the post of Barrancas until you talk."

Libby's eyes shot wide. He couldn't do that! Could he? She met his dark stare and decided instantly that the answer was yes, he could and would.

"I—I—" She tried to come up with a good story, but her imagination failed her. And telling him the truth, or what she thought might be the truth, was out of the question.

"Yes?" he said, quirking one blond eyebrow impatiently.

The gesture made him look rakish, like some conquering Viking. She assessed his overlong blond hair, streaked by the sun, his tall stature and muscular build, and decided the image fit him well. Too well. All her old insecurities rushed back to take advantage of her weakened position, and debilitating intimidation encompassed her. She wet her dry lips as nervous perspiration beaded her palms.

"I'm lost," she finally said, rolling her eyes at the inane lie.

He looked equally disgusted by her pitiful excuse. "Lost?" he repeated, the dissatisfaction in his tone laced with something else.

Amusement, Libby thought. She bristled. "Well, not lost exactly. I didn't know the island was off limits."

"I see," he said, his cinnamon eyes now bright with interest. "And how did you get here?"

"I—well, someone dropped me off." She breathed a sigh and met his stare steadfastly. This might not be so tough after all, she thought. If she just stuck as close to the truth as possible, she might actually pull it off. She had to. If he locked her up, she might never get back to the tree.

He nodded, propped his hands on his lean hips, and let his gaze wander over her figure once more.

"And this?" He motioned to her outfit.

"My clothes?" She realized that he and his men had been scandalized by her T-shirt and leggings. This man didn't try to hide his thoughts and Libby read censure and disapproval there.

What could she say? *They seemed appropriate at the time. My time.* She could no longer deny the blinding truth. Wherever she was, she was no longer in 1993.

But how? Was time travel really possible? Or had the fall knocked her unconscious? Was she, even now, lying on the ground having a bizarre nightmare?

She eased her hand down, pinched herself soundly on the thigh, and had to bite her lip to keep from crying out. This was no dream. She'd done something other people only wrote about in novels!

"Are you all right?" he asked, frowning at her. "Egad, you've gone completely white. What is it?"

"I'm so confused," she managed, feeling light-headed. The truth, the undeniable facts, came as a blow, and she reeled with shock. Instinctively she reached out and he caught her to him.

His whole body seemed to wrap around her, so big was he. His strength and tenderness further unbalanced her sensibilities, and a cold sweat covered her body.

"Relax." His warm voice soothed her. Libby detected a touch of a Texas accent in the soft drawl. She tried to block out the terror and dread her situation evoked. She'd never be able to fight her way out of this crazy farce if she panicked again.

"I'm fine," she said, pushing away from his embrace. "I think I hit my head when I fell."

"You're injured?" He held her at arm's length, took in the scrapes, bruises and torn trouser leg, and cursed beneath his breath.

51

"I wasn't informed you'd been in an accident. My apologies. I'll escort you to my quarters. You can at least sit down while we talk."

"No," Libby cried, taking advantage of his loosened grip to step back. "I have to return to the tree."

"Tree?" He shook his head. Several strands of hair came loose from the ribbon and swayed seductively against his hollowed cheeks.

Libby wondered if the sun was getting to her. A crazy tingle started in her stomach like the first notes of desire being played.

"Yes, the old oak. That's where the answer is."

He raised both eyebrows this time, apparently troubled by her sudden ramblings.

"Oh, I can't explain right now," she cried. "But I've got to get back to the tree where I fell. Something happened there—I don't know what, but I have to find out."

"You fell from a tree?" He looked suddenly enlightened.

"Yes, and I must get back there."

"You are obviously in no condition to go anywhere right now. Do you have family we could contact?"

At her silence, he frowned and continued. "What's your name? Where is your place of residence?" When she still didn't respond, he asked anxiously, "Do you remember anything?"

"My name's Libby Pfifer, and I live . . ." Her voice trailed off and she winced. What could she tell him? She lived in a condominium on the outskirts of Pensacola? He wouldn't even know what she was talking about.

"You don't remember, do you?"

Libby bit her lip and looked up into his odd-colored eyes. Compassion had replaced his distrust and anger. She hated lying, but what were her options? When he'd thought her an ambitious hooker, she'd seen how formidable a leader he could be. If he thought her in need of help, she might get him to cooperate.

"I know I have no family here," she said, comforted that at least that much of her story rang true.

"I see." He shifted, tucked his fingers into the pockets of his snug trousers, and considered her for a moment.

"Will you help me now?" she asked, unable to stand the tense silence.

"I can't allow you to stay here, you understand. Langdon will be enraged as it is when he learns you were here. But I suppose I could take you to Fort Barrancas. We have a medical officer there who could have a look at you. You can stay there until the ban is lifted and then, if you still want to, you can return to Pickens. Maybe by then you will be recovered enough that the area might refresh your memory."

53

"But I can't leave! Don't you understand, the key to this whole thing is here, on the island. If I could just go back to the tree . . ."

"Later." He straightened, his face lined with stern resolve. "I cannot allow you to remain here a moment longer than absolutely necessary. But I give you my word, I will see you are brought back as soon as Colonel Langdon lifts the ban."

Libby couldn't wait that long, however long it might be. She couldn't leave the island. What if the spell was broken and she never returned? What if she got stuck here, wherever here was?

No, she had to try and make a run for it. She had to—

"Do not force me to restrain you, Miss Pfifer." The Captain's voice broke into her thoughts, as if he'd read her intent. "I have my orders and I will see they are carried out."

He meant what he said. He might feel sorry for her, he might even help her eventually, but he would not disobey his commanding officer's instructions.

Libby realized that the Captain would only have to reach out and snatch her back if she tried to run. And she didn't doubt he'd carry out his threat to restrain her. She made her decision quickly.

The tree would have to wait. After all, it had survived hundreds of years—what difference could a few days make? If the Captain placed her in the guardhouse, she might be detained longer than necessary. Her best choice was to obey him, for now.

"Fine, Captain," she said, forcing a coquettish smile. She'd been an accomplished flirt in high school and college, her size immediately making men feel protective and masculine. She didn't like sinking to such measures, but right now she'd use whatever wiles were necessary to get the good Captain to do her bidding. "I'll just put myself in your capable hands. I know you'll take good care of me."

She fluttered her eyelashes and almost laughed outright at his astonished expression. He blinked, probably wondering where the little hellcat he'd first encountered had gone.

"I'll move heaven and earth to make sure you find your way back home," he said, a wealth of sarcasm telling her he suspected her sudden compliance.

Libby blew a heavy sigh and quickly smiled her appreciation. She hoped he could do it. Move heaven and earth. That might be just what it would take to get her out of this celestial mishap.

The distance across the bay from Fort Pickens to Fort Barrancas measured a mile. She could make out the buildings of the army post across the expanse of water. But that didn't help to ease Libby's apprehension as she stared down at the little skiff.

No waves formed on this side of the island, which had always been known as the sound, but the water deepened abruptly and the vegetation obscured the view and made the water appear almost black. She knew from experience that the bottom was slimy and reedy.

Faulk stepped one foot into the little craft and held out his hand for her. Libby swallowed hard and twisted her hands in front of her.

Faulk frowned. "Come along, it'll be fine," he said, coaxing her.

The other soldier, a pimply-faced young man about seventeen, glanced around to stare at her. The boat swayed with his movements and a lump of dread lodged in Libby's throat.

"Miss Pfifer?"

"Don't you have a bigger boat?"

He fought to suppress a smile and shook his head. "No, this is it." He bent down, knocked on the low side of the vessel, and nodded jerkily. "But it's seaworthy, and Franks here is a good sailor."

Libby forced a smile for the young man and then looked back at Faulk. "Still, it's awfully small."

"Nonsense, we make this trip several times a week. We only use the larger skiff when we bring supplies. It's perfectly safe, I assure you."

"But what if we capsize?" Libby knew all forms of ocean life inhabited the bay waters. Everything from eels to sharks routinely turned up there. Never fond of boating in the first place, she certainly didn't relish the idea of riding inches from the water's surface in a craft only slightly larger than a bathtub.

"What kind of boat did you travel to the island in?" Faulk asked, snagging Libby's attention.

She saw the anxious anticipation on his face and looked away. "I don't know," she lied, tempted to tell him that when she came to the island there was a perfectly good bridge to drive across. She'd done it so many times that she'd never even noticed the dark, rippling waters below.

"It couldn't have been too large, or my men would have spotted it."

"I said I don't know," she snapped, cross with the pretense she felt inadequate to carry off. "But I'm sure it was bigger than that one."

"Well, nevertheless, this is the one we'll be crossing in. Now, come on." He reached for her again and Libby backed away.

Faulk swore, stepped out of the boat and took her hand.

"There is nothing to fear," he said, his patience quickly wearing thin. "I've done this hundreds of times without incident."

57

"Well, there was that one time . . ." Franks looked thoughtful, and Faulk threw him a black look. He immediately broke off midsentence.

But Libby had caught the drift of his statement. She dug her heels into the deep sand and pulled back. "I don't think—"

Faulk cursed again, swept her off her feet and deposited her roughly on the seat of the little boat. It bobbed and swayed. Libby groaned.

"Close your eyes and we'll be there before you know it."

"I can't ride with my eyes closed," she mumbled, clutching the sides of the craft until her knuckles whitened. "I'll get car sick."

"Pardon?"

Both men stared at her with confusion and Libby quickly realized her mistake. "Motion sick," she amended, pretending she'd said that the first time. "I get motion sick."

"Wonderful," Faulk replied dryly, shaking his head and waving Franks to proceed.

The skiff bobbed across the wide expanse of water like a cork set adrift. Libby couldn't bear to look across the bay to Fort Barrancas, but she knew they skimmed the distance rather quickly by the slap of the paddles and the lap of the water against the sides of the boat. Franks was strong for his size and age, rowing effortlessly.

Soon Libby looked down and saw the weed-covered bottom beneath them. She gasped with relief.

Faulk glanced at her, shook his head, and cast her a knowing smile.

"To the right, Franks," he said. "Bypass the pier and dock in front of my quarters."

"But Cap'n, what about the Colonel?"

"Colonel Langdon can wait a few minutes, until the lady has had a chance to make herself presentable. To the right, Private."

"Yes, sir," Franks mumbled, flushing with embarrassment that he'd questioned an officer.

He turned the skiff slightly, and in a few minutes the boat scraped the sandy bottom of the shore. Libby closed her eyes and sighed, swallowing the taste of fear in her throat.

Franks leapt from the boat, pulled the bow closer to land, and stepped aside. Captain Faulk jumped out, landing in the shallow water up to his shins, and lifted Libby from the boat.

"I can walk, Captain," she said, pushing against his chest. A thrill raced from her fingertips up her arms and centered in her breasts as she felt the granite-hard surface of his chest. Like a smooth stone, it didn't give at all beneath her ineffectual push.

"Nonsense, no need to get your feet wet." He splashed to shore and set her down on the sand. She wobbled and he reached out to steady her.

"Thank you," she said, a breathless quality in her voice she'd never heard before. She swallowed and found that her mouth had gone suddenly dry. Rubbing the tingling tips of her fingers, she surveyed the surrounding area.

Surprisingly, it looked familiar. The area was a military post in her time as well, and only the absence of a few concrete buildings marked the passage of time. The houses, ten in all, were wooden structures much like the ones that occupied this section of the Pensacola Naval Air Station of 1993.

In fact, Libby thought, they might very well be the same structures. Oddly, that thought brought her a measure of comfort as she followed Faulk up the inclined lawn which led to the house nearest them.

The three-story, white and gray house, with wraparound verandas and huge ceiling-to-floor windows, nestled beneath a copse of live oaks. Shade from the trees shadowed the porches and filtered the sunlight. What beams managed to evade the moss-covered branches gleamed off the spotless windows and pristine white trim.

Libby stopped to study the house and Faulk followed her gaze.

"Is something the matter?"

"What?" She turned to see him watching her, an odd tightness now present along the full lips. "No, nothing. It's beautiful."

He turned toward the house once more, and she caught a glimpse of something cold and haunted in his eyes. His lean face tensed, and he seemed frighteningly rigid.

"Captain Faulk?"

He blinked and looked down at her hand, resting on his arm. A muscle worked in his cheek, signaling that he'd clenched his teeth, and he moved his arm out of her grasp.

"Come along," he said, walking ahead of her toward the wide front steps. His boots clumped up the wooden stairs and across the porch, and the door opened eerily as he approached it.

Libby stopped. Someone inside had heard his approach and waited to welcome him. A wife? An unreasonable pang of apprehension darted through her. She hadn't considered that he might be married.

What a ridiculous assumption, she thought belatedly. He was certainly handsome, had a measure of charm when he saw fit to exert it, and held a position of authority at the post. Of course he'd be married.

"Miss Pfifer?" he said, turning back to see why she'd stopped. "Come along."

Libby stepped forward and realized that she'd unconsciously obeyed his command. The observation unsettled her.

"Cap'n, who have you got there with you?" a woman's voice called out.

61

Libby stepped closer. The trees shaded her eyes, allowing her to see Faulk, the house, and the porch. But the shadows hid from view the owner of the voice she'd heard coming from the door.

Faulk turned back, leaned down, and grasped her elbow, pulling her onto the porch. She decided she'd had enough of his manhandling and shot him a fierce glare before yanking her arm free.

A throaty chuckle issued from the doorway, and a woman stepped into view. Momentarily startled, Libby stared. One word leapt to mind. *Buxom.* Another immediately followed. *Voluptuous.* And still another. *Older.* She latched on to the last, a wave of something akin to relief washing away her doubts.

The woman was tall and broad, the buttons of her blouse straining against her full breasts. Her skirt flared over full hips and settled on top of scuffed, brown, laced boots. Libby shut her eyes tight and felt another nail in the coffin of her hope. No one would dress like that in the Florida of her time. They'd collapse from heat stroke inside of an hour.

"Caroline, I'd like to present Miss Libby Pfifer. Miss Pfifer, my housekeeper, Caroline Cooper."

He eyed Libby, as though challenging her to accompany him to the door, now that he'd properly introduced her. She raised her chin and stepped forward. Extending her hand she said, "I'm pleased to meet you, Mrs. Cooper."

"Miss," the woman said, her husky voice again taking Libby aback. "And you can just call me Caro." She ran her palms down her skirt before taking Libby's proffered hand. But instead of shaking it, she tugged, leading Libby into the house. She glanced back to Faulk, nodding at Libby's leggings with wide-eyed shock.

"Colonel Langdon is expecting us, Caro, but I thought perhaps you could help Miss Pfifer freshen up a bit."

He tipped his head, drawing Caroline's attention away from Libby's outrageous clothing. The housekeeper's mouth snapped shut and she smiled. "Why, sure," she said, shaking her head with bemusement. "But nothing of mine is gonna fit her, Cap'n."

"Nevertheless, I can't take her across the post dressed like that. Anything will be fine."

"Yes, sir," the woman said, turning and leaving Libby and Faulk standing in the foyer.

Faulk dropped his gaze to study her T-shirt and leggings again. Embarrassed, Libby turned away.

The foyer was impeccably clean, the wooden floors gleaming and the furniture polished to a shine. A hint of lemon oil teased her nose.

"What do you think? I've found the perfect thing." Caroline's deep voice boomed down the stairs, and Libby and Faulk turned to watch her approach.

"If I tear the ruffle off the bottom, we can tie this ribbon around the waist and it'll be just right."

Over her arm she carried a yellow sprigged-cotton dress with ivory embroidered lace at the neck and half-sleeves. The ribbon she waved was brown satin.

"Oh, I can't let you ruin your dress," Libby said, eyeing the bulky garment warily. She always dressed casually—jeans, T-shirts, sneakers. She certainly didn't want to wear anything so cumbersome and weighty in the heat of the day.

"Never you mind," Caroline told her. "We'll have you fit to meet the Colonel in no time."

Steely determination etched Faulk's face; he awaited her protest. She remembered his threat to lock her in the guardhouse and her need to return to Pickens as soon as possible. She followed Caroline into the parlor.

The room resembled a picture of nineteenth-century domesticity, with its braided rug and soft floral brocade sofa and chairs. In the center sat an oval coffee table with a crystal bowl of dried flowers on top.

Caroline walked to the brass sconce on the wall and lit the wick of a tapered candle. She squinted at the six-inch ruffle around the bottom of the dress.

"This'll be fine," she murmured, tugging a thread with her teeth. "The skirt was basted before the ruffle was sewn on, so we can remove the ruffle and the hem will be neat as long as you're careful. We can get one of the laundrywomen to put a proper hem in it later. I can't sew a straight seam, or I'd offer to do it for you."

Caroline's heavily accented speech placed her as an area native. Her bronzed skin bore wrinkles from too much time in the sun. Stubby but clean nails tipped her big, callused hands.

Libby guessed she'd worked hard all her life, probably out in the open before becoming a housekeeper. That was all she could surmise without questioning the woman further. Since she didn't dare answer questions herself, she thought it best not to start asking them.

"I'm not going to be here that long," Libby finally answered. "I hope you can have them repair the dress later."

Caroline raised an eyebrow, bit off a piece of thread, and nodded. "No matter, it wasn't my favorite." She shook out the folds and held the dress in front of her.

"Come here and let's have a look."

Telling herself she had no other choice at the moment, Libby stripped and donned the yellow dress.

Caro glanced at Libby's bikini panties and lace underwire bra. Her eyebrows climbed, but she refrained from questioning Libby about them. Libby was thankful, since she had no adequate answer.

Soon enough, she'd return to Pickens and, hopefully, her own time. This nightmare of nature would be over.

"My, my," the older woman said, clucking her tongue. "Aren't you a beauty. Where did you say you were from?"

"I didn't," Libby said, biting her lip and hoping the woman wouldn't take offense.

"Well, are you married?" She glanced toward the parlor door.

Libby fought back a grin. The woman was matchmaking! Mercy, what an awful thought. Her, with Captain Neanderthal of the bygone army.

She bit back a laugh and turned toward Faulk's housekeeper again. The woman tied the ribbon snugly around her waist, fashioning a bow at the back. She pulled a thin yellow cord out of her pocket, looped it around Libby's head, and tied it above one ear.

"There now," she said. "You're fit to meet President Cleveland himself." She dabbed the scrapes on Libby's hands with the corner of her apron and bobbed her head once.

Libby barely grasped what Caro had said before a knock sounded behind her. She whirled around just as Caroline called for Faulk to enter. The door swung wide and he stood, more handsome than she'd remembered, staring at her.

Brass buttons gleamed on his chest, and his silver shoulder epaulets sparkled. A ribbon the same color blue as his uniform secured his long hair at the nape. He'd brushed back the loose strands and dampened them to hold them in place.

His strange eyes widened in astonishment. Desire lit the cinnamon-colored orbs and he swallowed hard.

Libby's throat tightened in response. She remembered the feel of his chest against hers, the strength of his arms around her. Heat spread over her beneath the heavy fabric of the dress, but she suspected that its cause lay with Faulk's fiery perusal and not the temperature in the room.

"Shall we go, then?" he said, a richness now evident in the timbre of his voice.

"Yes," she breathed.

He stepped forward, smiled his pleasure at her appearance, and took her hand. This time when he placed it in the crook of his elbow, she didn't object.

As they stepped out of the parlor, Libby heard the housekeeper breathe a self-satisfied sigh.

Chapter Four

Smells of hair tonic and shaving soap lightly scented the air as Faulk led Libby back into the bright sunshine. He didn't speak as they walked along the shelled walkway and met the road up a small incline. A wagon passed, and the driver transferred the reins to one hand, smartly saluting Faulk with the other. Faulk nodded in return, his face unreadable.

"Is it far?" Libby asked, for want of anything better to say and as a means to break the growing silence encircling them like a living creature.

"No."

Well, so much for small talk, Libby thought. Obviously he was a man of few words. She walked on quietly for a several yards, but her natural openness could not be suppressed.

"Have you been here long?"

Without even blinking, he replied only, "No."

Libby kicked the long skirt out in front of her as she walked, frustrated with the weighty clothes and sweltering beneath the yards of fabric. Determined not to utter so much as another pleasantry to the obstinate man, she strode on.

When Faulk suddenly stopped, his hold on her arm yanked her back and she stumbled.

"What did you do that for? I nearly fell," she accused him hotly.

"Why are you walking like that?" Faulk stood on the side of the road, his brow furrowed. The slight breeze loosened a few strands of his hair from the neat ponytail. Libby wondered how a soldier got away with wearing such a rakish style. Obviously the Army hadn't always held such a rigid dress code as they did in her time.

Still, there was something to be said for the style. It gave him a dashing Errol Flynn look. Of course, in the looks department, he loomed head and shoulders over the old-movie star.

"Walking?" she asked, shaking off the crazy flicker of attraction that had briefly threatened to tie her tongue.

"You were walking as if your legs were made of pine planks," he said.

"I'm afraid my feet are going to get tangled

in all this cloth if I walk normally. Besides, do you have any idea how hot it is under here?"

Faulk's eyes widened, and a wicked grin tipped the corners of his full mouth. A chuckle escaped his lips, and he coughed to cover it.

"No, I'm sure I have no idea."

Libby realized that her question had sounded loaded, and she cringed. *Idiot*, she called herself. If she didn't watch out he'd be mistaking her for a prostitute again. Embarrassed, she couldn't meet his gaze. Instead she focused on his mouth. Instantly she realized what a mistake that was.

The man had a mouth built for kissing. Just looking at the well-defined lips put her in mind of long, wet kisses that lingered and licked and teased until a woman could only cry out her desire. Kisses that went on forever, and yet not long enough.

"Miss Pfifer?"

The lips parted to form her name. Her mouth went dry, and she touched her tongue to her own lips. The sensation made her wonder what his tongue would feel like caressing her hot mouth. She swayed toward him before she caught herself and flushed. Lord, the heat must have fried her brain.

"Can we just get this over with?" she asked, desperate to get out of the sun and out of this man's presence.

"As you wish," he said, taking her arm once

more and turning toward the post grounds.

Heat radiated from Faulk's strong fingers through the sleeve of her dress. Libby stared down at the square tips, the big knuckles, and the smattering of gold hair on the back of his hand. Another wave of awareness raised her temperature by degrees.

"Excuse me," she croaked, wondering if this intense reaction to Faulk was part of the cosmic force that had brought her here. Certainly she'd never gone softheaded over a man like this before. Even his fingernails drove her wild.

"I can walk by myself," she said curtly, angry with the situation and venting her frustration on the nearest candidate. What was happening to her? Was she caught in an electrical force field of some kind? That would explain the tingling coursing along her nerve endings.

"As you wish," he repeated, nodding blandly. He took another step, realized she hadn't followed, and turned back. "Are you coming?"

Did a current of awareness arc between them, causing this pull she felt? Could he feel the draw? Even now, did he wonder how her lips would feel on his? His stance remained stiff, his back unnaturally straight. Except for the hair, he looked every inch the picture of starched military rigidity. She finally looked into his eyes, and the moment of madness died like a match in a whirlwind.

71

His look reflected annoyance and irritation. A tight line appeared around his mouth, erasing the tempting fullness and thinning his lips.

"I'm coming," she whispered, collecting her control and wrapping it around her like a shawl. Electric currents and cosmic awareness. What a crock. She was obviously losing her mind and if she needed any proof, she had only to consider her acceptance of this situation. Who would believe such a thing?

Less than ten hours ago, she'd driven her car to Fort Pickens in the hope of securing the big break of her career. Now, she blithely followed a man, who by all laws of time should be dead, across a parade ground which should no longer exist, to an extinct army post. And, odder still, it seemed the most logical thing to do.

Slat-railed fences separated the stretch of officers' houses from the parade ground. Cannons, no longer in use, sat rusting, their dull black surfaces attracting the sun's rays until you could almost see the heat rising above them. Brick supporters, now empty of cannonballs, sprouted weeds. Across the way she saw a huge brick building with three levels of windows, a structure as familiar to her as her own face. The breath lodged painfully in her chest, and she stopped short.

"Are you all right? Miss Pfifer?"

Libby studied the building which housed the school of photography on the modern-day base.

Other than a few small details, it looked the same. But, when Libby read the hand-lettered sign over the door, her doubts fell away at last. *Barracks*. Yes, she thought, it had been the barracks way back when this area was an army post. *Now*, she corrected herself.

Anger filled her. Never given to tears and pity, she considered herself strong and resilient. This situation had her doubting her own sanity, but she wouldn't fall apart. Whatever this was, nightmare or hallucination, she didn't know at this point. But Libby knew that her own inner strength would see her through.

Her rage grew at the bizarre circumstances she found herself in. Again she wanted to scream, *Why me?* She felt like shouting out her frustration, but she couldn't afford that luxury as long as she was under Faulk's close scrutiny. No, she had to remain in control, while playing on his need to protect and defend. That would be her advantage. As long as he thought of her as helpless, she stood a better chance of his complying with her wishes.

And right now she wished he'd take her back to Pickens. That tree, Old Patriot, held all the answers. If she could just . . .

"Miss Pfifer?"

Libby's gaze snapped from the old building to Faulk's face. A few dots of perspiration had beaded on his forehead and upper lip. The day promised to be hot, especially for May. That

73

much hadn't changed over the years. Northwest Florida held a reputation for unpredictability when it came to weather.

"I'm sorry, did you say something?" A patch of moisture dampened her own brow, and she dabbed at it with her fingers.

"We'd better hurry. The Colonel is waiting."

"Yes, of course."

They started across the grounds once more, and Libby tried to shut out the other differences she encountered. No purpose would be served by cataloging the oddities, and it would only drive her nuts at this point. The less she dwelled on it, the better.

She should have known it wouldn't be that easy, Libby thought as Faulk led her up a set of steps and into the building housing the offices of the commander. Soldiers, dressed in the now familiar blue uniforms of the Federal Army, snapped to attention and saluted as they passed. Faulk returned the salutes without breaking stride and escorted her past the men.

A desk sat outside a heavy oak door at the end of the hall. The young man behind it, wearing tiny round spectacles and holding a curious-looking pen, stood as they approached.

"Captain Faulk," the man snapped crisply. Another salute followed.

"Is Colonel Langdon in?"

"Yes, sir, and waiting for you."

The man eyed Libby curiously and attempted a hesitant smile. Faulk cleared his throat, and the soldier jumped back. Hard fingers clasped her elbow and propelled her forward through the now opened doorway.

An aging man, skin dark from the sun and hair glistening white, rose to greet them. Faulk saluted—Libby was getting tired of all the stiff formality—and the Colonel returned it, then motioned for them to be seated.

"I see you've collected our little trespasser without difficulty."

"Yes, sir," Faulk said, his fingers on the small of Libby's back, directing her to the chair in front of the Colonel's desk.

"Come, sit down, Miss . . ."

Libby opened her mouth only to shut it again when Faulk answered for her.

"Well, Miss Pfifer, make yourself comfortable. Would you like something? Tea perhaps, or coffee?"

"No, thank you," Libby said, warily eyeing the two men squaring off before her.

"Now then, did you ask Miss Pfifer what she was doing on Pickens during the ban?" Langdon asked the Captain.

"I was—"

"She doesn't know, sir," Faulk cut in, shooting Libby a hard glare. She resented his attitude and didn't appreciate his answering for her as though she were impaired.

Faulk ignored her displeasure, shooting her another black look. He lowered himself into the chair next to hers and sat rigidly straight. Libby leaned forward, intending to speak to Langdon on her own behalf, when the Captain broke in again.

"I fear she lost her memory when she fell from the big oak on the tip of the island. She has no idea of how she came to be there or where her family might be. The only thing she remembers is her name."

Langdon looked sympathetically toward Libby and shook his head. The graying wisps of hair over his ears fluttered slightly, and his blue eyes held compassion.

"Unfortunate situation to find oneself in. You have my deepest sympathy."

Too soon the tender look disappeared. He wore a stern countenance as he once more addressed Faulk. "However, we can't be sure what she was doing there in the first place, can we?"

"No, sir," Faulk agreed.

Libby might as well be invisible for all the attention the men now paid her. A complication to be dealt with, nothing more. The feeling renewed her anger and she sat forward, thinking to give them both her two cents' worth, whether they wanted it or not.

Faulk's hand slid down between the two chairs and grasped her fingers in a painful clench. She started to cry out, then realized that Faulk was warning her to be silent. Every ounce of stubbornness in her threatened to rise up at that moment. What right did he have to order her about, even silently? But Libby remembered the threat he'd issued about the guardhouse, felt confident that he'd follow through with the pledge, and decided to hold her tongue.

"Of course I'll do whatever you think best, sir," Faulk said, managing to sound respectful yet forceful. "In my opinion, however, no good would be served by locking her in the guardhouse."

Again she felt the pressure. This time she knew his words were meant to force her silence.

"If she truly can't remember anything," the Captain continued, "we'll get no answers that way. Perhaps you could suggest a position for her, here on the post. The surgeon could work with her, try to find an answer to her memory loss. And, of course, I'll continue with the questioning and keep you informed."

"Splendid," Langdon crowed, sitting back as though a weight had been lifted from his shoulders. "Then I'll leave her care in your capable hands. You find her a position—maybe Sue in the laundry can help with that. And instruct Doctor Stern to conduct an examination and check regularly on her progress."

Faulk rose, saluted the Colonel, and reached for Libby's arm. Libby couldn't believe it. That was all? The meeting had concluded without her even uttering a word. The gall of these two!

Ignoring the Captain's repeated attempts to silence her, she refused to be cowed.

"Sir," she said, snatching her elbow out of Faulk's hand. "If I could just say something."

The Colonel frowned, apparently displeased that Libby had not followed the Captain. Faulk reached for her again, and she jerked away. "I understand your reasons for closing the island, and I can appreciate that I was trespassing this morning, but the circumstances . . ."

Libby broke off, and Faulk dropped his head slightly. She saw the gesture for what it was, annoyance. She'd spoken out of turn and now she would have to invent some lie in order to continue.

"Yes?" Langdon said impatiently.

"If I could just be allowed to go back to the island, only briefly," she hastened to assure him. "I feel sure I could remember something, and . . ." Her imagination failed her temporarily, and she searched frantically for a story that would convince the Colonel to let her return to Pickens. "And I could—could tell you then what I was doing there in the first place. Yes, that's it." She breathed a sigh and smiled tremulously.

"I'm sure I'd remember and then I could tell you what you want to know."

"I'm afraid that isn't possible, Miss Pfifer. The island will remain closed for at least a month." Langdon looked at the Captain and then back to her as though he disliked having to deal with her directly.

Faulk nodded and continued in the Colonel's stead. "You see, Miss Pfifer, if we let you go back, then the people of Pensacola would want to know why they can't go also. Then, of course, we'd have the reporters, the officials, and all the other thrill-seekers lining up for their turn to view the Indians. Chaos would result."

Libby's mind spun. A month! She couldn't possibly wait that long. "But if you—"

"When the ban is lifted, I assure you we will escort you to the island without delay."

"You don't understand." She leaned forward, placing her palms on the Colonel's desk. "I can't wait that long. I have to go back now. Surely you could make an exception."

Langdon shook his head. "I couldn't issue you a pass if I wanted to," he said, appearing relieved that he at least had an answer for her. "I don't issue the passes."

"Well, tell me who does and I'll speak with him. I'm sure if I explain the situation . . ."

Langdon's gaze traveled past her shoulder and rested on Faulk. The older man's graying eyebrows rose slightly.

"Don't tell me," Libby said wryly. She turned to face a grinning Faulk. "You issue the passes."

He nodded, took her elbow, and said a hasty good-bye to the Colonel, who appeared glad to see the back of the pair.

The soldier in the hall jumped to his feet, and Faulk waved him back to his chair impatiently, without returning the man's flustered salute. Libby allowed Faulk to propel her down the hall and back out into the bright sun.

"Where are you taking me?" she finally demanded, tugging her arm back.

Faulk kept his grip on her elbow and swung about to face her. "You heard the Colonel. I'm taking you to see Dr. Stern, and then I'll find something to keep you busy while you're here."

"You can't keep me here like a prisoner," she snapped.

"Lady, you *are* a prisoner. I managed to talk the Colonel into letting me oversee you while you're here, but make no mistake about your position. If you don't agree to the Colonel's generous offer, I'll take you to the guardhouse. You can stay there until the ban is lifted, if that's what you choose."

"Generous? He told you to find me a place in the laundry—you call that generous? I think you both see a way to get free labor while you hold me here. Well, let me tell you, you can forget that. I'm not going to stay here washing clothes and waiting for you to grant me permission to return to the island. I'll find my own way back."

She turned to storm away, thinking she'd scored a point over the arrogant Captain when he swept her off her feet and around the corner of the building. They faced away from the post, toward the southeastern corner of the fort. No one was out, it being the heat of the day, and the length of ground stretched empty before her.

"I don't know who the hell you are, madam, or what you were doing on Pickens this morning. Against my better judgment, I decided to give you the benefit of the doubt and help you through your interview with the Colonel. But I warn you, do not cause another scene like the one in there. Because if Langdon decides I can't handle you, he might just decide to put you in the guardhouse. For all I know you could be a spy, or a saboteur. And for that reason I don't intend to let you out of my sight until I'm sure you've told me everything you do know."

"I don't know anything," Libby said, her arms burning beneath his hands as he held her firmly against the wall of the building. Again the electricity between them crackled. She could almost see blue streaks dancing along their skin where they touched, consuming her in the current.

"I've told you everything I can." She met the fury in his eyes and stiffened her resolve. Whatever this link between them, she couldn't let

81

it interfere with her need to get back to Old Patriot. Somewhere out there *her* John, John Ferrell, waited for her. He must be frantic by now. She imagined him coming back to find her gone. He'd no doubt find her bag and the flashlight and think her kidnapped—or worse.

"I don't know anything," she continued when he still didn't release her. "Except that I have to get back to Pickens as soon as possible."

"Well, then," he drawled, his accent heavy once more. "I suggest you remember who holds the key, or in this case the pass, to grant your wish."

"What are you saying?" She tried to push him aside, but he only moved closer. His chest pressed against her breasts, his thighs spread on either side of hers. He pinned her to the wall, her body overwhelmed by the hard length of his. She swallowed hard.

"I'm saying that I have a proposition you might find more appealing than working in the laundry. And all you have to do is promise you'll be nice and not make me regret my decision."

A proposition? Libby's mind whirled with an explosive mixture of surprise and hostility. She couldn't believe her ears. She glared at the lazy grin he now wore. She couldn't believe her eyes! She longed to raise her knee and decline his offer in the way her self-defense teacher had instructed her. But her legs were pinned, so she settled for a blistering look that succeeded in wiping the smirk from his face.

"You son of a bitch. You're propositioning me?"

Chapter Five

Libby shoved at Faulk's chest, but she might as well have been trying to push a mountain. She tossed her head back and looked up into his face. The anger she saw was mixed with something else. Disappointment? Disgust? She didn't know.

"Stop acting so damned self-righteous," he said, shocking Libby into temporary silence.

When she could finally find her voice, she hoped it wouldn't reveal the level of anxiety she felt.

"Oh, nice talk for an honorable military man," she taunted.

Faulk's eyes darkened; his hands bit into her arms. "Who said I was honorable? For that matter, who said I was a military man? I put this uniform on when it became necessary to accomplish my goal. Now that objective has been met, and there is no longer a need for it."

Libby gulped, choking down a measure of fear. Had she put herself in the hands of a scoundrel? Could this wickedly handsome face hide the heart of a villain? She thought of all the pretty-faced criminals she'd seen on television and wondered what would happen to her now that she'd been turned over to him?

"I—I know you're honorable," she said, fighting another grip of apprehension threatening to close her throat.

Her words bolstered her flagging confidence and suddenly she knew she'd been right. He *was* an honorable man. He'd had the opportunity to make a move before now. And besides, he wouldn't have brought her to the Colonel if he planned something wicked. Would he?

And even if he had propositioned her, it could be for a number of reasons. Maybe he still believed she was a prostitute. She hadn't given a good reason for being dressed the way she had been. Or, he might have thought her comments earlier were suggestive.

"You know nothing about me." He looked as though he'd say more, then turned abruptly away. Libby rubbed her arms where he'd held her and felt the lingering heat his hands had left there. She glanced around, noting the

85

avenues of escape in case she decided to run.

"Just as I know nothing about you," he added belatedly. His tone sounded bewildered, and Libby eyed him closely as he stepped back and surveyed her. "I know less than nothing, and yet . . ."

He shook his head, but Libby finally understood. He *had* felt the thread of intimacy that seemed to connect them. He studied her another moment, then turned his head away as though in disgust.

"And yet . . . ?" she coaxed, wanting to hear him say that he'd experienced the same feelings she had.

But Faulk had regained control of his thoughts and he faced her. "I wasn't propositioning you in the manner you think. I was offering you another job, a position slightly better than working in the laundry."

"What kind of job are you talking about, Captain Faulk?"

He shook his head and chuckled dryly. "Nothing as debauched as you were thinking, I assure you. I thought perhaps you could help my housekeeper, Caroline, for a while."

"Your housekeeper?"

"Yes. She's had a few problems with her heart. Nothing too serious, but the doctor suggested she take it easy. Caro won't hear of it. She refuses to let me hire a girl to assist her."

"Then why would she allow me to help her?"

"Caro's stubborn, but she's also very caring. If I suggested it was you, rather than her, who needed help, I'm sure she'd agree."

Still confused, Libby shook her head. "I don't understand."

"If I told Caro you were suffering memory loss and needed a place to stay until you'd recovered, she'd insist we take you in. She's really a soft touch when it comes to strays."

"Thanks a lot," Libby said dryly, not liking the analogy.

"In any case, she'd allow you to help her if she thought she were the one helping you."

"I see." And she did. A small smile tipped the corner of her mouth and she glanced down, then back up, looking into his warm eyes. "I knew you were honorable."

He appeared slightly embarrassed, but he covered it with a brusque, "Well?"

"Sure, of course. Why would I refuse an offer to live in your big, beautiful house when my only other option is working every day in a laundry? I know I haven't exactly wowed you with my acumen up until now, but I'm nobody's fool, either."

Besides, she thought, it surpassed her other choices. The guardhouse, unpleasant at best, sounded unbreachable, making escape impossible. Likewise, occupying a room with a bunch of other women ensured the same result. And escape was just what she planned to do at the first opportunity. She'd get back to that island, one way or another. Her scheme relied on the Captain dropping his guard. And that relied on her going along with whatever he suggested.

"Fine," he said, ignoring her comment without any indication of his own thoughts. "Shall we see the doctor now that that's settled?"

"Do I have any choice?"

"None whatsoever."

Libby laughed at his frankness and placed her hand in the crook of his elbow once more. "Lead on," she told him smartly.

The post hospital was located about a half mile from the Colonel's office, and although Faulk offered to find her a carriage, Libby told him she'd rather walk. The long, narrow front room, furnished with a desk and several uncomfortable-looking chairs, was empty when they entered. Faulk called out the doctor's name.

Doctor Stein appeared, tall and reed-thin, and led them to an examination room. Libby's eyes skimmed over the cabinet of brown bottles, rolled bandages, and unfamiliar metal instruments. She politely declined his offer to sit on the polished examination table and took a chair in the corner.

He was friendly, with a good bedside manner, and Libby had no trouble liking him. He listened carefully to Faulk repeat the story of her accident.

He clucked concernedly during the story. "And you don't have any idea how you got to Fort Pickens?"

"No," she said, tiring of repeating the same details over again.

"This is an interesting problem," the doctor said, eyeing her like a fascinating specimen under a microscope. "Of course, I don't know much about amnesia, or memory loss as you'd call it."

"Could it be caused by a fall?" Faulk asked.

"Oh, most certainly. Damage to the sensitive tissue of the brain can cause any number of maladies."

"But there isn't any way to know for sure?"

Libby shot Faulk a black look. Just what was the man implying?

"A test, you mean? No, I'm afraid not."

"Is there a cure?"

Again she glanced over at Faulk, her eyes narrowed in irritation. The man was acting as if she wasn't even in the room.

"No, none that I'm aware of. If the damage is caused by swelling, it's possible she could regain her memory when and if the swelling goes down. However, if the tissue is permanently damaged, there is no way of reversing the impairment."

"But wouldn't a trip back to the tree where I

fell help?" Libby cut in. "It might jar my memory."

Stein put his finger to his lip and studied her. Finally he nodded. "It might, indeed. A familiar place, something to stir a remembrance. Yes, I'd say that was definitely possible."

She had the incredible urge to stick her tongue out at Faulk and shout *I told you so*. She resisted the childish gesture, hoping the self-satisfied smirk she wore conveyed her feelings.

He ignored her look, turning his attention back to the doctor as the man spoke up once more.

"Of course, I suppose anything like that will have to wait until Colonel Langdon reopens the Fort to visitors," he added. "I can't imagine how you came to be there without an official pass."

Faulk glanced in her direction. Nothing on his face revealed that he was gloating, but Libby felt certain he was enjoying her setback. Stein might be a doctor, but that made him no less a soldier.

As they left the hospital building, the afternoon sun had faded to a bright orange sphere. Libby and Faulk strolled leisurely back down the shelled road. A light breeze blew in off the Gulf, chasing away the mosquitoes and other pests.

Neither spoke, each absorbed in private thoughts, and Libby glanced up in surprise when his house appeared before them.

"Oh, are we here already?"

The comment was rhetorical, and Faulk simply touched her elbow as she stepped onto the porch.

Caroline met them with a pitcher of lemonade. "Sit and have a cool drink," she offered, her brusque tone making it sound more like an order.

They made themselves comfortable in the matching set of wicker rocking chairs flanking the door.

"So, how'd it go?" Caroline asked when they all had drinks and seats.

Faulk leaned back and sipped his lemonade. Libby thought he looked relaxed for the first time since she'd met him. She watched his lips close over the edge of the glass and then his tongue dabbed at the drop of lemonade in the corner of his mouth.

"Fine, fine. You know Langdon. He left the matter to me just as I thought he would."

"That's good," Caroline said, offering Libby a sharp nod and smiling as though to assure her it was indeed a point in her favor.

"He suggested I find her a place in the laundry with Sue and the others. I'm not sure, though, considering her condition. I thought," Faulk said, still retaining a casual expression, "perhaps we should let her stay here where it's cooler and more comfortable. You wouldn't mind, would you, Caro?"

"Why, of course not. The very idea of puttin' the girl in the laundry when she's still ailing is ridiculous. Whatever was the Colonel thinkin'?"

"She's got to have a job, though," he continued, looking thoughtful. "Tell me, Miss Pfifer, do you know of anything you can do? Something useful I can use to convince the Colonel?"

Libby hadn't been paying attention to the conversation. Her thoughts had drifted, replaying the morning's events. Something nagged the back of her mind. His words jarred her and she started, nearly upsetting her glass. The liquid sloshed onto her hand and she shook it off before looking from Faulk to his housekeeper and back again. "I—I could help out around here," she said, snapping her attention back to the matter at hand.

Caroline's back stiffened, and Libby could see the protest rise to her lips.

"Caro takes care of everything here," Faulk cut in. "I don't see how . . ."

"Well, just a minute now," Caro said, setting her glass on the porch floor. "You've mentioned hiring someone to help me out."

"But you said you could handle everything yourself."

"Well, you and I know I don't really need the help. But the Colonel don't have to know that. Besides, it might be nice to have another pair of hands around. For a while," she quickly added.

Libby struggled to keep from smiling. Lord, the man was incredible! Not only had he gotten his way, he'd made his housekeeper think it was her own idea. Her smile quickly faded. She'd have to remember how manipulative the man could be.

"Then that's settled," Faulk said, standing. "I'll let Colonel Langdon know what we decided in the morning. If you ladies will excuse me, I've got some work to do in the study."

He walked through the doorway and disappeared into the cool, shadowy interior of the house. The silence stretched out while Libby slowly raised the glass to her lips and sipped. What a multifaceted man. She couldn't figure him out, and yet she could no longer deny the feelings he brought out in her.

Call it attraction, desire, lust. Whatever, she had it bad. She'd dismissed the sensation earlier as an unnatural phenomenon brought about by the circumstances of her arrival here. But she recognized it now as pure sexual longing.

"Are you all right?"

Resisting the urge to fan her flushed face, Libby glanced at the housekeeper. "I'm just a little tired," she hedged.

"Sure you are," Caro said, collecting the pitcher and glasses. "You come on inside where it's cooler, and I'll show you where you can lie down and rest."

Libby suspected she'd get no rest until this whole crazy trip through time was over with. But she needed privacy to think and plan, so she followed Caro without comment. They disposed of the dishes in a kitchen at the back of the house. Libby barely had time to observe the cast-iron, wood-burning stove and dry sink before Caro led her up the stairs to a small bedroom.

The tiny rose-print wall covering looked charming and old-fashioned. Libby felt only a mild shock when she realized it was probably the latest style. The bed, devoid of cover, sported a hand-sewn, striped mattress. The polished wood floor gleamed, naked of rugs. Minimal furnishings proclaimed the room vacant.

"I'll get some linens and make up the bed."

Caro left the room and returned a few moments later with crisp white sheets still smelling of sunshine and soap. Together they spread the sheets, tucked them in, and finished the chore.

"Can I get you something to change into? You can't rest trussed up in that dress."

"No, thank you. You've done enough," Libby said. She fingered the material of Caro's altered dress and wondered if she'd be there long enough to need clothes like these of her own. And what about underwear? It was only a matter of time before Caro questioned the slinky bra and panties she wore. Especially if they did the laundry together.

The precariousness of her position hit her fresh. She had no money. She had no resources. Without the generosity of these people, she'd be on the street, destitute and alone. "I'm going to need a few things," Libby thought, not realizing she spoke aloud. "I have no money, nothing," she whispered, feeling more and more anxious now that she had time to consider her situation.

"Don't you worry," Caro said, surprising Libby from her musings. "We'll take care of everything later. You get some rest now."

Caro closed the door on her way out, and Libby sank to the bed, exhausted. She tugged the cord from her hair and ran her fingers through the short waves. It was cooler in the house than outside, but the breeze could not reach her on this side of the house. She unbuttoned the bodice of her dress and laid the fabric back to expose her damp chest. Still, she couldn't get comfortable. Finally, she stood and removed the dress altogether. With just her underthings on, she lay back down.

What a day! How could any of this be happening? How could it be happening to *her*? People did not dart across centuries. At least she hadn't thought they did, but apparently she'd been wrong. It made good fiction, but the reality was hardly the stuff of fairy tales.

She *had* traveled through time. Difficult to fathom, but unfortunately true. It was the only explanation, albeit the most bizarre. She figured admitting that to herself was the first step. With that done, she tried to concentrate on her next question. Like, how did she get here? How would she get along while here? And, most importantly, how the hell was she going to get back home again?

But hard as she tried to focus, her mind kept digressing. Thoughts of Captain Faulk nudged at her consciousness until she finally gave in and let his image come to mind.

A nice picture, she had to admit. The man was drop-dead gorgeous. Of course, some women might be put off by the ponytail, or the seriousness that made him seem hard. And when she thought about it, his features lacked classical good looks. The full mouth, the narrow eyes. Worry lines creased his forehead and bracketed his lips.

All in all, not really handsome in the fashion model, *GQ* way. But there was something about him, some element he possessed that those other men lacked. And whatever it was, it touched the deepest part of Libby's libido.

A bad case of the hots, she thought derisively. That's all. Possibly combined with the fact that she was stranded here, and he'd offered to help her. She'd probably projected some feelings of hero-worship onto him because of the stress of her predicament.

She could handle this situation rationally, she assured herself. She had iron control when she set her mind to something.

Hadn't she overcome the obstacles of her size and insecurities to make it in a profession usually reserved for men? Hadn't she gotten over her hurt feelings enough to complete her English class with an A even after her professor ended their affair? She'd even bolstered her willpower and attended his extra credit seminar.

She could fight a little lust attack until she made it back to Fort Pickens and Old Patriot. Besides, what a story she'd have to tell John when she got home. He might not believe her, so she'd try to take something along to prove her story. After all, how many people got to do what she did?

None, her mind cried, bringing on another wave of doubt. At least none who lived to tell about it.

"Oh, stop being so melodramatic," she chided herself, flopping onto her stomach and punching her pillow. But her mind refused to be put off. If time travel was possible, why hadn't she heard of it happening to anyone before?

"Because," she said, snapping her fingers, "no one in their right mind would tell such a story for fear of being thought crazy." That had to be the answer.

She pictured the antiquated hospital and kitchen, and cringed. People in her time took for granted things like miracle medicine and modern appliances. She shivered at the lack of antibiotics and even aspirin. A chill feathered her spine as she recalled the kitchen, without a refrigerator or microwave. She knew she'd never get used to such primitive accommodations.

Steadying her nerves, she assured herself that she wouldn't have to. She would get home; she refused to consider any other possibility.

Somehow, she'd get to Fort Pickens. And then she'd climb right up into that old tree and with any luck at all return to her own time before her whole life sank down the tubes. She'd probably lose the job on the old oak, especially if it took her very long to get back. But she still had her regular clients, and another opportunity would present itself. All she needed now . . .

She bolted up in the bed, her mind locking on the elusive thought that had evaded her earlier. The tree! She slapped her forehead. Fool! she chided herself, feeling her enthusiasm wither and die.

The oak had received major damage. Life-threatening damage. Severe enough to warrant cutting the oak down, if she guessed right. And then what? she asked her racing mind. What would happen to her, stuck here in the past, if Old Patriot ceased to exist in her time?

Chapter Six

John Faulk leaned against the gnarled trunk of the crooked pine and took a drag of the thin cigar he held. His body relaxed, but his mind continued to chase thoughts of his houseguest.

Who the hell slept in his upstairs bedroom? Where had she come from? Her odd speech and wild phraseology stumped him. She must be from another region. Somewhere he hadn't visited in his extensive travels, since he'd never met anyone quite like her.

The important question remained: what business did she have at Fort Pickens? Was she a spy? The thought seemed unlikely, but he knew better than to discount it hastily. Instead, he filed it at the back of his mind for closer consideration later.

Her tale, fanciful to say the least, somehow rang true. When she spoke to him, he recognized her apprehension and confusion. That corroborated the idea of memory loss. But a few times he'd caught a hint of something in her eyes, and it worried him. Cunning? Deceit?

He inhaled, savored the sharp taste of the smoke on his tongue, and blew it out again. He hoped she'd told the truth. For his sake as well as hers.

The cigar burned unnoticed in his hand while he replayed the bizarre events of the day. Something unfamiliar touched his mouth and he realized it was a smile. Libby Pfifer had accomplished in one morning what no one else had been able to in years. Humor had all but vanished from his life a long time ago. It felt foreign, but good somehow, to have it back.

A stirring of arousal followed closely on the heels of his remembrance. His hands again felt her skin beneath their rough palms. His chest burned where her breasts had pressed against him. His tongue ached to taste the mouth that had sassed him so soundly.

She had spirit and a certain innocent charm he found himself inexplicably drawn to. But it was more than simple attraction. Something powerful stirred between them whenever they came within touching distance. He'd experienced a fierce longing just watching the sun glint off her midnight hair.

And even that didn't completely encompass her effect on him. More than passion, she evoked tenderness in a heart he had thought long dead.

But who was she? And what the hell was she doing at Pickens? He had to know before he let himself get too deeply involved.

His gaze drifted upward, to the window of her room, and he took another deep drag on the cigar. The curtains swayed gently in and out of the opening, carrying the cool night breeze to her as she slept.

He pictured her in repose, her unfashionably cropped curls wreathing her head. The small body would barely make a dent in the cotton ticking, her arms and legs thrown out in wild abandonment like a guileless child. But not a child. A woman, fully developed, with a sensuality many prostitutes feigned but few possessed.

He swallowed, tossed the cigar aside, and immediately lit another to busy his restless hands. Sweat broke out along his spine and trickled to the waistband of his trousers. Beneath the hidden shadows of the tree, he stripped off his shirt and used it to dry his skin. The breeze couldn't reach him under the curtain of moss, and he considered walking to the water and diving in to relieve the heat building within him.

Just then he heard a muffled noise from his guest's room. The sound of furniture scraping the wooden floor was followed by a thump and an unladylike curse. Again, he smiled.

Through the opening in the parted curtains he saw her fumbling with something on the table beneath the windowsill. Suddenly a spark shot up and she cried out. He stiffened, preparing to run to her rescue, then fought a chuckle when she used a plate to extinguish the small flame. She must have turned down the wick, for when she attempted to light the lamp this time she had no trouble. You'd think she'd never put match to wick before. Another oddity to ponder.

But thoughts of her strange behavior fled as she stood, in the glow of the lamp, wearing nothing but two thin strips of lacy, peach-colored cloth. One covered her breasts, barely, and the other her privates. But instead of hiding her attributes, the bizarre garments teased his imagination and set fire to his loins.

He knew he shouldn't watch, but he did. Closely, intently. He saw her lift her short curls from her neck and accept a cool whisper of air from the open window. He gulped as the action lifted her breasts until he feared, hoped, they'd spill over the crest of the fabric.

She disappeared from view, and he choked on regret. But then she was back. He watched her pull a shirt over her head. It fell to her thighs and he recognized it as the one she'd worn when he first saw her. She tottered on one foot and then the other as she slid into the curious trousers. Fully clothed, she quickly doused the light. He straightened expectantly.

What could she be planning? The obvious answer came quickly to mind. Escape. Why else would she dress at midnight?

He listened and heard the soft sound of the back door opening and closing. Tossing the second, forgotten, cigar aside, he crept deeper into the shadows of the tree. She tiptoed into view around the side of the house and paused, scanning the moonlit terrain.

Her boots clutched in her hand, she darted across the yard toward the water. John kept her in his sight, but remained in hiding.

A few yards behind the carriage house she stopped, glanced around, then sprinted down the incline and out of sight.

The crushed shells cut into Libby's feet as she sped away from the house. But her boots would have made too much noise, so she clenched her teeth and endured. She had to make it to the shore and find a boat of some kind. The horror of crossing the bay, alone and in the dark, was surpassed only by her terror of being stuck in this place forever.

She had to get away. *Had to. Had to. Had to.*
The words, whispered like a litany, urged her
on, step by step, closer to the water.

The moon, full but for a sliver, streaked the
bay with slices of blue-silver light. The sugar-
white sands of the shore reflected the illumina-
tion and overpowered the darkness.

Her feet sank to the ankles in the shifting
sand, sucking her legs down. She stepped high
and continued on, searching up and down the
shore for a boat.

Finally, she spotted a dark shape bobbing
against the pier perhaps thirty feet away. It
was difficult to tell in the dim light, but she
didn't think it was the skiff they'd come across
in. However, it looked sound enough, so she
broke into a trot, sprinting awkwardly across
the unstable terrain.

As she drew close to the small pier, the sound
of crunching footsteps from behind alerted her
that she was no longer alone. She whirled, recognized her would-be captor, and cried out.
Frantically, she raced the last few feet.

But her short legs could not outdistance his
long ones, and he overtook her a moment before
she reached the pier, tackling her and bringing
them both down on the grainy ground.

Sand flew from beneath them as they fell.
He encircled her body and took the brunt of
the fall on his right shoulder. She heard the
breathy grunt expelled as he impacted and

rolled. She struggled to free herself, but he quickly positioned her beneath him.

He straddled her middle, his weight balanced on his knees. His hands flattened hers above her head. Libby bucked once, felt her lower region ram against the hard male part of him, and didn't repeat the action.

"Get off me," she said, tugging her restrained hands futilely.

"Be still," he hissed through deeply drawn breaths. She realized that he was winded from chasing her and again tried to dislodge him. This time he sank his crotch several inches until it pressed her arching hips into the sand.

She battled to control her own labored breathing, but the pressure on her pelvis caused a breathlessness all its own. Her chest heaved, her breasts straining against the thin T-shirt.

"Let—me—up," she said, noticing that his eyes had shifted to the low, scooped neckline of her shirt. He'd caught the tail of the tunic beneath his knees and the fabric had pulled down, exposing her chest all the way to the lacy top of her bra.

The pulse pounding at the side of his neck throbbed harder. The bulge pressed against the juncture of her thighs twitched and hardened.

Libby's eyes shot wide. What did he plan to do? She could see his face clearly in the bright moonlight, but his expression was unreadable.

"Where do you think you're going?" he finally asked, drawing his gaze back to hers.

For several seconds Libby didn't respond. Her mouth refused to form any reply. She licked dry lips, tasted the grit of sand, and tried to spit it out.

He transferred both her hands to one of his and surprised her by gently dabbing the sand from her lips. His thumb brushed her full bottom lip, dusted off the grains, and lingered.

"Where?" he softly demanded.

Libby tried to concentrate on her need for freedom but the pad of his thumb traced lazy patterns along her cottony mouth, robbing her of clear thought.

"Pickens," she finally managed to say. Her voice cracked and shook, and she knew by the way his hand stilled above her face that he noticed it too.

"Dammit, woman, I told you no one is allowed on the island. I explained . . ."

"I don't care about your rules," she said, cutting off his angry protest. "I have to get back there."

"Then you must wait until the closure is over."

"I can't," she cried, renewing her struggles. "You don't understand how important this is."

"Then explain it to me," he challenged.

Libby stilled. Her teeth clamped shut with an audible click. There was nothing she could say.

He'd never believe the truth. If she tried to tell him, he'd think she'd gone mad or he'd think she was lying.

Both prospects threatened her freedom. If he thought her insane, he'd have her locked away in an asylum, and if he thought she lied, he'd lock her in the guardhouse.

Their belief that she had temporary amnesia was the only thing keeping these people from pressing her for difficult answers. Lame as it seemed, she knew she had to continue the ruse.

"I must get back to the tree, tonight. Please," she said, forgetting any thought of pride in her desperation. "It's vital I don't wait."

The hard lines of his face softened, and he eased his hold slightly. "I wish I could help you, truly I do. And I will, if I can, once the ban is lifted. But until then . . ."

"No," she cried, bucking again. One hand came loose and sprang free, popping him in the jaw and snapping his head back. He cursed, pinned her easily, and shook his head once.

A drop of blood glistened on the corner of his mouth, and Libby gasped. She'd never hit anyone in her life. Fear rocketed through her. What would he do? How would he retaliate? Damn, she'd been a fool. He outweighed her by a good seventy pounds.

He sat, unmoving, for so long that Libby began to squirm. His eyes locked on her face, his jaw clenched, but otherwise he remained statue-still.

Unable to bear the silence and uncertainty any longer, she cleared her throat and said, "Your lip is bleeding."

His tongue came out and touched the drop of blood. She watched the movement, mesmerized by his tight control. He saw her gaze follow his tongue and he leaned closer. The breath lodged painfully in Libby's chest.

She'd feared him, wondered if he were capable of violence. None of her wild thoughts prepared her for his assault when it came, gently, caressingly against her mouth. His lips, warm and full, cajoled her. The silken strength of his siege stole the fight from her. Libby parted her lips, raising herself to deepen the kiss.

His hands ran down her arms, to her ribs, her waist, her hips. They slid back up and rested on either side of her neck as he set her afire with his machinations.

Shocked by her eager response, Libby shoved hard against his shoulders, succeeding in unbalancing him. He toppled to one side, his leg still stretched across her thighs.

Backhanding her mouth, she glared up at him. "What do you think you're doing?"

He chuckled. "Something I've been wanting to do all day. Something," he said, moving his hands from her breasts, where they'd fallen in the struggle, "I think you wanted also."

"You're nuts, buster. I want out of here. I want freedom."

He waved his hand in a half circle. "Freedom to go where? Do what? Under no circumstances will I allow you back on that island until Colonel Langdon repeals his orders. The closest town is Woolsey, a tiny little burg with very little to offer. Pensacola lies fifteen miles to the east, but without money or means, I shudder to think what you'd encounter there. Especially dressed as you are now."

Libby sprang to a sitting position, throwing off his heavy leg. "I'll get back to Pickens, one way or another."

"No, you won't. And if you persist in being stubborn about this, I'll have no choice but to lock you in the guardhouse. Why is that tree so damned important anyway? Is it a meeting place, perhaps? Does an accomplice wait for you, even now?"

"What accomplice? What are you talking about? I had an accident—I want a chance to try and figure out what happened."

His features softened and Libby knew he struggled to believe her. She needed his cooperation and so she pleaded. "Please, help me. Take me back, just for a few minutes. I promise I'm not up to anything. I'm no threat to anybody."

He shook his head, but his gaze continued to hold hers. "I want to help you. If I can, I will.

109

But you are going to have to cooperate. I can't go against Langdon's orders. But I will make you a promise. If you behave, and don't try any more tricks, I'll take you to the island myself just as soon as the closure is rescinded."

"*Ooohhh*," she cried, burying her face in her hands. "I can't wait that long." Pain etched her features as she glanced up at him. Desperation shone in her eyes. "I can't."

"That is the best I can do. If you refuse, I will have no choice but to see you safely confined behind lock and key." He sounded sincerely disturbed by the fact, but determined nevertheless. "What difference can a few weeks make? You can stay here in the meantime. Maybe you'll remember something and you won't need to return to the island."

Libby wasn't listening any longer. Her mind flew, trying to reassess her situation. "What did you say?" she murmured.

"I said, what difference can a few weeks make? And . . ."

"None," she said, her eyes lighting with sudden excitement. She'd been rash. Now that she thought it through, she knew she really had nothing to worry about. Some of her panic subsided. She remembered another case where an old tree had been vandalized, much like Old Patriot. Several years back, in another state, the same thing had happened. And, Libby recalled, it had taken months to cut through the red tape and ecologists' protests before the county had been allowed to cut the tree down.

The same thing would be true for Old Patriot. No one was going to do anything hasty. That oak resided on a national park, making the avenues of procedure even more complex. She had time. Knee-weakening relief engulfed her.

"Miss Pfifer?"

"Yes?"

The Captain stared down at her, compassion and confusion replacing the brief flash of desire she'd seen on his face earlier.

"Are you all right?"

"Yes, Captain. I'm fine now." She still wanted to get home as soon as possible, but she drew a small measure of comfort from her newest conclusions. She didn't have to risk his anger by trying to escape and possibly end up in the guardhouse indefinitely. She could afford to bide her time until Langdon lifted the ban. It wouldn't be easy. Her patience would be strained to the limit, but she could do it.

"And I accept your offer, Captain. I'll wait until you can take me back to the island. You have my promise I won't make another escape attempt."

He frowned, obviously baffled by her sudden change of attitude. "You're quite sure? I would not want to risk the Colonel's wrath should he find out what you've been up to."

Marti Jones

Libby noticed that the corner of his lip had swelled a bit, and she felt guilty for the way she'd behaved. Hysteria had driven her from the house in a mad rush to get away. But Captain Faulk could not know how she felt. He'd been kind to her, and she'd repaid him by betraying his trust.

She forced a smile and offered him her hand. As his big palm closed around hers, she again felt the magnetism that linked them.

"You have my word, Captain."

Chapter Seven

John's gaze swept over the men standing in a row before him awaiting the routine morning inspection. He tried to concentrate on the shine of their buttons and the condition of their weapons, but his usually rigidly disciplined mind refused to focus.

He couldn't seem to get Libby Pfifer out of his thoughts. She'd stumbled into his life much the way she'd staggered into his arms at the fort. Without purpose or intent. But he found she was firmly fixed there now. Dislodging her was proving to be more difficult than he'd imagined.

A noisy buzzing caught his attention as a large bee hovered around the nose of one of the men. The young sergeant refused to acknowledge the insect's presence, but his eyes were focused on the tip of his nose in a comical manner.

John tried once more to put his mind to the matter of morning inspection. He moved on a few steps and paused, instructing the soldier before him to step forward. He checked the man's weapon and, satisfied, allowed him back in line.

As he reached the end of the formation, he noticed a restlessness in the men. Their eyes were struggling to remain fixed straight ahead, and a few had strained looks on their faces.

Abruptly he swung about, and they snapped back to attention. Following one slow-moving Sergeant's gaze, he turned and stared.

His jaw snapped tight, and he ground a fist into his palm as he watched the subject of his wayward thoughts sashay across the parade grounds. The hem of her dark skirt was clutched in her hand, revealing her shapely legs from the knee down as she balanced a wicker basket on her outthrust hip. What the devil did the woman think she was doing? he wondered.

His first reaction was to run to her and force her to properly cover herself. More than a hundred men were openly gawking at her as if she were a sideshow in a traveling circus. But something held him back. She looked so innocent as she strolled along, her feet barely stirring dust and her wild hair flying loose around her head in its unusual manner. She had no idea of the effect she had on the men—or on him for that matter.

Again he wondered where this odd woman had come from. Who had raised her to be so innocent, while at the same time dangerously seductive? Didn't she have any female relatives to instruct her in proper carriage and deportment? Or perhaps a male relation to warn her of the baser attitudes of men?

The wind blew and her skirt fluttered up in front. He gulped hard, watching her, but she only seemed to enjoy the sensation.

Finally, the sounds behind him penetrated his lusty thoughts, and he turned to see a sea of hungry faces hovering over his shoulder.

"Take charge of your men, Lieutenant Garvey," he shouted, causing the men to jump guiltily. "A reminder of the finer points of being gentlemen and military personnel seems to be in order."

A sudden anger overtook him and he lit out across the field while the feeling was strong. He didn't like the idea of constantly berating the woman, but he had to keep Libby Pfifer in line or the Colonel would surely find someone who could.

"Miss Pfifer," he called out to her, his voice hard-edged, his long legs hastily eating up the distance between them. His boot heels pounded mercilessly on the packed earth. "Miss Pfifer, will you wait, please?"

"Oh, hello, Captain," she said, turning so sharply that she knocked into him with the basket.

"What do you think you're doing?" he demanded, releasing his jacket hem from the prickly fingers of wicker sticking out on the side of the hamper.

"I'm taking the dirty clothes over to the laundry. Caroline said they do all the washing and ironing for the post."

"I'm aware of the post routine, Miss Pfifer. What I meant was, what are you doing walking in front of my men like *that?*" He pointed an accusing finger at her trim calves encased in black stockings.

"Caroline told me to wear this," she said, her expression clearly indicating a fact that she was less than happy about. "I told her I didn't need all these doo-dads, but she insisted. I'd have been happy with my socks. Of course they're in the basket here. They need to be washed after all the walking around. . . ."

"Miss Pfifer, need I remind you this is an Army post? The only females allowed here are the officers' wives and a few miscellaneous women employed as cooks or laundresses for the benefit of the soldiers. You cannot be so naive as to think these men will not notice you parading around with your limbs on display. So that leads me to believe you are purposely trying to entice them. Well, let me tell you. Colonel Langdon will not tolerate a troublemaker. And neither will I."

"Entice them! I was doing nothing of the sort," she told him hotly. "And I am certainly not a troublemaker. I was minding my own business, trying to help Caroline—just as you said."

"And exhibiting your legs like chicken parts at a banquet."

John watched the crimson flush wash over Libby's dimpled cheeks. Her full, red mouth thinned in irritation, and her green eyes shone like bottle glass.

She dropped the wicker basket with more force than was necessary, barely missing his booted foot. "Now look here, you," she said, slapping her hands on her hips. "I'm trying my best to fit in here with all these cumbersome clothes, formal speech, and old-fashioned male chauvinism. After all, we did make a bargain. I agreed to it and I intend to keep my word. But don't think for a minute that you can come down on me like I'm one of your soldiers, Captain Faulk, because I won't stand for it. So, just cut me some slack, why don't you?"

John eyed the petite tornado warily. What on earth had set her off like that? And what on earth was she going on about? Her speech sometimes seemed like a foreign language to him, so difficult was it to understand. Her temper was nothing to sneer at either.

He couldn't help noticing that she was even more beautiful with the color rising in her cheeks and the wild flash of fire in her bright eyes.

Could she be deranged? Maybe they were mistaken on their diagnosis. She didn't look hurt or vulnerable now. She looked as mad as a March hare.

"Now, just settle down there, Miss Pfifer," he soothed, belatedly realizing that it might not have been a good idea to confront her openly. "There's no need to get so upset. Would you like to go and talk to Doctor Stein?"

"I don't need therapy, you oaf," she said, shaking off the hand he tried to lay on her arm. "I just want to do my time here and go home."

His eyes widened, and he stared at her for a moment in surprise. "Home? Do you mean you know where you live?" John's excitement soared. If she'd remembered that much, he might be rid of her soon. And frankly, the way he'd been reacting to her presence it wouldn't be soon enough to suit him.

"Of course I know where—"

Suddenly she clamped her mouth shut. A look of frustrated annoyance crossed her face and she looked away from him.

"I mean, I'm sure I'll be ready to go home when the ban is lifted."

John didn't miss the way she carefully avoided looking at him. She stared at the ground, nudging the basket with the toe of her boot.

"Humph." He frowned. He should have known it wouldn't be that easy. "Well, until then, you had better stay away from the men and remember to keep yourself properly covered at all times."

She shot him an annoyed look and mocked a salute. "Whatever you say, Captain."

Ignoring her sarcasm, he bent to collect the basket. "Let me carry this for you," he said.

"I can carry it myself," she told him, although he'd already hoisted it into his arms.

John dismissed her protests with a shrug, but didn't relinquish his hold on the stiff handles. "No doubt. However, I know what the word chauvinism means, Miss Pfifer. And while I don't quite understand your accusation, if I'm to be accused of something, I'd just as soon have the pleasure of doing it."

They faced off beneath the rising sun as the temperature climbed in equal measure with the fireball's ascent. Her hands were clasped over his on the basket handles. For a minute she stood still, watching his impassive expression.

Then, to his surprise and amazement, she smiled at him as she released the basket. Motioning him ahead with a wave of her hand,

119

she offered him a snappy grin.

"Lead the way, Captain," she said, her voice almost teasing. "And for the record, I never was much of a woman's libber."

"Do you have a minute, Doc?" John poked his head into the hospital building.

Stein was busy scratching notes in a journal, but he quickly finished up and, after blowing the damp ink dry, closed the book.

"What can I do for you, Captain?"

"I was wondering how everything went at Caro's last appointment. I tried to ask her about it, but she wouldn't tell me anything."

"You know Caroline, Captain Faulk. She refuses to accept the fact that she has a weak heart. She keeps insisting she's in perfect health. But I can tell you that little lady has got to slow down or I'm afraid she'll soon kill herself."

"Damn, I was afraid of that. You know, that was the main reason I took Libby Pfifer in," he said, stretching the truth a bit. He'd done it for that reason, but not solely to help Caroline. He needed to keep his eye on Miss Pfifer and try to determine what she was up to. "I knew Caro would pity the girl and let her stay with us, and Miss Pfifer has agreed to lend a hand with some of the chores Caroline has been doing."

"Good, good," the doctor said, nodding briskly. "At least you're making progress. Perhaps she'll realize she needs the assistance and you can get her permanent help after Miss Pfifer is gone."

John stepped farther into the building, glancing furtively over his shoulder.

"That's another thing I wanted to talk to you about, Doc. What do you really think about Miss Pfifer and her story?"

"I'm not sure I know what you mean. I'm aware of her memory loss, but as you know, I haven't spoken with her since you first brought her in."

There was something accusatory in the doctor's tone, but John chose to ignore it. Langdon hadn't insisted on daily visits and he hadn't seen any reason to bring Libby over again so soon.

"So you still believe she lost her memory in that fall from the tree?"

The lanky doctor stretched his long, thin legs out beside the desk and scratched his rough cheeks. Leaning back in his chair, he folded his hands behind his head. "You've spent more time with her than anyone else has. What do you think?"

"Well, I'm no doctor. But I'd say she remembers a lot more than she's telling us. Could it be partial memory loss?"

The doctor shrugged. "Anything with the mind is possible, I suppose. Modern medicine knows very little of its workings."

"Could it be she doesn't have memory loss at all? Could she be making it up?"

"I don't know why anyone would do that," the doctor said, gingerly sidestepping the direct question.

Why indeed, John thought. A hundred reasons crossed his mind every time he thought of Libby Pfifer. And he thought of her a lot. Could she be a spy? If so, who would be interested in the goings on at Barrancas? Or, maybe she was another zealot from the Indian Rights Association, poking around in the hopes of finding evidence that the poor savages were being mistreated despite Langdon's constant reports to the contrary.

It was certainly a possibility worth considering, but somehow John couldn't see Libby Pfifer in the role of government investigator.

"What about her mental stability?" he asked, deciding it was more likely that she was a lunatic than a clever operative.

"Are you asking me if she's addlepated?"

John stared across the yard to the laundry building. He'd come here hoping to find some answer to the puzzle of Libby Pfifer. Now, speaking all his thoughts aloud, he was more confused than ever.

There was a lot more to Miss Pfifer than he'd first thought. He'd almost bet a double eagle that she knew where she lived and who her family was. Which would seem to add weight to the spy theory. However, when he'd asked her about her presence at Fort Pickens, she'd been truly confused and frightened. He wanted the truth, but didn't know how to go about finding it.

"No," he said, almost to himself. "I don't think she's touched." He was surprised to discover that he made that statement with more certainly than he'd expected.

She might be strange and out of tune, but she wasn't insane. And he'd bet she was no spy either. Somehow he felt certain of that. Since he'd taken responsibility for her and even allowed her into his house, he hoped his conclusions were correct.

"Perhaps we're looking at this whole thing from the wrong end of the stick," Stein said.

"What do you mean?"

"Maybe it isn't a physical injury at all. Perhaps Miss Pfifer is suffering from a problem unconnected with her health."

"I'm not sure I follow you."

"It's possible the young lady knows very well who she is and where she's from. She might even be withholding the names of her family intentionally."

"Why?"

The doctor shrugged. "I'm not a fancy city head doctor. I'm a military physician. But it doesn't take a doctor's degree to know when someone's in trouble. Maybe she doesn't feel she can go home for some reason. Maybe she's frightened."

"Of what?" John asked, leaning over the doctor's cluttered desk.

"How should I know?" Stein glanced up at him, baffled. "I'm just guessing. Maybe she's got a mean daddy or a jealous husband. Hell, for all we know she could have both. A woman's troubles are many, take my word for it. And most of them never make sense to us men even when we know what they are."

John thought that an ignorant statement for a doctor to make. Of course he'd never been married, or even had any dealings with women that lasted more than the few hours he usually paid for. But he felt certain he could help Libby if only he knew what troubled her.

It occurred to him then to wonder why he should care. But the plain fact was, he did. And he'd never been one to sit around bemoaning what he didn't understand. He usually just accepted things the way they were and didn't dwell on the why's and wherefore's.

"By the way," Stein cut into his thoughts. "The Colonel sent word I'm to go out and give the prisoners the once-over. You got any idea what's up?"

Once more, John's mind went to the driving force of his life. The Apache. He'd spent the better part of his adulthood tracking them down and capturing them so they could be brought to justice. He'd lost count of the years of running and chasing he'd done.

Accepting that they'd never stand trial for the deaths of his family, or any other brutalities, had been a bitter pill to swallow. Hearing the doctor's question didn't ease his frustration.

"No, I don't know what's going on."

He wasn't sure he cared any more. Damn, but hate and anger took a lot out of you. Sometimes he wasn't sure he was even a whole man anymore. He didn't feel things the way other men did. He no longer mourned the lost love of his parents. It seemed, in the long hours before morning when his demons refused him rest, that somewhere along the way he'd died inside. All things considered, he thought it was probably best that way.

Look what a fool he'd almost made of himself over Libby Pfifer. First on the parade ground and now, questioning the doctor as if she meant something to him. Hell, he was the crazy one.

"See you around, Doc."

He left the hospital with his cold mask of apathy securely in place. Cursing himself for the momentary lapse, he regained his iron control before heading to Langdon's office.

Chapter Eight

A crisp spring breeze temporarily relieved the unseasonably warm weather. Grateful for the cool respite, Libby dunked her rag into the bucket of vinegar and lemon juice. She straightened and scrubbed another pane of the huge front window.

For two days she'd scrubbed, polished, and dusted everything in sight. It kept her mind from exploding with thoughts of her situation, her intriguing host, and her unreasonable infatuation with him.

She'd noticed in the last forty-eight hours that Caroline kept equally busy. That fact, accompanied by the sad, secretive smile she sometimes caught on the woman's face, made Libby wonder what interesting facets of the housekeeper's personality were hidden behind the friendly face.

It would do no good to ask, she knew, for the woman remained tight-lipped, almost to a fault. She never gossiped about anyone, Faulk included, and her silence sometimes drove Libby mad with curiosity, for she would have liked to inquire about every aspect of the Captain's life.

Faulk had kept busy with his post duties, and they'd seen each other only briefly since Libby had officially moved in. Occasionally he'd be at the breakfast table when she came down, but he'd excuse himself quickly and leave for the post. He usually took dinner in his study, while she and Caroline dined together informally in the kitchen. Libby wondered if he were avoiding her.

She'd also noticed that his somber moods had worsened. She'd thought several times of trying to get him to talk, but always backed down at the last moment. As long as she held secrets of her own, she didn't dare ask anyone else to reveal theirs.

"Time for a rest," Caro said, coming onto the porch carrying a pitcher of tea and two glasses.

"I won't argue with you about that," Libby said, sinking onto the nearest wicker rocker. Her skirt flared over the arms of the chair, and she gathered it into her lap with an irritated

127

sigh. She'd never, not in a million years, get used to wearing so many clothes.

"If you'd let me have them clothes taken in, you wouldn't all the time be wrestling with 'em."

Libby took the glass Caro offered her and smiled. "You've done enough just lending me your clothes. I can't have you ruining all your clothing making it fit me."

"I've give you one skirt and a couple of blouses I long ago outgrew. It ain't gonna hurt nothin' for you to take a tuck and a hem here and there."

"They're just fine with the belt to hold them in," Libby said.

"Stubborn," Caro muttered.

"Remind you of anyone," Libby countered, enjoying their banter. Caro often compared Libby to herself at twenty, and she smiled now at Libby's reference.

Chuckling, she sipped her tea. "Sure does," she admitted.

Libby heard the sound of horses's hooves and glanced up to see Faulk riding into the yard. Her answering smile stiffened. Even from a distance, she detected the anger on his face and the tension in his body.

"Something's wrong," she whispered, not taking her eyes off him.

Caro turned to look, then walked to the edge of the porch. "Cap'n," she greeted him.

"Don't wait dinner on me, Caro. I'll be late."

"Yes, sir," she said, hastily glancing back at Libby.

Libby joined her at the steps, and Faulk paused a minute to offer her a nod. "Miss Pfifer."

"Is everything all right, Captain?"

Caro shot her a hard look, and Libby knew she'd overstepped her bounds. Faulk stiffened, covered his reaction, and replied simply, "Nothing for you to worry about."

He swung around and nudged the horse with his boot heels, darting out of the yard in a cloud of white dust from the oyster-shell drive.

"That's the second time this week he's left here in a fine temper. Somethin's up," Caro observed.

"I'm sorry if I butted in where I shouldn't have, but do you know what's bothering him?"

"I suspect it has to do with that Indian."

"Geronimo?"

Caro nodded.

"Wasn't Captain Faulk part of the company who brought him in?"

"That's right. For all the good it's done. The man ain't gonna have to pay for his crimes."

"I don't understand," Libby said. "Isn't he being held prisoner?"

"Sure, if you call having the run of an island being a prisoner. What I meant is, he won't be hanged like the men were told he'd be."

"Geronimo hanged?" Libby gasped, wondering why she'd never heard that possibility mentioned in the reference material she'd read.

"Sure." Caro turned to face her. "When they set out after him, they'd been told he'd stand trial in San Antonio for his crimes. Instead, General Nelson Miles agreed to forgive the Apaches' crimes if they surrendered. He hustled 'em here to Florida, under President Cleveland's orders, before they could be turned over to the civil authorities. Now the Indians have the run of the island there," she said, pointing to Fort Pickens. "And they've been reunited with their families. It's hard for John to accept the Army's decisions."

"Why, if those were the terms of surrender? They've ended his raids. Wasn't that their goal?"

Caro looked thoughtful for a minute, then she turned back to the rocker and collected their glasses. "Maybe, for some of them. Some had personal reasons for wantin' to see the Apache dealt with stronger."

"Are you saying Captain Faulk had personal reasons for fighting the Apache?" Her interest might put Caro off, but she had to ask.

Caro heaved a sigh. "He does. I don't know the details, but I know he lost his whole family in an Apache raid when he was a boy. He don't talk about it, and I wouldn't dream of askin'."

She took the dirtied dishes and disappeared into the house.

Libby sat staring after her, aghast at what she'd just heard. His whole family had been murdered when he was a little boy? No wonder she'd found his personality brooding, even morose. So many things made sense to her now.

She wanted to question Caroline further about Captain John Faulk, but again she recognized the futility. Caroline might like her, but the housekeeper's first loyalty was to Faulk. And the woman simply didn't believe in betraying trusts.

No, if she ever heard any more of the Captain's story, she knew she'd have to hear it from Faulk. And, although she suspected he wouldn't tell her anything, she knew she'd try to draw him out. Her heart ached for the tragedy he'd suffered.

Already she was planning, in her usual go-getter fashion, just what she could do about it.

Sometime after midnight, Libby heard the Captain ride into the yard. She jumped from the bed and threw on the robe Caroline had lent her. As she passed the small window in her bedroom, she caught a glimpse of Faulk leading his horse into the small carriage house behind the row of officers' quarters.

She eased her door open and slipped down the back stairs to the kitchen, where she knew he would enter.

131

Caro had left the Captain's dinner in the warming shelf as she did whenever he was going to be late. Libby knew the housekeeper slept like the dead and wouldn't know when Faulk returned.

In the kitchen, Libby put coffee on to boil and set a place at the small wooden table. She'd decided, against her own better judgment, to wait up and talk with him tonight. Her curiosity refused to be appeased until she learned more about the man. The fact that she'd never experienced such intense feelings for a man only added to her desperate need for answers. And she was determined that she'd get them tonight.

The back door opened. She trembled at the sound of boots scraping on the stone step. Tensing, she steadied her hands and poured a cup of coffee.

"What's this?" Faulk asked, closing the door behind him as he stared at Libby.

She held up the cup. "Coffee."

Faulk eyed her warily. Reaching up, he removed his hat and hung it on the peg by the door. Raking the loose hair back from his face, he stepped closer and accepted the mug she offered.

"I don't expect you to wait up for me, Miss Pfifer. Nor serve me."

"That's all right. I was awake." It was the truth, she told herself. She didn't add that she'd

132

purposely lain in bed, forcing her eyes to stay open, planning this moment. She removed his food from the warmer and waved him toward the table.

"Are you having trouble sleeping?" he asked, his face instantly marked with genuine concern. "We could speak to the doctor."

"It's all right. I suppose under the circumstances it'd be strange if I didn't have some trouble sleeping."

Faulk nodded. "You have a point."

The solicitude disappeared, immediately replaced by the hardened lines of bitterness she'd noticed etched permanently into his face. She understood their presence better now. He had lived the kind of life she could never understand. Seen things she'd only read about in history books. And, even then, she'd sat cringing at the pictures the horrid tales wove in her mind. What must it have been like to live through such an experience when you were still very young?

She wished there was some way she could help him, which was why she'd waited up for him. But now she realized that it had been a foolish notion. She had no idea what this man needed. As usual, her curiosity and impulsiveness had gotten the better of her. Only now did she realize the impact of what she'd almost done.

Whatever Captain Faulk's troubles were, she

didn't have the answers. God, she couldn't even solve her own problems. Besides, she reminded herself, she meant to leave here just as soon as possible. There was no reason for her to become involved in this man's life.

Suddenly Libby felt she had to get away before she became entangled any deeper. She stood and tugged at the wide sash of her robe. "Well, if you don't need anything else, I think I'll go on to bed now. Good night, Captain."

She reached for the door. He called her name. Libby stopped, her hand frozen in midair.

He'd never called her Libby before. He'd always treated her with the utmost respect and courtesy. Hearing her name on his lips made her heart flutter, then race.

Slowly she turned back. Several emotions played across his face—curiosity, doubt, interest. The last slipped into what might have been desire, but he quickly covered it.

"You wanted something?"

Did I? she thought. Another kiss? More? Had her decision to talk to him tonight been a ruse to throw the two of them together, alone? If she'd wondered whether the sparks would still be flying, the gooseflesh on her arms assured her they were. She had to escape before she made an even greater error in judgment, and stayed.

"No, I just couldn't sleep and I thought perhaps we could talk. But I'm feeling tired now."

They stared at each other for another long moment. Finally he nodded his head, and she thought she heard him sigh.

"Good night, then," he whispered.

"Good night," she said. Her knees trembled as she fled up the stairs. In the silence of her room, she closed the door and leaned against it, breathing deeply.

What had almost happened? More importantly, what had she .wanted to happen? She imagined him calling her back into the shadows of the kitchen and into the hard strength of his arms. Would she have gone willingly? The answer resounded. Yes!

Pushing away from the door, she thrust the thought aside.

Love at first sight was not a concept she believed in. What had happened between them on the beach constituted instant attraction. But she knew that wasn't all that had her libido doing back flips. His honor, his devotion, his concern for his housekeeper, and the ease with which he accepted responsibility combined to give her a clear picture of the whole man. And the effect left her much the way she suspected someone felt who had been run over by a large moving vehicle.

She had to get a grip on herself. Wasn't it enough that she had to accept time travel without being bombarded with sexual energy from a man she feared had a lot of inner turmoil?

She simply didn't have the time or inclination to get involved with him. She knew nothing about his generation or their ways and, frankly, she didn't want to learn. She wanted to go home, the sooner the better, without leaving any emotional entanglements behind. Not with Caroline, and especially not with Faulk. Gorgeous hunk or not.

Faulk slapped his forehead with his palms and raked his fingers violently through his hair. Damn. Why now?

He'd never regretted his decision, not in all the years since he'd first imposed it on himself. Why now, with the Indians' reign over and the end of his quest so close at hand, did he have to feel this way? Why did she have to come into his life before he could close, once and for all, the book on that raw time?

Not that the timing mattered all that much. A month from now, a year, it wouldn't make a difference. He had nothing to offer a woman. Nothing external, and less than nothing inside. He'd been emotionally barren for too long to try and change now. And Libby Pfifer, whoever she was, deserved better than that.

Libby Pfifer was not your average young woman. She'd intrigued and mystified him since the first time she stumbled pell-mell into his arms. She'd defied him, stood up to him, taunted him. Her size made her courage all the more admirable. He could have crushed her with his bare hands, but all he really wanted to do was crush her in his embrace.

He took a gulp of the coffee she'd poured him and grimaced. Stone cold. Like his heart, his soul. He'd been dead in all the ways that mattered for a long time. Why did he have to come alive now? Why with her?

As Libby entered the kitchen the next morning, Caroline looked up from the stove. She held out a cup of thick black coffee, remembering how Libby liked it, and smiled a greeting.

"Where's the Captain?" Libby couldn't help asking, even though it would only get her a raised eyebrow from the housekeeper. She wasn't disappointed.

"Done gone," Caro told her, plopping a saucer of fried bread on the table. They'd already established a routine and Libby wondered again how wise it was to let herself get attached to these people.

They nibbled toast and drank their coffee in silence as Libby tried to figure a way around the emotional entanglements she felt encompassing her.

After cleanup, Libby considered ways of keeping busy so her thoughts couldn't dwell on Faulk, but nothing immediately came to mind. Between them, she and Caroline had spit-and-polished the whole house. The yard and the carriage house were neatly kept by a young soldier from the post. Her heavy sigh drew Caro's attention. "I thought I'd let you take Miz Boudreax's basket over to her this mornin'," the housekeeper said, nodding toward the large wicker hamper on the floor. Caroline took the basket over every other day, and Libby had wondered what it contained.

"I told her about you the other mornin', and she'd like to meet you. Miz Boudreax likes meetin' folks, and she's about your age, so you two ought to get along fine. Besides, she needs the company and I was goin' visiting elsewhere, so it'll give you something to fill the mornin'."

A hint of something resembling apprehension lit in Caroline's eyes before she looked away. Libby knew from what Faulk had told her that Caroline was seeing the doctor regularly. She wondered if the housekeeper had a medical appointment scheduled that she didn't want Libby to know about. If so, did Faulk know about it? Should she mention it to him?

Caro looked back at her expectantly, and Libby stammered, "I'd be happy to."

"Miz Boudreax, she's a beauty. One of the French from up Canada way. And she's the sweetest thing you'd ever want to know most of the time." Caro linked her hands together on the table in front of her, and Libby knew she was uncomfortable relaying what she considered gossip. But at the same time, she felt

Libby needed the information.

"She's not healthy. Real frail, you know. Suffers god-awful headaches that no one can do anythin' about. Most days she spends in her room, curtains drawn. You'll have to go in without knocking 'cause she won't hear you otherwise. It's the first door on the right when you get upstairs. There's some food I fixed up for Miz Boudreax's lunch and a set of pillow cases. Miz Boudreax embroiders on 'em for me when she's feeling up to it, to repay me for helping her. She does the finest needlework I've ever laid eyes on."

"I look forward to meeting her," Libby said, pretending she wasn't madly curious about the woman. Caro clapped her palms on the table's surface and pushed herself up. A gray pallor suddenly crossed her face, and tiny beads of sweat popped out on her upper lip. Libby nearly jumped to her feet, but then the color flooded back into Caroline's cheeks and she smiled hesitantly.

"I reckon I'll go on and get my visitin' done. I'll be back before lunch and you can tell me how your mornin' went."

Libby struggled to remain in her seat until Caroline left the room. Just how bad was Caroline's heart condition? My God, the woman might be in danger of a massive heart attack. If so, she shouldn't be doing any of the work around the house. Libby decided she'd keep her eye on Caro, and from now on she'd do all the heavy work, including the visits to their neighbor, Captain Boudreax's ailing wife.

The humidity outside nearly stole her breath away when she stepped onto the back porch. Even after all the years she'd lived in the area, it never failed to amaze her how humid it could be along the coast. The brisk spring breeze blowing in off the Gulf barely eased the discomfort.

The basket wasn't heavy, but perspiration coated her face by the time she reached the Boudreax house. Feeling intrusive, she opened the door and let herself in. The tidy house surprised her until she realized that the Captain's wife must have someone come in and clean up for her. Surely she, an invalid, didn't do the work herself.

The stairs were padded with a tapestried runner to muffle footsteps, and the shades and drapes made the interior of the house dark and cool. She touched the wall as she balanced the basket on her hip, and the plaster chilled her fingertips. The shadows and silence were almost creepy in the big old place. Certainly it lacked the bright cheeriness of Faulk's home.

Or maybe it was the absence of Faulk himself she felt. She suspected that the man influenced his surroundings so much that you felt his presence even when he wasn't there. One of the reasons she couldn't stop thinking about him was that his essence permeated every room in his house.

"Mrs. Boudreax?" she called softly as she reached the top of the stairs. "It's Libby Pfifer, from next door."

A slightly muffled noise came from the bedroom Caro had specified as the right one, so Libby proceeded, hoping the sound she'd heard had been an acknowledgment. She didn't want to frighten the woman.

With the basket propped under one arm, she eased the door open a crack.

"Come in," a voice called softly.

Libby pushed the door open the rest of the way and peeked around the edge. Her eyes adjusted to the dark interior of the room, and she followed the wall past a large wardrobe, an elaborate chaise covered in some sort of shiny brocade fabric, and a dressing table littered with bottles and vials.

"Mrs. Boudreax, I'm Libby Pfifer. Caroline sent me over with your things."

"Yes, Miss Pfifer, do come in," the disembodied voice invited her.

Libby's gaze quickly followed the voice across the large room to a huge four-poster in the opposite corner. Her eyes found the lump under the covers, traveled up to the head of the bed, and widened in surprise.

Chapter Nine

The woman was beautiful all right, Libby thought. Other than her pale complexion, however, she didn't look as sickly as Libby had expected her to. Stepping lightly across the floor, she squinted to see better.

Waves of black hair flowed over creamy shoulders and framed a face as white and smooth as a porcelain doll's. Huge amethyst eyes were circled with long, thick dark lashes.

"Come in, come in," the softly accented voice urged her. She sounded slightly French, her tones clear and bell-like. "I was so happy when Caroline told me to expect you. I receive so few callers."

Despite the situation and her supine position in the bed, one might have thought she was entertaining by the way she addressed Libby. Libby set the basket down by the bed and eased closer.

"How do you do, Mrs. Boudreax," she said and extended her hand. The woman took it and smiled.

"You can call me Pilar, please. I tell Caroline to call me that, too, but"—she waved her hand—"she is strange."

"Hello, Pilar. I'm Libby."

"I wish I could see you better, Libby, but I am not having a good day." She looked toward the curtained window, and a soft frown marked her pale forehead.

Libby took another careful step, wishing for more light in the room. But she knew all about migraines. Her brother had suffered them for years and he'd always insisted on darkness, coolness, and quiet. She lowered her voice even more.

"Caro sent you some lunch. Should I put it downstairs?"

"No, just set the basket here by the bed. Christopher will be home today at noon, and he'll know what to do with it."

"Is there anything else you need? Can I get you something?" Libby felt slightly awkward as she fidgeted where she stood.

Pilar Boudreax looked suddenly lonely and sad. "Company is what I crave most. Even when the headaches are at their worst, they cannot

143

compete with the loneliness."

Libby's discomfort fled. Loneliness she understood. She went to the corner and pulled a heavy chair over to the bed.

"I'd be happy to stay a while. If you're sure I won't bother you."

"Oh, not at all. It's good to meet someone on the post who is close to my own age. John and Christopher are the youngest officers here, so most of the wives are older, or widowed, or single women like Caro who are working here. Everyone is usually too busy to visit often, except Caro. She comes to see me almost every day."

"You know, my brother, Gene, used to get terrible headaches and he always wanted to be alone." Libby laughed and settled closer to the bed. "Of course, he considered me his tagalong little sister, so that was the case most of the time where I was concerned. Do you have brothers or sisters?"

"Eleven," Pilar said, a small smile tipping the full red lips.

"Eleven! Goodness, no wonder you're lonely. You probably never had a moment to yourself when you were growing up."

"No, I never did. But it was really wonderful having so many brothers and sisters."

"How many of each?"

"Nine sisters and two brothers."

"Nine sisters!" Again Libby laughed, careful

to keep her voice low. "Well, I always wanted a sister. But nine. . . ."

The morning flew by. She and Pilar hit it off right away and Libby suspected that they shared a lot in common. Foremost, they both were living in environments alien to them. If Pilar did not understand everything Libby referred to, she made no comment. And if Libby found Pilar's references to Canada and antiquated travel odd, it didn't hinder their budding relationship.

Libby loved hearing about Pilar's life before she married Christopher Boudreax and they moved south. In return, Libby told Pilar what it was like to be raised so near the Gulf with its beautiful emerald-green waters and the sugar-white sands. She carefully avoided any references to time or things that had not been invented in Pilar's lifetime. Since Libby's first love had always been nature, that task proved easier than she'd first thought.

Pilar told of her large family and how she'd never lived in a house with fewer than twelve people. Libby could understand why the woman's isolation made life on the post exceptionally hard for her.

Pilar's voice began to fade; she'd tired herself out. With the promise that she'd return the next day, Libby reluctantly took her leave.

When Libby arrived back at Captain Faulk's house, Caroline still hadn't returned, so she decided to take a walk down to the water. The breeze had picked up, and it blew her tangled crop of hair wildly. She reached into her pocket for a handkerchief, took it by two corners, and twirled it into a rope. Then she wrapped it around her hair and fashioned it into a scarf.

She still wore her boots, so the sand didn't bother her, and she tromped out to the edge of the water. With the weight of her skirt and the long sleeves on her blouse, the slight breeze helped. But she knew she'd never adjust to the styles. She didn't belong here. And not just because the clothing bothered her. Everything about the past felt foreign to her.

She kept her sanity by assuring herself that all this was only temporary and soon she'd be home. She'd go back to her job, maybe call her brother and mother, or even go visit them, and her time here would begin to seem like a dream. Until then, it didn't make sense to get involved with any of the people she met.

But Libby's gregarious nature didn't lend itself to reclusiveness. She'd already grown close to Caroline; she worried about her health and wondered about the mysterious past she seemed to be hiding. She and Pilar had quickly become friends, and she'd already decided to try to help her with the headaches if she could. And Faulk . . .

Oh, yes, Faulk. Well, Libby knew how she felt about Faulk. Just being near him made her feel sixteen again. All breathy and excited and ready to fly in the face of adventure. He made her heart pound and her palms sweat and she dreamed of throwing caution to the wind and setting her emotions free. The only difference was that she had more experience than a sixteen-year-old and she knew what she wanted with Faulk. She wanted a very grown-up relationship, with all the passion and fervor he made her feel.

She strolled along the beach, her sane side debating with her wild side. To get involved with Faulk would be a big mistake. Huge, in fact. They only had a few weeks together before she returned, and she couldn't very well tell him where she would be returning to. And that was assuming he even wanted a relationship with her. He hadn't said a word that could be taken as forward since the night on the beach. He hadn't made a move even slightly resembling a pass. And yet, Libby knew he felt the same things she did. She'd seen him watching her, his eyes soft. She'd noticed the tremor that shook him when they touched accidentally or brushed too closely in the hall. His austere manner couldn't hide the attraction they shared.

Whispered voices reached her, and Libby paused. A large dune stood between her and the row of officers' houses farther up the hill. She walked closer and could make out a small horseshoe-shaped cavity in the side of the dune. She inched nearer, her curiosity getting the better of her as usual. As she peered around the sand enclosure, she flushed with embarrassment. Lovers! A giggle threatened to escape and she turned away, intending to make a hasty exit. But the woman's hushed exclamation stunned her, and she froze.

"Again," the unknown woman whispered. "Oh, Boudreax, I can't . . . I don't . . ."

"Easy, *chere*," her ardent companion soothed.

Libby choked down revulsion and looked back at the couple once more. God, it was the man in the picture beside Pilar's bed. Christopher Boudreax! Bile rushed up in a hot wave to replace the giggle Libby had suppressed only a moment ago. The man had the woman's skirt clutched in one hand as his other hand disappeared beneath the crumpled folds. The woman's plain face twisted in a grimace as she swayed against his questing fingers. When the Captain's companion fumbled for the buttons on his trousers, Libby turned away from the scene in disgust. Darting across the sand to the shore, she clutched her side, fearing she might throw up.

She couldn't quite believe what she'd seen, and she glanced back toward the dune and then up at the house directly above where she stood.

Another wave of loathing swept over her.

How could he carry on like that with a drab, dirty-looking woman when his beautiful wife waited for him not twenty yards from where he stood? Her gaze darted to the house once more and she gasped. Pilar's bedroom window faced the shore, and Libby was certain she'd just seen the curtain move!

When she reached Faulk's house, she was panting breathlessly. She pressed her side, her hands gripping the length of her skirt to keep it out from under her flying feet. The hand-kerchief had flown loose somewhere along the way, but she hadn't stopped to pick it up.

As Libby entered the kitchen, Caroline looked up with a start. Seeing Libby's flushed face and wide eyes, she rushed to her.

"What is it, girl? What's happened?"

"Is the Captain here?" she asked, struggling to catch her breath.

Caroline nodded. "He came in a few minutes ago for lunch. Where have you been?"

"I went for a walk," Libby said, already heading out of the kitchen and up the stairs toward Faulk's room.

The door was closed and Libby pounded on it. Faulk's muffled voice called out, and she turned the knob and barreled into the room.

"I need to speak with you," she said, ignoring the startled look on his face. She vaguely noticed the damp sheen on his face and the

Marti Jones

towel in his hands, but her attention caught immediately on the way he was dressed. He'd removed his jacket, and his shirtsleeves were rolled to the elbow. The buttons down the front were undone, revealing a wide expanse of muscular chest, deeply tanned and covered with whorls of golden hair. A trickle of water ran slowly over one pectoral muscle, and her eyes followed it down to the center of his stomach where it caught on the waistband of his trousers.

Libby gulped and met his narrowed gaze.

"I said just a minute. If you had waited . . ."

"I—I'm sorry," she lied. She wasn't a bit sorry. She wouldn't have missed seeing him like this for the world. She swallowed hard and tried to remember what had sent her racing recklessly into his bedroom in the first place. "I need to talk to you."

"If you'll give me a minute, I'll join you downstairs."

Libby knew she'd made an error. He seemed composed, standing there rolling his sleeves down casually. But she saw his eyes darken as they briefly lit on the big bed centered in the room.

"I would rather Caroline not know about this," she said, taking another step forward. "It's a very personal matter."

His eyebrow shot up, whether because of her statement or her bold move she didn't know.

150

Then he nodded and shrugged, as if to say it was her choice.

Libby took another step and pushed the door partly closed, so that it gave them a measure of privacy.

"I met Pilar Boudreax this morning."

Faulk didn't reply, and after a moment, Libby knew he was waiting for her to make her point.

"She's a very nice lady. I liked her a lot."

He nodded and finished buttoning his sleeves into place. As she searched her mind for the right words to tell him what she needed to say, he began fastening his shirt across his chest.

"Anyway, I went for a walk down by the shore afterward and while I was there I saw . . . that is, I came upon . . ."

"Yes?" he said, retrieving his jacket from the back of the chair where it hung and sliding his arms into it.

"I saw Pilar's husband in the dunes with another woman. She was kind of grubby, with dirty blond hair, and she wore a brown dress."

"I know who you mean."

His words stopped her. Libby couldn't help wondering how Faulk knew the woman. In what sense of the word did he *know* her?

Her surprise must have shown. "She works in the laundry," he said. "Her name is Rose." His lips twitched, and he rubbed a finger over

151

them as though to hide it. "At least, that's what she says."

"You mean she's a . . ."

"She takes care of the men's laundry. As far as the Army is concerned, that's all she does."

"Well, that isn't what she was doing in the dunes this afternoon," Libby said heatedly, her mind once more able to focus on her anger now that Faulk was fully clothed.

"I don't see how that is any of my concern—or yours either, I might add." He stood, stiff and rigid, but Libby could see him eyeing the door as though he would have liked to escape.

Libby turned away, her cheeks burning. What a fool she'd been! Why had she come to Faulk? Had she thought his erstwhile code of honor somehow made him more chivalrous? Or had she thought he could help this time because she'd come to depend on him since her arrival? No matter; what was done was done. There was no sense backing down now.

"Can't you at least speak to the man? You're an officer—just tell him to knock it off or something. Remind him he's got a great wife and she needs him now, especially with those headaches she gets."

"Look, Libby," Faulk said, taking her arm and turning her toward the door. "I don't like what the man's doing any more than you do, but I can't tell him to stop. He's a Captain, the same rank as I am. I'm not his commanding officer, and I can tell you Langdon doesn't want to be bothered by his officers' private lives."

"But it's wrong. Besides, I think Pilar can see him from her window. I saw the curtains move in her room, and the angle would have given her a clear view of the two of them."

She stepped into the hall with him and he closed the door behind them. Libby was aware of the feel of his hand on her arm and the tension in his touch. She looked up. His cinnamon eyes had turned dark, and it occured to her that he'd called her by her first name again. His gaze locked on her mouth, and she knew he was thinking of kissing her. She wanted him to, she even leaned in a little closer, but he blinked, his eyes met hers, and the moment slipped away.

He'd fought their attraction since that first kiss, even avoiding her at times. Libby understood and agreed that his approach was best, all things considered. However, at times like these when they were alone, she wished they could throw their doubts into the wind and relive the feelings they'd shared on the beach.

His hands settled gently on her shoulders. "Look, I can warn him to keep his liaisons confined to Rose's cottage if that will make you feel better. And I can hint that I'll speak to Langdon if he doesn't, but that's about all I can do," Faulk told her frankly.

Libby nodded mutely, wanting to hold on

to the intimate moment a bit longer. "Well, that's something anyway. Thank you," she said, clearing her throat of the desire lodged there. "I really appreciate it."

"Let's go down and enjoy the lunch Caro's prepared, shall we?"

"Oh," Libby cried, suddenly remembering that she'd wanted to discuss Caro's health with him, too. "I wanted to talk to you about Caroline."

Instantly Faulk's face tensed, the familiar lines of worry returning to crease his features. "Has something happened?"

"Yes, she had some kind of a spell at the table this morning. She turned gray and broke out in a sweat. And she gave me a story about going visiting, but I think she really had an appointment with the doctor today."

"Yes," he said, glancing toward the stairs and the kitchen beyond. "I knew about the visit to the doctor. Stein keeps me informed. But I'm sure she didn't tell him about the episode this morning. He didn't mention it to me, in any case. I'll be sure to speak with him about it as soon as possible."

"I thought I'd take over going to Pilar's house and some of Caroline's other chores. As much as she'll let me, that is."

Faulk nodded in understanding. "She won't allow it, you know. Not if she's aware of what you're doing. That is one stubborn woman."

"I'll try to be subtle, but what about when I'm gone? What will you do then?"

He looked uncomfortable at the mention of her leaving, and Libby felt equally unsettled. She was glad he hadn't kissed her in the bedroom. It would only complicate matters if they became involved. And she didn't want anything standing in the way of her return to the island and her own time.

"I'll have to insist that she allow me to hire help. It will hurt her pride, but it might just save her life."

"Maybe she should retire," Libby said, a picture of Caroline's sickly pallor returning to haunt her.

Faulk smiled ruefully and shook his head. "People like Caroline don't retire. They live to work, and they work until they die."

Libby didn't want to think of Caroline working herself into a heart attack and dying. The fact that these people were all dead in her time, and had been for a hundred years, still bothered her. Seeing them every day, talking, smiling, living, she could almost pretend they would go on that way after she left them.

The heat from Faulk's hand penetrated her sleeve, and she reached out her fingers to touch his arm. His skin was warm beneath her hand, and she felt the muscles in his forearm bunch.

She couldn't imagine him any way except like this, healthy and strong and virile. She didn't want to think of him growing old, alone and probably still bitter over the Apache.

But what could she do? She belonged in the twentieth century and he belonged here. If she hadn't gotten caught in that time warp, she'd never even have heard of him.

Her gaze met his, and her heart lurched. Overwhelming sadness consumed her, and she longed to throw herself against that massive chest she'd glimpsed earlier.

Her mind cried out with the question never far from her thoughts. *How did she get here in the first place? And why had she come?*

Chapter Ten

Libby hesitated a moment, then set off across the yard. Detachment just wasn't a word she understood. Pilar, Caroline, maybe even Faulk needed her. And since she'd found herself stuck here for the time being, she might as well make herself useful.

After a great deal of thought, she decided to start with Pilar. Armed with another basket, this one filled with more than food and pillowcases, she put her plan into action.

Caro had decided to polish the silver, a relatively sedate chore, so Libby felt safe leaving her alone for the afternoon. What she had in mind for Pilar might take a while.

The heat swept across the Gulf once more, and a trickle of sweat ran down her spine.

She'd become accustomed to maneuvering the cumbersome skirt, but with the temperature in the eighties, she longed for a pair of jogging shorts and a tank top.

Knowing Pilar's house would be cooler, she felt grateful for that at least. She had her work cut out for her, and the brief respite from the heat of the day was welcome.

Her conversation with Faulk had not gone as well as she'd liked, but she had to admit he was right. There wasn't anything he could do about Captain Boudreax's infidelity. For some reason she'd gone to him without even thinking through her request. She'd decided to ponder the Freudian implications of that later. First, she had to help Pilar get back on her feet so she could deal with her wayward husband in her own way.

Inside the house, she took a moment to let her eyes adjust to the darkness after being exposed to the brilliant sunshine outside. She made her way through the kitchen and up the stairs, pausing outside the bedroom door.

"Pilar," she called softly, again afraid of frightening the woman by sneaking into her house unannounced.

"Come in, Libby," Pilar called.

Libby pushed open the door and entered. Pilar sat up in bed, her eyes focused on a circle of fabric held within the bounds of an embroidery hoop. The drapes, partially open to allow in a sliver of light, illuminated the white cloth.

"Well, you must be having a good day," Libby said, setting her basket aside for later.

"Better than most," Pilar admitted. "Alas, it won't last long, I fear. Already I feel the pressure." She touched her cheek lightly.

Pilar's words confirmed what Libby had suspected, and she felt like cheering. "Your headaches start there, in your cheeks?"

"Or behind my eyes," Pilar told her.

"Pilar." Libby leaned close. "What would you say if I told you I thought I could help you with your headaches?"

"You are sweet to want to help, Libby, but it is hopeless. I've seen doctors, and they all say I must live with the pain."

"I don't agree with that, Pilar. My brother had terrible headaches, much like yours. And he isn't suffering anymore."

Pilar set aside the embroidery, her attention on the words Libby spoke.

"I told you about Gene. He's in the Navy now. But when we were younger, he suffered from horrible migraines. All the doctors could do for him was prescribe drugs. He had to choose between being in pain or being doped up all the time. It was no choice for Gene. And so he kept searching for an answer."

Pilar's eyes were hungry with hope as she asked, "Did he find one?"

Libby grinned. "Yep, he sure did. And I

thought maybe, if you were willing to give it a go, we'd see if it would help you."

A huge sigh slipped past the red, pursed lips, and Pilar sank back against the pillow. "I don't think there is anything that can help me, Libby. But I appreciate that you care enough to want to try."

"I care enough. Do you?"

"If I thought it would work . . ."

"You'll never know unless you let me try. What have you got to lose?"

"The headaches will get worse if I don't follow the doctor's orders. It might take months to get them under control again."

"That is a possibility, and I know you're scared. But just maybe they'll be gone forever. It's worth the risk, don't you think?"

Libby waited, her breath suspended and her bottom lip caught between her teeth. She'd thought Pilar would jump at the chance to let her help. But she understood the woman's hesitation. She was asking a lot, and Pilar had no reason to trust her.

Finally Pilar smiled and Libby released her breath. "All right," she said. "Let's do it."

Libby made a fist, bent her elbow, and drew her arm down sharply in a triumphant gesture. "Yes," she cried.

Pilar blinked at the odd reaction, made a fist, and repeated Libby's actions. Together they laughed.

"First thing," Libby said, going to the table beside Pilar's bed and picking up a small brown bottle. "No more of this."

"But, Libby, that's . . ."

"It's laudanum, Pilar. And believe me when I tell you you don't need what's in there."

"But . . ."

"I know, honey, it dulls the pain. But it's a drug, Pilar. A major narcotic. And all it does is keep you doped up. It doesn't cure the head-ache."

"Don't throw it away," Pilar said, lowering her head as though ashamed of her demand.

"No, I wouldn't do that. If my ideas don't work, you might need it again." She bright-ened and smiled at Pilar. "But I don't think you will."

Pilar nodded, but continued to eye the corked bottle of medicine.

"First," Libby said, drawing her attention back to the matter at hand. "I thought about what you told me the other day. You came from Canada, right? And you never suffered headaches like this before you and Christopher moved to the South?"

"Yes, that's right."

"I think what's causing your headaches is the climate down here. It's different than any-where else, and we have all the things that cause sinus problems like ragweed and mold spores."

"What . . . mold . . . ?"

"I know, it sounds complicated. All I mean is that we have a lot of plants and stuff that irritate your sinuses." She traced circles around Pilar's cheekbones. "These things in here you breathe with. And we also have high humidity which, simplified, means thick air."

Pilar laughed. "Thick air?"

"I know it sounds funny, but didn't you feel the difference when you first moved here? The air is heavy with moisture."

Pilar's eyes brightened. "Yes, I do remember. The air bothered me from the first moment we arrived."

"You're not alone there. A lot of people feel the same way. My mother wrote me from New Mexico after she first moved there. She said the temperature was several degrees hotter there, but she felt better. It's because the air is dry and easier to breathe."

"So what do we do to dry the air?"

Libby chuckled. "Unfortunately there isn't any way to dry the air. Not when you live so close to the water."

"So what *do* we do?"

"Well, it wasn't easy, but Caroline and I managed to find most of what I need. There are several herbal remedies that you can use to open the sinuses and make breathing easier. That releases the pressure, and the headache goes away. Most of the time." She didn't add that a cold tablet would come in handy, since that would convince Pilar she'd lost her mind.

"Herbs? I don't know, Libby."

"Let's give it a try, okay? I'll go down and brew up the first one. We'll try them one at a time until something helps."

After nearly an hour of sipping everything from ginger and turmeric to a cayenne pepper mixture, the one that finally did the trick was a form of horseradish root. Pilar took a sip, gasped, and started to sneeze. But within seconds, her sinuses began to drain, and she laughed as she dabbed at her nose.

"Now," Libby said, setting aside the cooling brew. "You're going to have to trust me on this next part, Pilar. It's going to seem kind of— well, bizarre—but I promise you it will help."

"More bizarre than drinking that?" she asked, still dabbing her nose.

"Yes."

"Well, go ahead. So far you've done all right."

"Can you lie down on the floor?"

"On the—" She bit off the rest of the exclamation and smiled. "The floor it is."

She swept the covers aside and took a few steps into the middle of a huge Aubusson rug. "Here?"

Libby nodded. When Pilar had stretched out on the rug, Libby went to her head and sat. "Don't panic. I'm not going to hurt you. I used to do this to my brother all the time." She took

Pilar's head in her hands and gently turned her neck from side to side.

"Relax," she coaxed. "I told you my brother went to doctor after doctor. Well, he finally got help from a chiropractor. That's a doctor who practices manipulation of the spine to cure certain ailments. Normally only a chiropractor would do this, but without the yellow pages I don't have the slightest idea where to find one."

"What are the yell—"

Without warning Libby snapped Pilar's head to one side. A series of pops and alarming cracks erupted. Pilar cried out.

"I didn't hurt you, did I?" Libby asked, massaging her fingers over Pilar's slender neck.

Pilar looked frightened and confused for a moment, then her face relaxed into a smile. "No, you didn't hurt me at all. But how did you do that?"

"I watched the chiropractor adjust my brother all the time. One time when we went camping, Gene got a headache. He was in so much pain that he asked me to try and duplicate what I'd seen the doctor do. I was terrified I'd hurt him, but I didn't. Once you do it, you can feel the right positions. After that, I got pretty good at doing this for Gene. Are you ready for the other side?"

Apprehension tightened Pilar's face, and she cringed. "Maybe in a minute?"

Libby laughed. "Take two. I need you relaxed."

After a moment Pilar nodded. "All right. I'm ready."

Libby gently moved Pilar's head from side to side and then repeated the procedure. Again Pilar cried out, but Libby knew the response was from surprise this time, not pain.

They stayed on the floor, Pilar lying supine, Libby massaging the cords in her neck for several minutes. Finally Pilar's eyes popped open.

"Oh, Libby, I don't believe it." She spun around to a sitting position facing Libby. "It's gone."

Libby laughed. "I know. It works like magic, doesn't it?"

"It's not . . . ?" Pilar's face fell.

"Magic? No, just good sense."

Pilar turned her head from side to side, forward and then back. She touched her cheeks experimentally and pushed gently on her eyes. "I can't believe it. Oh, Libby, it's a miracle."

Libby smiled and took Pilar's hand, helping her stand. "Lie down for a minute while I get you a cool cloth."

"But I don't want to lie down. I've been doing nothing but lying in that bed for months. I want to go out, see things, talk to people."

"In time," Libby told her chuckling. "You'll do it all in time. But not all your first day."

Pilar accepted the cool cloth Libby pressed

against her neck and reclined against her pillows, but she refused to rest. She talked and laughed, and they even planned an outing for the next day.

"We could go down to the shore and have a picnic, couldn't we?" she asked. Without waiting for an answer, she rushed on. "Oh, there is a lovely spot by the lighthouse I've been wanting to visit."

"Providing you don't overdo," Libby warned her.

"Oh, I won't. I promise. But there are so many things I want to do that I haven't been able to for a long time. Can I cook?" Pilar asked her anxiously.

"Cook?"

"Yes, I would like to make dinner. I used to love to cook, and I've really missed it."

"Are you planning something special for Christopher?" Libby couldn't help asking, a frown quickly replacing her smile.

Pilar glanced away and shook her head. "Christopher has late watch at the Fort tonight. He won't be home until morning. I thought—I hoped maybe you'd join me."

Libby's smile rushed back. "I'd love to."

She left Pilar happily dressing in a bright pink day dress of soft voile. The woman hummed a cheerful tune as Libby collected her things and started down the hall.

Next door, she set the basket in the corner of

the kitchen and called out Caroline's name.

"In here," the housekeeper called back. Libby went into the dining room and tipped her head to see Caro's face past the pile of shining silver. Everything from teapots to serving trays big enough for a turkey littered the table which was carefully covered with an old cloth.

"My goodness, you have been busy."

"How did it go with Miz Boudreax?" she asked, pushing away the punch bowl cups she'd been working on. "Did your remedies work?"

Libby grinned. "Like magic," she said, her voice brimming with the pride and excitement she still felt. "At this moment Pilar is cooking dinner for us. How about that?"

"That's wonderful!"

"You don't mind if I go over there, do you?"

"Not at all. Captain sent word he wouldn't be home for dinner again. I thought I'd just fix a bite and get on with some mending I've been puttin' off."

Good, Libby thought. Nothing too strenuous there. "Well, I'll go on back, then. See you later."

"Bye now."

As she made her way back across the stretch of rocky yard between the two houses, Libby thought about what Caro had told her. The Captain wouldn't be home for dinner. Again.

Since the scene in his bedroom, he'd increased his efforts to avoid her, apparently deciding that close contact might be dangerous. Libby didn't mind, really. She knew the feelings he evoked in her could only lead to disaster for them both.

She anticipated the evening with her new friend, finding that she liked spending time with Pilar Boudreax. But she had to admit she'd miss seeing John.

Everything about the man brought on an orgy of awareness. She didn't know how she was going to manage to keep her hands off him for the next few weeks.

It was late by the time Libby and Pilar said good night. Pilar had been confined for so long, she'd been about to burst with the need to talk to another human being. She never mentioned Christopher's unfaithfulness, but Libby could tell things were strained between the two. Whether Pilar had seen her husband from her window, Libby couldn't be sure. She would never ask.

Pilar walked her to the door and spontaneously hugged her. Libby didn't know what to say. Success had always been her drug of choice. She was so high on it by the time she reached the kitchen door of Faulk's house that she floated three feet off the ground.

As she entered the kitchen, her eyes widened and she froze. John stood by the stove, a mug in his hand and the smell of fresh-brewed coffee permeating the night air.

"What's this?" Libby asked, a shiver of desire coursing through her. His hair was loose, the customary ponytail gone. Barefoot, and with his shirtsleeves rolled to the elbow, he looked so damned good that she found it suddenly hard to swallow.

With a grin that nearly stopped her heart in its tracks, he held up the mug. "Coffee?" he asked, mimicking her words the night she'd waited up for him.

Libby made an effort to appear calm, although she felt far from it. She closed the door behind her and forced a casual smile. "Thanks, I could use it."

He reached out and their hands touched. He closed his fingers over hers and held her hand in place for a long minute before letting go.

"You didn't have to wait up for me," she said, when she could speak clearly.

"I know."

She sipped her coffee and tried not to grimace. He might be gorgeous, but his coffee left something to be desired.

"So, why did you?"

He shrugged as though his answer weren't the most important thing she'd ever waited to hear.

"Caro told me what you did for Pilar Boudreax."

169

She nodded.

"I just wanted to tell you I thought it was very kind of you. First Caro, now Pilar. Do you make it a habit to help everyone you come in contact with?"

Libby set the coffee aside, an excuse to break eye contact with John. "If I can."

She turned back and found him standing right behind her. She sucked in a deep, settling breath.

"Why? Do you need my help?" she asked, thinking he was leading up to something and wanting to get it out in the open.

"Very much," he admitted, letting his fingers drift up the side of her arm. She followed his movements with her eyes, and the sight of his tanned hand against her pale blouse stirred her.

"What can I do?"

One eyebrow rose slowly and he grinned at her. She blushed.

"You can start," he said, his other hand coming up to clasp her arm, "by telling me what the devil is happening between us."

"What—what do you mean?"

He cocked his head to one side. "I think you know what I mean. Ever since you first came into my arms at Pickens, I've been wanting to hold you. Ever since you first opened your beautiful mouth, I can think of nothing but kissing you. I gave in once to the temptation

170

and nearly died from the pleasure. Tell me now if you didn't feel the same."

"I—I did," she confessed, secretly thrilled to hear him say he was as affected by the attraction between them as she had been.

"I thought you had." His eyes narrowed and he shook his head, a wry grin tipping his lips. "I tried to tell myself you were nothing but trouble. I stayed away from you until the Colonel got tired of seeing me and ordered me home." He shrugged. "So here I am. Tell me, what are we going to do?"

"What do you want to do?" she hedged, still unable to admit out loud the wild fantasies she'd had about the two of them.

"This is mad. We barely know one another. You could be married," he said, only half-teasing.

"I'm not," she told him, wishing she could drop the amnesia bit and tell him the whole truth.

Again an eyebrow rose. "You've remembered something?"

"No, not the way you mean. But I know if I were married, I'd feel it somehow."

"Engaged then?"

She shook her head. "I'm not involved with anyone. Don't ask me to explain, but I assure you there's no one else."

"There's still the problem of your memory. What if you feel differently about me, about

171

us, when you remember your other life?"

"I won't."

"You're sure? How can you be?"

"Because I've never felt this way before, with anyone. I know I wouldn't have forgotten it if I had."

Her confidence must have convinced him. He smiled, sending a warm vibration all the way to her toes.

"Well, that covers all my questions. What about you?"

"I only have one," she said.

He looked apprehensive for a moment and then he stepped closer. The warmth from his chest quickly seeped through her thin blouse, and she tipped her head to look into his half-closed eyes.

"What's your question?" he asked.

Libby touched her lips with her tongue and smiled at John. "When," she said, stepping fully into his arms, "are you going to kiss me again?"

Chapter Eleven

His lips claimed hers, their kiss immediately deep and full of need. She opened to him and heard, with satisfaction, his groan of longing. All the new sensations washed over Libby: the feel of his mouth, the smell of his skin, the taste of coffee on his tongue. She clutched his back and tried to deepen the kiss even more.

She'd have been happy to go on kissing him until she collapsed from lack of oxygen. But too soon, John drew back. The fire in his cinnamon-colored eyes only fueled her passion more.

"Libby. . . ."

His lips trailed over her jaw to her neck, and he bent low over her throat, keeping their bodies pressed tightly together.

Libby ached to take his hand and lead him

173

upstairs to her room, but she felt his reluctant withdrawal. Loss and disappointment filled her.

"Libby, I didn't mean for this to happen, I swear it." He lifted his head and pressed his forehead against hers. "I told myself I wanted only to talk to you for a while. To try to get to know you better. But somehow I feel as if I know you better than I've ever known anyone in my life."

"Yes," she whispered, her fingertips trailing lightly down his back to his waist. She felt the warmth of his skin and the solid strength of him beneath his shirt.

"My life is complicated right now. I can't promise you anything," he said, regret lacing every word.

Libby heard the pain and frustration in his voice and she did what she'd wanted to do since Caroline told her about his family. She tucked her head into his chest and cuddled him close.

"I don't need promises, John. God knows I can't offer any."

He clutched her to him, almost desperately, then set her away. "Where does that leave us?"

Libby wanted to tell him that they could enjoy this incredible magic between them for whatever time they had together. But she remembered where she was and decided she'd better not. She wasn't too sure about these things, but she suspected women from his time didn't offer themselves up lightly.

His hands gripped her shoulders briefly before he turned away. "I wish . . ."

He stopped and Libby saw the struggle on his face as he battled inner demons. "What? What do you wish?" she asked softly.

He looked back at her and grinned, and the hot rush of desire flamed to life. Running his hands through his hair, he chuckled.

"I can't tell you what I really wish," he said, lifting his mug from the table and sipping the forgotten coffee. "But sometimes"—the grin disappeared and the familiar tension slid back into place—"I wish I were someone else, anyone else."

How odd, Libby thought. She was certain he'd been about to admit he wanted her, no matter what. The way she wanted him, the way she wanted him to feel. But something had stopped him, turned him back into the austere soldier. What would make him say such a thing?

"I don't understand," she told him, following him across the kitchen to the cast-iron cookstove.

He smiled again, but Libby suspected that his light mood was feigned now.

"Never mind," he said, touching her fingers gently. He stared down at their clasped hands

175

for a moment, then released her abruptly. "You must be tired. Why don't you go on to bed?"

Why don't you come with me? she wanted to say. But his expression told her he needed time alone right now. Their encounter had disturbed him, and more than his chivalrous nature had him troubled.

She wanted to talk, to learn what ghosts from his past refused to give him peace. Caro had hinted at the reasons for his sadness and mood swings, but had refused to discuss the details. Reluctantly, Libby nodded.

"If you decide you want to talk . . ." She let the invitation trail off. He wouldn't come to her room. No matter how much he might want to.

"Good night, Libby."

Libby touched his arm lightly when she passed him. "Good night, John."

John had left for the post by the time Libby awoke the next morning. She missed seeing him at breakfast and remembered the coffee, and the kiss, they'd shared the night before. She couldn't help herself; she was falling hard for the Captain. And no matter how many times she told herself it was a mistake to get involved, she couldn't convince herself. She wanted to get involved with John, deeply involved.

"What did you say?" she asked Caroline. Her mind had wandered and she struggled to keep her attention on the conversation.

"Would you and Miz Boudreax like to have your lunch here after your outing this mornin'? I thought I'd whip up something fine."

Libby glanced up. "Oh, that would be nice. Pilar wants to visit you. She told me that was at the top of her list of things to do. But don't go to any trouble, Caro," she added quickly, thinking of Caroline's spell a few days ago.

"Ah, pshaw," the housekeeper muttered. "What trouble is lunch?"

Libby heard the irritation in Caro's voice and suspected that she'd upset her. "Well, I better get a move on. I told Pilar I'd be over early. We're going for a walk along the shore, down to the lighthouse and back."

"You give Miz Boudreax my greetings and be sure and tell her how glad I am she's up and about. You surely are somethin', Libby girl."

Libby smiled and finished off her coffee. It felt good to do something useful. It meant a lot to her to be able to help these people in some way. Almost as though her trip here weren't a complete waste.

She thought of John and shook her head. Traveling through time was a lot of things. Confusing, irritating, frightening. But since she'd met John, it could never be described as a waste of time.

Thoughts of the previous night's events lent a lightness to her step as she reached Pilar's back door. Out of habit, she twisted the knob and sailed in. She crossed through the kitchen in a rush, but stopped abruptly at the bottom of the staircase.

She heard voices. Angry voices.

Glancing up the stairs, she saw the door to Pilar's bedroom standing open. A woman's voice—Pilar's?—was raised in agitation. A man's deep tones answered.

"What did you expect me to think? I brought you here. You didn't want to come. You're always talking about your family and how they did this and that."

"I love my family. What is wrong with that? You act as though it's a crime to have loved ones."

"Not a crime Pilar, a burden. Your love for your family has always been a burden. One we couldn't get past. Or so I thought."

"You thought," she cried. "You thought? What about what I thought? Did you ever wonder what I thought when I saw you with that woman?"

Libby gasped and stepped back toward the kitchen, but Pilar and her husband were now shouting and she could hear the conversation clearly.

"You didn't know I saw you, Christopher? Or you didn't care?" Only silence answered her, and she quickly continued. "No, I think you intended for me to see. You wanted me to know what you were doing."

"No."

The strangled response startled Libby. Another long, brittle silence followed. Libby's cheeks burned with shame, but she stood rooted in place, not knowing what to do, as Pilar reclaimed her pride.

"Yes, you wanted me to know you had other women. Why, Christopher? Did you want me to find you out? Or were you punishing me for some reason? How could you bring me here and then treat me so cruelly? We were in love not so long ago. I was, at least."

Libby wanted to run from the house. She didn't want to hear Pilar and Christopher arguing. But she was afraid to leave Pilar alone with her husband. She had no idea what kind of man he was, or how he might react to being accused of infidelity.

Besides, if the couple heard her leave, Pilar would know who'd been in the house. She was, after all, expecting Libby.

"I thought *you* were punishing *me* for bringing you here, Pilar. You were never sick a day before we came here, and you never tried to hide how you felt about leaving your family. I thought . . ."

"You thought I was pretending to be sick? You thought I wanted to hurt you for bringing me with you? How could you, Christopher? I loved you. I would have gone anywhere with you. Yes, I missed my family, my home. But

179

you are my family now. My home is wherever you are."

"God, Pilar, I've made such a mess of things. When I came home and saw you this morning, just like you used to be, I thought my heart would burst. It was so good to have you back. Now I fear I've lost you for good."

"I just don't know, Christopher. I don't know anything anymore."

Her voice sounded weaker now, Libby noticed, concern making her step forward again.

"Is your head hurting again?" Christopher asked. "Perhaps we should finish this later. I'll get you the tea Libby left for you."

Libby tiptoed back into the kitchen and glanced around frantically. What could she do? How was she going to get away without being seen? Hearing footsteps on the stairs, she rushed to the back door and opened it, banging it shut with more force than necessary.

"Pilar," she called out, pretending she'd only just entered the house.

Christopher Boudreax reached the door to the kitchen just as Libby turned around. She pasted on a smile of greeting.

"Oh, hello," she said, trying to catch her breath.

"Hullo," he said, eyeing her warily.

"Pilar and I were planning an outing," she said, her gaze darting nervously away from his.

"Oh. I'll tell her you're here."

They both fell silent. The moment dragged on, and the room filled with nervous tension.

"How . . ."

"I . . ."

They both spoke at once and then immediately stopped.

"Go ahead," Christopher told her.

"I was just going to say that something has come up unexpectedly, and I really should postpone our plans until another day."

He nodded. "Well, I'll tell Pilar. I'm sure she'll be disappointed."

Libby saw him glance quickly over his shoulder toward the stairs. She suspected that he knew exactly what had come up. But she stood silently meeting his gaze.

"I wanted to thank you for what you did for Pilar," he said, his tone congenial. "She told you she's been to several doctors and none of them could help her."

Libby nodded.

"I see. I wonder, how did you know what to do?"

Libby cleared her throat and smoothed the cuffs of her blouse. "I—um, I told Pilar my brother had the same condition. That's how I knew what to do."

"Yes, but who diagnosed your brother's case? Certainly not a physician from around here. Pilar has been examined by all the local doctors. And yet, if what Pilar said about the climate being the culprit is true, your brother must have been living somewhere nearby."

An alarm sounded in Libby's head. Christopher Boudreax was suspicious of her! Obviously he'd heard about her and her supposed amnesia and he knew she wasn't telling the whole truth. Damn, she should have told Pilar not to repeat all she'd told her.

She searched frantically for a plausible explanation, but couldn't think of a single thing to say. She shrugged helplessly and was saved from having to make excuses by Pilar's timely entrance.

"Libby," she cried, her expression going from dour to surprised. Obviously she'd forgotten about the outing. Libby was glad she'd decided to postpone it.

Pilar passed Christopher in a swirl of soft cotton skirts. She hugged Libby and turned back to her husband. Immediately her smile disappeared, and a wounded frown turned down the red lips.

"I forgot that Libby and I had made plans for today," she said.

Christopher leaned against the doorframe and nodded, his eyes still pinned on Libby.

"Actually," Libby said. "I was just telling Captain Boudreax that something has come up. I think I really should put off our outing until another day."

"Oh, that's too bad. Nothing serious, I hope."

"No, just a few little things I need to take care of. I hope you're not too disappointed."

She watched the estranged couple exchange tense glances. Would Pilar rather not continue the heated discussion? Or would she want to get everything out in the open once and for all? Her pale face looked strained, but there was a determination in her eyes that Libby hadn't seen before.

Libby shifted nervously. She didn't know if she'd done them more harm than good with her interference.

"Maybe tomorrow, then," Pilar said, seeming to feel some reply was in order.

"Tomorrow," Libby confirmed, stepping backward toward the door. "Bye now."

She left the house, releasing a huge sigh. If the strain between Pilar and her husband wasn't bad enough, she'd almost been caught in a lie by the curious Captain. Why hadn't she thought someone would question her about what she'd done?

She'd have to be more careful. If John and Colonel Langdon thought she'd regained her memory, she knew they'd want to question her extensively. And there were still no answers she could give them. Not without sounding like a mental case.

The day was bright and cool and, thankfully, the humidity low. Libby decided to take the walk to the lighthouse after all. Despite all that had happened, she couldn't help feeling proud of her accomplishments with Pilar. No matter how things turned out with her marriage, at least the woman had her health back.

As Libby walked along, she reached up to run her fingers over the feathery moss draped on the trees. Her boots made soft crunching noises in the blanket of dry leaves covering the ground.

Her thoughts couldn't seem to leave Pilar, though, and she wondered how prevalent divorce was in this century. In Libby's time, Pilar's choices would be vast and relatively uncomplicated. But here, Libby just didn't know. Even if divorce was legal and acceptable, she didn't imagine it was too common. People married and stayed married. For better or worse.

As she came out of the brush into the clearing, the sun momentarily blinded her. She stopped to collect her thoughts and looked around. Amazingly, she had found the lighthouse by herself. Stunned, she stared up at it.

It looked just like it did in 1993!

The two–hundred-and-ten-foot, black-and-white brick structure which had been one hundred and seventy years old the last time she saw it, was now a mere sixty-four years old. Of course, it had recently been renovated in her time, as so many historical attractions had. But this lighthouse, the one she was standing in front of, had yet to suffer the ravages of time

and hurricanes which no face lift can completely obscure. To see it fully operational as well
came as quite a blow.

Up on the walkway, polishing the windows,
the caretaker saw her and waved his white towel in greeting. For a long moment she could
only stare. There hadn't been a caretaker at the
lighthouse since 1953. He waved again, and
finally she regained enough presence of mind
to wave back. She watched as he went back to
his work.

Libby shook her head and turned to stare out
at the still water. The bay was calm today, a
clear, crystal green. Not a ripple disturbed the
glassy surface.

She ambled toward a group of rocks clus-
tered nearby and sank down on one to let
the sun warm her cheeks. Closing her eyes,
her thoughts traveled the now familiar path
straight to John.

Complicated didn't begin to cover her feelings. She now understood his need to bring
the Apache to justice. She'd accepted his bitterness at their light punishment. She even recognized the pain that drove him, made him
seem cold and unapproachable. And there her
problem mounted. How could she ask John to
get involved with her and then leave him in a
few short weeks? The answer was simple. She
couldn't. She could not ask him to open doors
to her that he'd slammed shut years ago.

She rose and brushed off her skirt. Battling her troubled thoughts and dilemmas made the walk back seem shorter somehow. Before Libby realized it, she stood at the back of Faulk's house. She hoped that for once he wouldn't be joining them for lunch. She wasn't sure she could face him without giving her feelings away.

As she stepped up to the porch, she heard footsteps behind her. Turning, she saw Pilar crossing the yard.

"Hello," she called, waving.

"Hello." Pilar hurried the last few steps. "I was just bringing these back to Caroline," she said, holding out a handful of dishes.

Apparently the couple had finished their talk, or Pilar had decided they'd said enough for one day. Either way, Libby was glad to see her looking chipper now.

"How about staying for lunch?" she asked.

Pilar grinned. "I'd love it. If you don't think it will be any trouble."

"Not at all. Caro was fixing something when I left, and she always makes enough for the whole Army."

"Caroline?" she called, as they entered the kitchen.

She smelled seafood and went to the counter beside the dry sink. Some kind of shrimp dish waited to be served, along with crusty bread and fried tomatoes.

"I wonder where she is?" Libby said, bending to savor the aroma of the tomatoes.

Pilar had walked to the door leading to the dining room and Libby heard her gasp. Spinning around, she hurried to Pilar's side. Immediately her heart plunged to her stomach, and her knees threatened to fold beneath her.

On the dining room floor, amid a tray of broken glasses and spilled lemonade, lay Caroline's still body.

Chapter Twelve

"The doctor," Pilar cried. "You must get the doctor."

Libby stared down in horror at Caroline's blue lips and earlobes. She couldn't think. Fear controlled her movements and she stood for a second, paralyzed. Pilar knelt beside the housekeeper and began patting her wrist.

Libby whirled and ran for the door. She would have killed for a telephone and 911. But she didn't waste time cursing their absence. She had to get help.

Snatching open the kitchen door, she flew out and plowed right into John on his way in for lunch. He grasped her shoulders, steadying them both as they teetered on the small porch.

"The doctor," she panted. "Caro's collapsed."

John didn't need any further instruction. He knew what had happened. He disappeared around the corner of the house in the direction of the post before she could finish her sentence.

Libby ran back to the dining room, calmer now that help was on the way. She knelt beside Caroline and put her ear to the housekeeper's chest.

"Quick," she cried, yanking the bodice of Caro's dress open. She positioned the woman's head and told Pilar, "When I say go, blow into her mouth like this." She demonstrated and then waited for Pilar to nod her understanding.

Rapidly she compressed Caroline's chest five times and shouted, "Now, do it."

Pilar hesitated for an instant, then did as Libby instructed. Libby waited, silently counting until it was her turn to repeat the procedure.

"Don't stop," she said breathlessly. "Keep going."

Over and over the two women performed the lifesaving technique on their friend. Sweat popped out on Libby's forehead and ran into her eyes, but she never slowed her efforts. Together they worked for what seemed like hours. Libby's back ached and her hands were cramping by the time John came crashing into the house, the flustered doctor in tow.

"What are you doing?" Doctor Stein cried, pushing Pilar aside. "Here, here, you're going to hurt her doing that."

"No," Libby told him, gasping for air herself. "Helps, helps her heart."

From his bag he brought out a small brown vial and twisted the cork out. He dumped several pills into his hand and fished one out, placing it beneath Caro's tongue.

"Stop that, I say," he repeated to Libby, who had continued the heart compressions.

"No, not until you get a rhythm."

John and the doctor exchanged startled glances.

"Listen to her," Pilar cried, scrambling to her knees. "When we found Caroline, her lips were blue. Look at them now."

All eyes turned to the housekeeper's face, which was regaining some of its color as they spoke. The doctor frowned deeply and withdrew his stethoscope. He pressed it to Caro's chest and listened.

"Nothing," he said.

Libby continued the CPR and Pilar bent to breathe into Caro's mouth as she'd been told. Another minute passed, and the doctor pushed the stethoscope back into place.

"There, there, I hear it. It's faint, but regular."

Libby and Pilar both collapsed on the floor, exhausted but elated.

"We did it!" Libby laughed through tears. "She's going to be okay."

"Well, I don't know about that," the doctor said. "She's not out of the woods yet."

His words couldn't dim Libby's happiness, though. She knew beyond a doubt that Caro wouldn't have lasted until the doctor arrived if not for the CPR. God bless modern procedures!

John's hand appeared before her face, and she looked up into his eyes. He smiled, his gaze overbright. She took his hand, and he pulled her to her feet. Silently, he tucked his arm about her waist and squeezed gently.

Pilar stood shakily and joined them. Libby put her arm around Pilar's waist and pulled her into the embrace.

"Can you get her upstairs, John?" the doctor asked, tucking his tools back into his battered black bag. "I can examine her there."

John released Libby and scooped Caro into his arms. She wasn't a small woman, and the veins in his arms pushed against his tanned skin, but he never faltered. He strode up the stairs and deposited her on her bed.

"If one of you ladies would stay and assist me?" Stein said.

Libby quickly volunteered, and John and Pilar stepped silently out of the room.

"Just what do you think you were doing down there, little lady?" Stein spoke without

191

looking at Libby, all the while performing his examination.

"Trying to save her life," Libby said sharply. And she'd succeeded, too. Caro was alive and breathing on her own. It occurred to Libby that she might have screwed up the time continuum or something—she'd seen all three *Back to the Future* movies—but she didn't care. If Caro was supposed to die today, Libby was glad she'd messed things up.

"By crushing her chest?" Stein snorted derisively.

"No," Libby said, her anger taking over. "By restarting her heart."

"The digitalis did that."

"She wouldn't have lived long enough for the digitalis to take effect if it hadn't been for the CPR."

"CPR?"

"Cardiopulmonary resuscitation," she explained glibly, delighted to see the look of startled disbelief on the doctor's face. "It restores normal breathing after a heart attack, so the patient doesn't die from lack of oxygen."

Libby knew she might be digging her own grave, but how could she remain silent when she alone had lifesaving information?

Stein, finished with his exam, turned to stare at Libby. "How do you know about all this?" he asked suspiciously.

Libby considered telling him the truth. She'd

saved Caro's life, dammit. The fact that she was from the future shouldn't matter after what she'd done for her friend.

But Libby knew it would matter, a great deal. They'd all think she'd really flipped if she told them she learned CPR in 1990 when she taught swimming at the Y to supplement her income.

"I just know it, that's all." She couldn't think of a witty reply and she could see her answer didn't satisfy the curious doctor. Caro mumbled and shifted, and Stein's attention focused once more on his patient. Libby breathed a shaky sigh.

Doctor Stein stayed for the next several hours, then left the vial of digitalis along with instructions for Libby. She listened closely to everything he said. After all, she might have helped Caro temporarily, but she was in 1887, not 1993, and this doctor knew the best treatments available at the moment.

John brought her lunch on a tray, and she ate every bite with relish. Food had never tasted so good, and she polished off the last crumb. Saving a life took a lot out of a person.

But it gave back an equal measure of satisfaction, and she couldn't help feeling jubilant. There was a reason she'd come back to the past, she decided. And if that wasn't the case, at least she'd made a difference by being here. When she returned to 1993, she'd never again regret her odd voyage.

"She's resting peacefully," John said, breaking into her thoughts. Libby nodded.

"You might as well go and get some rest," he told her. "I'll stay with her for a while."

"Thanks, but I'd like to stay."

"Always the caretaker," he said with a smile, and Libby felt a glow of pleasure.

He pulled a chair over to the side of the bed opposite Libby and sank into it. For the first time, she noticed the lines of worry and fatigue etched into his face. He really cared about Caroline. He'd been elated when Caro rallied. And he'd believed Libby partially responsible, no matter what the doctor said.

She leaned her head back against the cushioned chair and closed her eyes, a small smile curving her lips.

Three days later, Caro was grouchy and restless and driving them both crazy. Libby pleaded with her for the hundredth time to stay in bed as the doctor instructed, but Caro tried to get up despite Libby's pleas.

John came in and frowned at the two struggling women. "What in the name of Sam's cat are you two doing?"

"Tell her she has to stay in bed," Libby said, pushing the housekeeper back against the pillows.

"I ain't gonna do it," Caro told them both, swatting Libby's hands away.

194

"Yes, you are," John said. He settled the light quilt around his housekeeper's waist and successfully ended the discussion.

He'd already dressed for work in his uniform, with his hair properly slicked back and tied. But Libby remembered his bare feet, loose hair, and relaxed manner from their encounter in the kitchen. And she'd never forget that kiss. His uniform made him appear stoical and indifferent, but it only hid the real man. A man with passions and desires. A man who could be tender and remain virile.

Her body grew heavy and warm, and her heart skittered and raced. Lord, how she wanted him. Not even her professor, the great love of her life until now, had caused a reaction like this one. He might have been handsome and charming, but he lacked the other qualities she'd come to recognize in John—compassion, vulnerability, and trustworthiness.

A cross between a Greek god and a boy scout. What a combination!

He caught her staring, and a slight grin tipped his lips. She smiled as he returned the perusal, his gaze slowly taking in the loosened curls around her face, the unfastened buttons at the collar of her shirtwaist, her own bare feet. Her toes curled instinctively, and a hot flush swept over her chest and neck. Caro caught the exchange and raised an eyebrow.

"Well, I better get going," he said, reluctant

to leave. "You behave yourself and quit giving Libby a hard time," he told Caro. He stood staring at the two women for another moment, then turned to go.

The temperature in the room dropped ten degrees with the loss of John's presence. Libby missed the warmth which always seemed to accompany him.

"What was that all about?" Caro asked frankly, as soon as they heard the door close downstairs.

Libby straightened the bedding and shrugged her shoulders, avoiding Caro's eyes. "I don't know what you mean," she lied.

"Huh," her patient snorted. "I ain't blind. And even if I was, I could feel the heat you two put off. And that's with an old woman, a bed, and half a room between you."

Libby turned away, picked up a hand towel, and folded it.

"I ain't tryin' to pry," Caro told her. "I make it a point not to stick my big nose in where it don't belong. But . . ."

The word was leading, and Libby was sure it had been meant that way. She wanted to talk to someone about John, but there wasn't anything to say. She couldn't hurt him by getting involved with him and then leaving. He'd never understand if she told him she couldn't stay without giving him a good reason why. And reasoning played no part in her life right now.

"All right," Caro said behind her. "I'll mind my own business."

Libby turned around and smiled. "I would tell you, if there was anything to tell," she said. "There isn't. John and I are . . ."

"Friends?" Caro's brows climbed higher.

"No," Libby laughed dryly. "I wouldn't call it that. In fact," she said, sitting on the edge of Caro's bed, "I think it's probably hard for John to make friends. I don't suppose he has many."

"I reckon not," the housekeeper agreed. "But he seemed interested in you, and I can't help thinking how good it is to see him interested in something besides that Indian."

"Geronimo?"

"Yeah, Geronimo. He don't talk much about it, but you can bet that's where his thoughts are most times."

A sad sigh escaped Libby's lips, and she stared out the window at the rising sun. Soon the temperature in the room would escalate and, along with it, Caro's temper.

"I wish I could get his mind off the Apache for a while."

"Not much chance of that," Caro stated without hesitation. "He's been running that same rail too long to switch track now."

Libby wondered if that were really true. If she could get him away from the post and the Apache for a time, maybe he could begin

197

to get over his bitterness. Soon the Apache would be sent to Alabama, and from there on to Oklahoma, where they would stay. Would John go along with the guard or stay in the area? She realized she knew very little about the man she'd quickly lost her heart to.

She looked up and noticed that Caroline was deep in thought. Absently, the housekeeper rubbed the locket hanging from a silver chain around her neck. Apparently Caro wore it all the time, even when she slept. Libby's curiosity blossomed.

"That's very pretty," she said, leaning forward to inspect the piece.

For once Caro didn't withdraw from questions. She proudly showed off the tiny filigree locket in her fingers.

"It must be very special to you," Libby hinted.

Caro smiled and nodded. "Oh, yes, it is. I don't mind telling you this is my most prized possession."

Libby feared seeing Caro's expression shut down if she pushed too hard, but she couldn't resist asking her next question.

"Where did you get it?"

The now familiar sadness filled Caro's eyes, and a bittersweet smile curved her mouth.

"There was a man, a sailor. He used to come into my pub all the time before I sold out."

"You owned a pub?" Libby asked, amazed.

Caro grinned. "Sure. You didn't think I'd been

a housekeeper all my life, did you? Anyway, Thomas, that was his name. Thomas Kane. A good-looking man with shoulders out to here," she said, motioning with her hands, "and hair the color of the sun. He gave it to me after one of his voyages. I almost lost my breath when I first saw it."

"He was your beau?" Libby asked, trying to hide the excitement in her voice. She couldn't quite get over Caroline talking openly about her past. She'd never done so before. Perhaps coming close to death had loosened her tongue.

Caro's throaty chuckle surprised Libby. She'd gotten used to the woman's husky tones, but her laugh always took Libby aback.

"No, Libby," Caro said, looking her friend in the eye with aplomb. "He was my lover. For nine years."

"Nine years?" Libby nearly tumbled backward off the bed. She couldn't have been more surprised if Caro had announced she was an alien from outer space. She sat, mouth agape, in stunned silence.

Caro laughed and slapped the mattress beside her. "Close your mouth, girl, you're catching flies."

Libby snapped her mouth shut and realized, belatedly, how rude her reaction must have seemed. "I'm sorry. But you really surprised me, Caro. I never thought . . ."

She stopped, realizing that her next words

wouldn't have sounded any better.

Caroline laughed again, obviously unoffended. "That's all right. I suppose most young girls would feel the same. But the truth is, Libby, a lot of people find the right person in the wrong circumstances. It don't mean you turn your back on that love. You just rearrange your thinkin' a bit."

"And you loved him?"

"Lord, how I loved that man. I thought no one had ever loved deeper. Of course, I suppose everybody feels that way when it's happenin' to them."

Libby nodded. She'd never felt that way before, but she'd always assumed she would when the real thing came along. Her thoughts jumped directly to John. Maybe, in time . . .

"But Thomas had another mistress," Caro said, grabbing Libby's attention and wrenching it back to the present.

"What? You mean there was another woman?" Libby cried, appalled.

"No, not a woman," Caro told her. "That would have been easier to take. Thomas's love was sailing. I was the only woman for him, and I know he loved me as much as a man ever loved a woman. But he couldn't give up the sea. He had to be on the water. And so, I waited. I waited while he traveled to Spain and brought back this," she said, motioning to the chain and locket. "And I waited while he traveled to the Orient and brought me back silk and jade. And I waited."

A lump lodged itself in Libby's throat. The love light faded from Caro's eyes, replaced with longing.

"But Thomas couldn't give it up, and I couldn't go on letting him go. Every time he came and went, I died a little more inside. I'd worry and stew until he returned. We'd have a wonderful reunion and then I'd begin to worry about the next trip. The good times got shorter and the hard times longer until, finally, I told him I couldn't do it anymore."

Libby read every emotion in Caro's eyes, as though it were happening right now. The love, the longing, the pain, the loss. No wonder Caro never talked about her past. She had only to open the door a crack, and the world could see her life laid bare.

"Thomas's ship, the *Wild Card*, planned to sail to Constantinople. The men were crazy with anticipation. And the more they carried on, the worse I felt. I couldn't beg him to stay, Libby. I loved him too much to take away the one thing he needed more than life itself. But I couldn't take the months of waiting either. We had a wonderful last night together, and he left before dawn the next day. I left that day, too. That was five years ago."

"But you had a tavern, right? Where was it? What happened to it?"

"Sold it," Caro said, all the emotions wiped from her expression now. "It was a nice place, right on the docks in Pensacola. About fifteen miles from here. There was a man, a customer, who'd always wanted my place. I let him have it."

"And Thomas?" Libby couldn't help herself. She had to know what happened.

But Caro only shrugged. "I don't know. I never went back. I hope he returned safely. I hope he's happy."

"But what about you? Don't you miss him?"

Such a hurt look entered Caro's gaze that Libby wished she'd kept her mouth shut for once. Obviously the woman had never gotten over her lover.

"I missed him all the time, even when he was with me. This way is easier. I can put him out of my mind for days at a time and, if I tell myself he's well and happy, I can truly believe that's the way it is."

Libby watched her caress the locket and realized that Caroline lied. She'd never put Thomas Kane out of her mind, not for a moment. She'd only put him out of reach.

Trying to get Caro's mind off the pain of her loss, Libby struggled to make casual conversation.

"So, how'd you come to be here, working as a housekeeper?"

"I work because I need to stay busy. I couldn't

sit around doin' nothing all day. Why, I'd shrivel up and die in no time."

Libby knew why Caroline kept busy—to keep Thomas's memory at bay. The pain must be strong enough that, if she let it have free rein, it would consume her. But she was killing herself. Her heart couldn't take the strain of continuous physical labor any longer. She had to slow down.

But Libby knew Caro would never slow down. She'd work until she had another attack. And if Libby, or someone else, wasn't there when it happened, she'd die.

All the good feelings Libby had experienced when she'd helped Pilar and Caroline dissipated like fog beneath the Florida sun. She hadn't really helped Caroline at all. She'd only postponed what would inevitably happen once she left.

The ache in her chest told Libby how much Caro had come to mean to her. She couldn't leave knowing her friend's death was imminent. She had to do something, and fast.

And, just like that, Libby knew what she had to do. The term *kill two birds with one stone* had never been more appropriate.

She'd find Thomas Kane, or someone who knew where he was, and she'd tell him about Caroline and how she still felt about him. She'd see the two lovers reunited before she returned to her own time. And she'd enlist John's help in doing it. Because, in order for them to find Thomas Kane, they'd have to travel to Pensacola. And that would take John away from the post, the Apache, and his constant turmoil for a time.

Yes, Libby thought, confident in her plan. She'd get John to go with her to Pensacola. He and Caro both would benefit from the trip.

A small voice whispered that it could be dangerous to get away alone with John, but Libby only smiled. What ever happened in Pensacola would happen. And damn the consequences.

Chapter Thirteen

"Dammit, Libby, you can't fix everything."

Libby glanced up the stairs and then back to face John. "I know that," she said, careful to keep her voice down. Caro was sleeping, and Libby didn't want her getting wind of her plan. "But I think I can do this."

"Look." He lowered his voice and took Libby by the arm, leading her farther from the stairs. "No one appreciates what you did for Caro and Pilar more than I do. But you've done enough. I can't let you do this."

"It's the only way, John. You said yourself she's never going to retire. She'll keep right on working until she drops dead. And that probably won't take too long. I have less than three weeks left before Langdon lifts the ban and I can go back to the island. I won't be here to help Caro after that."

"How can you be sure your memory will return just because you go back to the tree?"

It wasn't the time to tell him she'd never really had amnesia. Libby longed to confide in him but knew she couldn't. And so she said, "I have to go back to my life."

An odd light lit his eyes and he stepped closer. Taking her by the shoulders, he bent slightly. Thinking he was going to kiss her, Libby leaned in eagerly for the touch of his mouth against hers. But he stopped and drew back, and she released a frustrated sigh.

"I've been thinking about that," he said, looking away and tucking his hands into his trouser pockets. "Maybe . . ."

Libby knew what he was about to say and quickly shook her head, silencing him. She couldn't let him say it. Couldn't even let him think it. Although, Lord knows, the same thought had crossed her mind. But it was impossible, and she refused to mislead him.

"I *will* leave when the time comes," she told him, her words laced with painful determination. "I can't stay here. But I want to know Caro is going to be all right. She told me about Thomas Kane, and I know if we could find him, bring them together, she'd slow down."

"You can't be sure of that, Libby," he said, any disappointment he felt at her statement carefully masked. "He might be married."

"No. No way." Libby shook her head. "He loved Caro deeply. He wouldn't have just found someone else. I'm certain."

She could see he wasn't so sure, but he didn't argue the point. "He wouldn't give up the sea for Caro five years ago. What makes you think he'll give it up now? Nothing will have changed. We might end up doing Caro more harm than good by resurrecting an old hurt."

"It isn't an old hurt, John. Caro's pain is still fresh, and very much alive." She tried to understand how it felt to lose someone you loved so much and found it wasn't hard to do at all. Already she was preparing herself for the time when she and John would part. And already her heart felt the heavy weight of loss. They'd never made love, had never even discussed their feelings. But she knew without a doubt that she loved him. More than she'd ever loved anyone in her life. And she knew, with a deep, dark certainly, that she'd never get over him.

"I don't know, Libby. I don't like interfering in other people's lives."

The emotion he felt was fear; she could see it clearly in his eyes now. He was afraid to get involved in people's lives because that would make him too close to them. And she suspected he'd spent a great deal of time and energy making sure he didn't get too close to anyone.

"You care about Caroline, you can't deny that. Please, John," she pleaded. "Help me do this. I can't leave without doing something. I feel like I'll be signing her death certificate if I do."

A multitude of emotions played across his usually impassive face. She'd seen the hard shell crack over the last few days, and now the mask fell away. He couldn't hide his concern for Caro. And, as he looked into her eyes, he couldn't hide his feelings for her.

"How are you going to convince Caro?" he said, giving in reluctantly.

"Let me handle that. I have an idea," she told him.

Libby didn't know whether to cry or cheer. He was going to help her. She'd broken through his wall of indifference and made him feel again. It would have been a victory except for one thing. If her plan worked and Caro and Thomas got together, the housekeeper would probably leave. And in less than three weeks, so would she.

Back to her own life, her own time, she'd go. And once more John would be alone. But this time it would be worse. Because she'd made him feel again. And what he'd feel would be pain and loneliness.

"I can't believe you got him to agree to this, Libby," Caro said as she slowly rose to her feet and made her way across the room. Libby wished she'd take a few more days and rest, but Caro was eager to be up, and so the doctor had agreed to allow her out of bed for a few hours each day.

She sank into the chair by the window, already short of breath. Libby stood back, fighting the urge to rush to Caro's aid. The housekeeper refused to be fussed over, so Libby tried to allow her to do things herself. But sometimes it was hard to suppress the natural desire to help.

"I suggested that a trip to Pensacola might be a good way to find out if someone knows me and is possibly looking for me," Libby said. "But the truth is, I want to get John away for a couple of days. He's been even more somber lately, and I think something is up with Geronimo. Whatever it is, it's eating at John and he needs to get away before it destroys him."

That much of her tale was the truth, and she knew her voice sounded convincing. Caro nodded.

"Pilar said she would be glad to come and stay over here for a day or two," Libby added. She saw Caro's face tighten and she added quickly, "I think she needs the time to sort out her own troubles. I thought maybe you could help her with that since I'll be busy with John."

A sparkle of animation danced suddenly in Caro's eyes, and Libby knew she'd just leapt the last hurdle with ease. If there was one thing

Caro couldn't resist, she thought with a bubble of exuberance, it was a soul in need. Libby knew the fact well from her own experience.

"I told you about her and Christopher. She needs time to decide what she's going to do, and I think she feels she could think more clearly if they weren't living under the same roof. This way she can get away for a brief time without anyone knowing they're having problems."

"Yes, yes," Caro said, her loving spirit springing to life instantly. She had something to put her mind to and someone who needed her— two very important things to Caro's mental, as well as physical, health.

"That's settled, then," Libby said, backing toward the door. "I'll go and tell her she can come over first thing in the morning when John and I leave."

She slipped sedately out the door and closed it behind her. Then, lifting her skirts high to keep them away from her feet, she dashed down the stairs and slid breathlessly into the kitchen, where Pilar and John waited impatiently to learn if she'd succeeded or failed.

Pilar spun around as Libby flew into the room. John leapt to his feet by the table.

"She bought it," Libby crowed. "Hook, line and sinker." With a great giggle, she lifted her hand high into the air. Pilar knew the gesture by now; she lifted her hand up and slapped Libby's palm with unladylike enthusiasm.

210

"High five," they shouted together. John stepped back, startled by their odd behavior. But Libby was too excited to care whether he thought she'd gone mad. She resisted the urge to hug him breathless and, with a full-throated laugh, she turned and held her hand up in front of him. He paused and she read the amusement mixed with bewilderment on his face.

"High five," he shouted back, slapping his big hard palm against hers. "Whatever that means," he added with a chuckle as the two women hugged with self-satisfied glee.

They arrived in Pensacola the following afternoon, dusty and weary from a morning riding. Libby had chosen to ride astride, much to John's amazement. Having had very little experience with horses, she told him she was nervous enough without having to balance sideways on the saddle. He raised an eyebrow but acquiesced, and she'd worn her leggings under her skirt so she'd be adequately covered.

Libby's first look at her hometown sent a wave of trembling panic through her. John led the way to the City Hotel on Government Street. Wide-eyed, Libby saw Baylen and Palafox Streets and other familiar names, but other than that, the place looked completely foreign to her. Her breath came in short,

211

quick gasps as she saw the busy port and a harbor full of ships. In her time, the harbor was nearly empty, most large vessels choosing the more commercial ports of Mobile or New Orleans.

"Recognize anything?" John asked quietly.

Without thinking, Libby choked out, "No." Tears welled in her eyes as she struggled to find something familiar amidst the brick and wooden structures. But with the exception of one church and the courthouse, she didn't recognize anything.

"It's all right," he said, his large hand covering hers where they rested on the pommel of her saddle. "You will, in time."

She blinked back the moisture in her eyes and turned to him. With a grimace, she realized what he'd asked and how her answer had sounded. And suddenly she couldn't stand the deception any longer.

"This was my hometown," she told him, glancing around at the horse-drawn trolley and the light carriages rolling briskly by.

John's eyes shot wide. "You remember something."

"Yes, I remember. But I remember it the way it was before."

"Before?"

"Before I went to Fort Pickens that day."

"Well, it can't have changed much in less than a week."

He seemed encouraged rather than confused by her cryptic statement, and Libby could only shake her head as she realized once again just how far from home she really was.

"You have no idea," she told him despondently. "You have no idea."

The hotel he'd chosen did not even exist in Libby's time, and she stared at it in dismay as they went in. How could something so big and solid vanish from existence? She'd never even heard of the place, yet it brimmed with people as they passed through the lobby.

John registered and collected the keys for two adjoining rooms. She followed him stiffly to an old-fashioned elevator and held her breath as they chugged to the third floor. She felt like someone was cranking them up every inch of the way, and she didn't breathe easy until they were out of the contraption. She'd never much cared for modern elevators, and she decided she'd just as soon take the stairs the next time than chance this one again.

The rooms were nice enough and, surprisingly, looked much like all the other hotel rooms she'd ever been in. The big difference, of course, was the lack of a bathroom. You had to go down the hall to the water closet, which was shared by a number of guests.

John had tucked her belongings into a leather satchel. Dumping them on the bed, she shook out the wrinkles. Pegs lined the wall by the

213

door and she assumed they served as hangers. She hung up her only other dress, then put the underthings Caro had given her in the bureau drawer. A washbasin held fresh water, and she washed her face and tidied her curls.

Minutes later John knocked on her door and she opened it to him. "Come in," she said.

His gaze darted nervously down the hall and then around her room as he stepped inside.

"I thought we'd get something to eat before we start our search," John said, obviously uncomfortable at their being alone together in her room.

Libby wanted to tell him that she'd rather not venture out into the alien streets, but she couldn't do that without offering explanations she wasn't ready to give. So she smiled and nodded. "Sounds great," she lied.

They took the stairs this time, and John walked along silently beside her until they reached a small cafe at the corner of the street.

"How's this?" he asked.

Again Libby had to fight back her reaction to the unfamiliar place. There was no cafe here in her time. In fact, the main branch of her bank sat on this very corner.

"Fine."

They went in and took a seat at a white wrought-iron table that resembled something from a modern-day ice cream parlor. A woman

214

in a black skirt and white blouse came out and took their order, then disappeared through swinging doors into what Libby assumed was the kitchen.

"So, did you remember anything else?" John asked after the waitress left them alone.

Libby started, and looked up at him. "Huh? Oh, no, not anything important."

"Anything at all? Maybe it seems unimportant to you, but it could be vital."

Libby hated deceiving him. How could she pretend to be unaffected by her surroundings? And why hadn't she realized how difficult it would be to see her home this way? She hadn't noticed it before, but she'd been living in a dream world at the post. Because there was no Army post in her time, she hadn't had to face the reality of what had happened to her. She'd let herself be lulled by the ease with which she'd adjusted to life on the post. But facing her old stomping ground and finding it foreign to her was almost too much to bear.

"Are you sure you're all right?" John asked, noticing her pallor. "Maybe this wasn't such a good idea after all."

"I'm fine," Libby croaked, looking around at the signs lining the wall. Ads for everything from baby food to tooth powder hung between the plate-glass windows. The posters looked bizarre, all the people with apple-red cheeks and softly painted features. The women wore what must have been considered high fashion, but to Libby they looked like portraits out of a museum.

"I don't get it," she said, swiveling her head around to examine all the ads. "The women all look alike in the paintings, but the women I've met don't resemble each other in the slightest."

John didn't seem surprised by her question. "That's because the women want to be endowed with whatever features are popular at the time. For instance, if they don't have deep-set eyes, they have the artist paint them like that anyway."

"You're not serious!" Libby cried, her eyes going from one picture to the next. Sure enough, the same features could be seen on every female presented. "But that's terrible. How will people ever know what they really looked like?"

A chuckle escaped John as the waitress came back carrying two large glasses of tea. He waited until she'd gone again and then continued. "They don't want to be remembered as they were. They want to be remembered as they *wished* they were."

Libby's mouth fell open. "That's crazy. We'll never know who really looked that way and who had their portraits touched up."

"We?" John said, his eyes narrowing in confusion.

Libby snapped to attention and sipped her tea to wet her suddenly dry throat. "I mean, future generations will never know what anyone really looked like."

"I don't suppose that'll be a problem for long. They've opened a portrait studio just down the road and a gentleman from Boston has been taking photographs. An artist might retouch his paintings, but the photographs show the people just the way they are."

Libby didn't even want to consider the implications of that statement. She refused to accept that she was living in a time when photographs were rare and special things. She wanted the days of Polaroids and disposable cameras back. She longed for a one-hour photo booth on every other corner.

The waitress arrived with their meal, but Libby barely tasted the boiled vegetables and fried chicken. She doubted her ability to see this plan through. The thought of facing Palafox Street, the wharf, and the harbor again nearly sent her running back to Barrancas. She only had a few weeks left until she could put this nightmare behind her. Why should she torture herself this way?

But she'd practically begged John to help her, and she couldn't back out now. He'd already noticed something was wrong, so she had to be more careful. Before she knew it, she'd be blurting out the truth to him and that would

217

never do. He'd pack her right back to the base surgeon and that could delay her being allowed back on the island.

"Ready?"

John's voice brought her back to the task at hand, and Libby quickly pulled herself together. She had to get a grip. Facing downtown Pensacola couldn't be any harder than admitting she'd traveled through time in the first place. She was strong. She could handle this. For Caroline's sake, she told herself, if not for her own.

Chapter Fourteen

Libby stared up at the wooden tavern doors. The weathered shingle overhead swayed slightly in the breeze off the harbor. Wave after wave of emotion pounded her senses—shock, dismay, nervous tension.

The tavern Caro told her she'd once owned had been purchased by Joe Fisher. Libby knew this because she'd celebrated her twenty-first birthday in the well-known dive everybody called Trader Joe's. She'd met the proprietor that night, a man named Sidney, who'd told her the story of the old tavern's history.

The thought came to her that she could tell old Sidney a thing or two. The original owner of the tavern was not Joe Fisher, former accountant. No indeed. The original owner of Trader Joe's was her good friend, Caroline Cooper.

A tremulous smile tipped her lips as she finally let herself consider what she'd truly experienced. Time travel! An idea scoffed at and ridiculed. A phenomenon so incredible the human mind couldn't comprehend its possibilities. And she, ordinary Libby Pfifer, had somehow been chosen to experience it.

"What's so amusing?" John asked, his own mouth going easily into a soft grin.

Libby read the changes in his demeanor, and her smile broadened. He was loosening up. Her presence had disturbed him at first, but since their kiss in the kitchen he'd been inching closer to her. Little things alerted her at first. A hesitant touch, a shared look. But since they'd left the post, his smile had come more easily and with more frequency.

Knowing how badly they might both be hurt, she knew she should pull back. But she loved his smile and wanted to see more of it. And, despite her better judgment, she longed to nurture the growing camaraderie between them. Grinning, she tucked her arm into his.

"I'll tell you all about it one day," she said, deciding in that moment that she would. He might never believe her, but she vowed to confide the truth to John before she left.

"Right now," she added, "let's go inside and see what we can find out."

Libby started forward, only to be drawn back

sharply when John didn't move. His eyebrows were raised so that the worry lines on his forehead returned.

"I don't think you should go in there," he told her, placing his hand over hers where it lay in the curve of his elbow.

His warmth thrilled her and she let her skin absorb the feel of him. He was so real! Not a ghost from the past or a figment of her imagination, but a hot-blooded, boldly handsome, powerfully built, flesh-and-blood man. To the people of her century, he was no more than a footnote on time's page. But Libby knew he would always be much more than that to her.

"Libby?"

She savored the precious moment a second longer, then smiled. "Caroline owned this place. She worked here for years. I think I'll be safe, with you, for a few minutes."

He hesitated a long minute, then nodded. "All right, let's go."

The interior of the tavern was constructed of planked wood walls, floor, and ceiling. An odd assortment of metal tools and gadgets hung from the walls and scarred, rough tables were set about with short barrels for seats. But the eye-catching main attraction was the mahogany Brunswick back bar with a stained-glass canopy and the wraparound, L-shaped front bar topped with black marble and sporting a gleaming brass foot rack.

Libby whistled softly.

"I hadn't expected anything like this," John murmured, for some reason keeping his own voice subdued.

"You've never been here, then?"

He scanned the ornate tavern and shook his head, obviously still stunned. "She never told me about her past. Until you asked me to help you the other day, I had no idea where Caroline was from or how she'd come to be working as a housekeeper on the post. She was already there when I arrived."

"Really?" Libby started to ask him when that was, but a shuffling sounded from the door at the back of the room and they both turned to see what it was.

"Howdy, folks." A lanky man with mutton-chop whiskers struggling valiantly to cover his ruddy cheeks paused behind the bar. He wore an apron over soiled brown trousers and a once-white shirt which was missing several buttons.

"Can't get you a horn, I'm feared. Not open to business."

Libby frowned up at John, who squinted in the dim light of the room. "We didn't come here for a drink," he said, clarifying the man's odd words.

"I wonder if we could ask you a few questions?"

The barkeep tugged an oily rag from his waist

and polished a spot on the black marble.

"'Bout what?"

John led Libby farther into the room and up to the bar. "About the previous owner of the tavern," John said.

The man continued to polish the spot though it was obvious the bar shone. He shrugged.

Libby was about to speak when John pulled a coin from his pocket and tossed it onto the shiny marble. It looked like a half-dollar, with a Liberty head wearing a wreath on one side.

The man's eyes brightened and Libby thought dryly how some things never change. A thin-boned hand reached for the coin, but John's covered it first.

"Whatcha wanna know?" the man asked, suddenly very cooperative.

Libby congratulated herself on her brilliance in bringing John along. No doubt she'd never have gotten anywhere with her frank, volatile personality, not to mention her lack of funds.

"Everything you know about Caroline Cooper."

The man leaned against the back bar and fiddled with his rag as his pale eyes studied the ceiling. "Well," he said. "I know she was a real g'hal."

"A what?" Libby said, stepping forward.

"He means she was wild, rowdy."

Libby nodded and the barkeep looked at her as if to ask if she were ready to hear more.

223

He added, "And she run this here doggery without a kick."

"John?"

"She operated the tavern without any trouble."

"Yep, until she pulled foot."

"John!?" Libby hissed, agitated by the foreign language the man seemed to be speaking.

John turned to her and frowned oddly. "She ran off, left."

"And I figure, although this ain't gospel, that she fled off the reel on account of that sailor boy she hankered after."

"I got the hanker part," she told John dryly as he turned to interpret the latest gibberish.

John grinned and told her, "He suspects Caroline left so suddenly because she was in love with Thomas Kane."

"Got it." Libby turned to the barkeep. "But we knew that much."

"Well, you didn't ask me what *you* knew. You asked me what *I* knew. And I'm a'telling you."

"Sorry," Libby muttered grumpily. She ignored the chuckle John couldn't muffle.

"So like I was saying, she hightailed it and no one knew where she set down. Her sailor, the man named Kane, he come back to get her and acknowledge the corn."

"Hold it," Libby cried, throwing her hand up.

The barkeep shot her an exasperated look, and John stifled another laugh as he explained, "Kane was going to admit something."

"That he loved Caroline?" she asked eagerly.

"Now how should I know?" the barkeep snapped irascibly. "He come in here looking for the boss lady and you could tell he was knocked into a cocked hat when he heared she'd gone. He ordered one horn after t'other until he left with a brick in his hat."

"Aaarrgh." Libby pressed her hands against her head and moaned. John's laughter could no longer be controlled, and he guffawed loudly. Libby had longed to hear him laugh and nearly missed the joy of the sound out of frustration. But finally his humor penetrated, and she couldn't help joining in.

"All right, very funny. Just tell me what he said."

John looked from her to the confused barkeep. "Kane came back to get Caroline and was shocked to find her gone. He drank heavily and then left, drunk."

"And that's all? You don't know where he went or what happened to him?"

"He come from a family of crackers, so I reckon he went back to sea."

"Oh, this is ridiculous. He came from a family of crackers? What was he, a saltine or a Ritz?"

Now the two men exchanged baffled looks.

"And she thinks I talk funny?" the barkeep said, scratching his head.

"Crackers are poor whites, Libby. He means Kane would have had to return to what he did for a living, which was sailing."

Libby ran frustrated fingers through her hair, forgetting she'd pinned it up under the snood before she and John went to eat. The pins popped loose and several strands fell into her eyes. With a low growl, she stabbed the pins back into place.

"What about his ship?" John asked. "Do you know anything about the *Wild Card*?"

"Sure 'nough. It come into port at candlelight three day ago. The sailors moseyed in and got corned first thing."

"Wait," Libby said. "Let me guess. The ship docked at sunset, and the men came here and got drunk."

"That's what I just said."

Libby grinned. "So you did."

"Is it still here?" She felt her first bit of relief since entering the tavern. Was it possible they could have found Thomas Kane so easily?

"Far's I know," he said with a nod. "Say, why do you want to know all this?"

Libby and John exchanged looks, and finally Libby turned back to the barkeep. "I'm trying to reunite Caroline and Thomas Kane."

"You mean the boss lady's still cuttin' didoes somewheres?"

226

"Well, if that means is she still alive and well, the answer is yes. For the time being at least."

"That's good to hear. I thought sure she was a gone coon when she disappeared that-a-way."

"She might be *a gone coon* if we don't find Thomas Kane." Libby felt her adrenaline pump. They just had to find Caro's beau. She wouldn't even consider the possibility that they might fail.

"Thank you for the information," John was saying, shaking the man's hand. Libby reached out to do likewise, and he lifted her fingers to his hair-covered mouth.

"It was a pure pleasure," the barkeep told her, meeting her gaze with a twinkle in his rheumy eyes. "Even if you are crazy as a loon."

Libby burst out laughing. "Now wouldn't you know it—that one I understood."

John took her arm and they left the barkeep polishing his immaculate black marble and chuckling. She saw him casually tuck the coin John left into his pocket.

"Can it be this easy?" she asked warily as they strolled toward the dock. Nervous excitement had her bouncing on her toes with every step.

"Don't get your hopes up, Libby. Sailors aren't known for staying with the same ship long."

"But you have to admit it was a stroke of luck that the *Wild Card* just happened to be in port."

He grinned down at her bobbing form. "Yeah, it was a stroke of luck."

They turned the corner and came parallel with the docks. Libby stopped, her mouth dropping open.

"Holy cow!"

"What?"

"Look at this place." She did, closely. Everywhere she turned there were piers and quays reaching iron tentacles out into the bay. Countless ships, boats, and tugs lined the wharf and dotted the emerald water. A railway station had been built out over the water, and a railcar was being loaded directly from the ship.

"Yes?"

"Oh, John. If you only knew how deserted and run-down all this is now."

"Now?"

Libby didn't hear his query. She walked slowly toward the bay. It was beautiful, vibrant and alive. All around her people hustled to and fro loading and unloading cargo. The air smelled of fish and salt and damp wood. Burly men who could put Arnold Schwarzenegger to shame hoisted crates like pieces of cordwood.

"Libby." John's voice drifted to her on the wet breeze, and she glanced up into his dancing eyes. "Look."

She followed the direction he pointed, and a broad grin split both their faces.

The *Wild Card* rode the tide, just three berths

down from where they stood.

"Suddenly I'm afraid to go closer," Libby admitted, stepping back toward John. Her shoulder bumped his chest and his hands came up to cup her arms. They stood there, silently, for several minutes watching the *Wild Card* dip and sway. It was a long, sharp-bowed clipper ship, its wooden bow gleaming in the afternoon sunlight. Stevedores lined the dock in a human chain, hauling crates and barrels from its hull.

"Its too bad we don't know what Thomas Kane looks like," Libby said, enjoying the comfort of John's closeness another moment before turning to face him. "He could be right in front of us and we'd never know it."

"Not one of them," he told her, indicating the stevedores. "They only unload the ships. They're not part of the crew."

"Oh, well then, I guess we'd better find out where the crew is."

John slipped his arm around her shoulder as they started toward the boat. Libby fought the overwhelming urge to cuddle into his arms despite the crowded dock. The mixture of urgent anticipation and sexual magnetism had her feeling as if she'd overdosed on caffeine. Her stomach fluttered, and sweat broke out on her palms and forehead.

"Are you all right?" he asked, his arm instinctively drawing her closer to the hard strength of his side.

Libby resisted the need to fan herself and forced a brittle smile. "Just nervous," she said.

"Yeah, me too," he confessed, his own smile less than jubilant.

Libby studied his tense brow and hardened mouth. She wondered if his nervousness stemmed from their close contact as much as their mission. Never one to mince words, she stepped toward him. "Why are you nervous?"

He looked as though he'd offer some glib reply, then thought better of it. His fingers tightened on her arms, and she couldn't tell if he was longing to pull her closer or considering pushing her away.

"I haven't allowed myself to really care about anyone for years, Libby," he finally said, his usually closed expression now revealing more than she was ready to see. "For the first time in a long time I care. About Caroline—and you." For a moment his face looked tortured, then he rolled his eyes away from her. "I care so much sometimes that I ache. I want Caro to be happy and healthy. And I want . . ." He allowed his gaze to settle on her face and he seemed to individually assess every feature. "I want you."

Libby's heart rolled over in her chest, sucking every morsel of air from her lungs. The intensity in his unusual brown eyes scorched her. His hands burned on her arms. Suddenly she felt on fire. Her heated skin tingled with electric awareness.

"Oh, John, I . . ."

Just then a beefy stevedore bumped into them. John tightened his hold on Libby as the startled stranger tried to steady the pair.

"Sorry, folks, I guess I wasn't looking where I was going."

John scanned Libby quickly. "Are you all right?" She nodded.

"No harm done," he told the man, though his voice held a definite note of disappointment that the moment had been cut short. The man slapped John's shoulder and started to walk away.

"Hey, wait," Libby called. "We were looking for Thomas Kane. Can you help us?"

"Ask over there," the man shouted back, his long legs having carried him several yards already.

Libby and John turned to see where he'd pointed. A group of men were gathered around four barrels at the end of the gangplank.

Once more Libby's heart turned over. Could one of those men standing so close to her be Thomas Kane? All her life she'd fought her fear of failure. She wasn't a stranger to disappointment. But this meant so much. This was one of the most important things she'd ever done in her life.

"Shall we go?" he said, seeming to notice her hesitation. Libby looked from John to the group of men and clasped her nervous fingers

231

together in front of her.

"Let's do it," she said, her voice rife with false enthusiasm.

Side by side they walked over to the group of men. Raucous talk and loud laughter flowed from the group in such a jumble that Libby couldn't make out a single word.

"Excuse me." John stepped forward into the small cluster and held out his hand to the man closest to him. "I'm Captain John Faulk, and I was wondering if any of you know a sailor by the name of Thomas Kane."

They all looked simultaneously to an older man standing propped against a barrel. As he eyed his companions, they looked away one by one and stepped back.

Libby soaked up all the details of the sailor hurriedly. He was about the right age, she guessed. Early to mid-fifties. His salt-and-pepper hair hugged his head and looked ragged at the ends, as though it had been cut with a knife. A faded red shirt scarcely covered a herculean chest and thick arms. His buff trousers fit like a second skin across trunk-like legs.

"Are you Thomas Kane?" Libby couldn't help asking.

The man's eyes cut to her, and she sucked in her breath. Lines fanned out from the corners of crystal-blue eyes. They might have been laugh lines, but she didn't think they were, for the deepest sadness seemed to convey itself in the clear depths she looked into.

"Who wants to know?" he asked, rising to his full, intimidating height.

Chapter Fifteen

The wary tone of the man's voice couldn't stop Libby from stepping forward. The other men moved on, shuffling down the warped planks of the dock, mumbling and stealing glances over their shoulders as they went. She looked up into the man's haunting blue eyes with what she knew must look like pleading.

"We need to find him," she said. "I have a good friend who once knew him very well. She's extremely ill now, and I thought he should know." Libby didn't consider her words a lie. If they didn't find Thomas Kane, Caro's future looked bleak.

The man's eyes widened and filled with concern. "What did you say your friend's name was?"

Libby knew he was fishing for information, but she didn't care. If this man was Thomas Kane, and her heart raced at the very thought, he deserved to know the whole truth. And even if he wasn't, she knew she'd have to tell him to get his cooperation.

"Her name is Caroline Cooper," she announced. The expressive eyes blinked rapidly in recognition, and Libby cheered inwardly. "She used to own the tavern around the corner."

"I know who she is," he admitted. "Every man on this dock knows Caro. We didn't know what had happened to her, though. You say she's poorly?"

"Yes, it's her heart." Feeling she'd given enough details to expect a few in return, she added, "Do you know Thomas Kane?"

"I do."

John met her eyes, and she knew he thought the same thing she did. She turned to the sailor and voiced their question aloud. "*Are* you Thomas Kane?"

A wry grin split his leathered face, and he shook his ragged head. "No, I'm not."

Disappointment settled over Libby like a wet wool blanket, locking in the humid, smelly air around her. Suddenly the dock seemed less than picturesque. Her shoulders slumped, and she felt John lay a sympathetic hand against them. Deep down, Libby had known that hope was too good to be true.

235

"But Thomas used to sail with us on the *Wild Card*, up until two years ago. Then he went to a ship named the *Elise Marie*."

"Do you know where we can find that ship?" John sensed Libby's despair and took up the conversation.

"Sure, it's on a run to the Orient. Passed us a week ago on the way out."

A cry of anguish broke from Libby's tightened lips. She saw their plan die before it had even begun. For the first time, she found she needed John's strength. He seemed to sense her pain and put a supporting arm around her, drawing her into a half-embrace.

The sailor saw Libby's reaction and hurried on. "He wasn't on the *Elise Marie* when we made contact with her. I know because I asked. We were shorthanded the last leg of the trip on account of an epidemic of influenza, and I was going to ask him to come aboard and lend a hand bringing the *Wild Card* into port."

"Do you have any idea where he might have gone?"

The man shook his head, his look of distress plainly written on the weathered face. Libby knew he'd help them if he could. She wanted to ask him if he'd been close to Thomas and Caro, but she didn't. If the sailor didn't know where Thomas was now, it didn't matter anyway.

"I took on a few of the hands from the *Elise*, though. Maybe one of them could tell you something. If you can find them. I paid them full wages for volunteering to switch ships, and they lit out as soon as we docked to find other work. I'm afraid I have no idea where they went, but I can give you their names."

The man's concern touched Libby. She almost wished he had been Caro's beau. He didn't lack anything in looks, he certainly had compassion, and he seemed very interested in Caroline's well-being. But all that hardly mattered. He wasn't Thomas Kane, and he'd never be able to take the other man's place.

"Thank you, we'd appreciate that," John was saying.

The man took a scrap of paper from his pocket and picked up the stub of an old charcoal pencil he'd been marking invoices with. Licking the tip of the lead, he scribbled something on the paper. John took the names and stashed them in his coat.

Libby shook off her dismal mood and managed a smile for the man. "Thank you," she said. "You've been very helpful." It wasn't wholly true, but she could see that it made him feel better.

"My pleasure," he said, his doleful eyes unusually bright. "And when you see Caro, would you give her a message for me?"

Libby nodded.

"Tell her—tell her Beck says hello. And tell her we sure do miss her around here."

"I will, I promise."

He started to walk off, then turned back. "You said she was ill?"

Again Libby could only nod.

"Let me know if there's anything I can do. I'll be in port a while. The owner of Trader Joe's knows where to find me most all the time."

"Thank you," Libby whispered, watching him walk away, his massive shoulders slightly stooped. When he disappeared out of sight, she looked up at John.

"He was in love with her, too."

John smiled and brushed a strand of hair away from her forehead. "Yes, I'd say Caro left behind more than one broken heart when she left Pensacola."

Libby sat sipping a cool glass of lemonade in the cafe on the corner. Most of the taverns known to be frequented by the sailors were within a four-block radius of the main docks. John had deposited her in the cafe while he made inquiries at each of the taverns.

He was gone less than an hour, and Libby immediately noticed the disappointed look as he approached her table.

"No luck?"

He shook his head. The same waitress who had served them earlier hurried to the table, but

John waved her away. "Nothing definite. One of the barkeeps suggested a boardinghouse on Alcaniz Street, three blocks east of here. He said the owner sometimes lets rooms to the sailors waiting to sign on a ship."

Libby pushed her glass aside. "Shall we go?"

John dropped some coins on the table and they left the cafe. He took her arm as they crossed the street, and she noticed for the first time the uniformed man directing the various conveyances through the intersection.

They waited until he waved them across. So many changes, Libby thought. Cars, traffic lights, things she hardly noticed in her time these people had never even heard of.

"Libby?"

"Coming," she said, dragging her gaze away from the congested intersection.

They strolled three blocks along the bricked walkway the without speaking. John instinctively seemed to know she needed time to think, to consider everything she'd seen since their arrival.

The clatter of wooden wheels on the uneven brick road made a *chu-wump chu-wump* sound as the buggies and carriages passed by, their passengers oblivious to the turmoil inside Libby.

They approached the corner of Alcaniz and Government Streets and Libby stopped and stared, a tight smile on her lips.

"What is it?" John asked, looking past her to the grassy lot which encompassed the entire block.

"Seville Square," she whispered.

A quick flash of surprise crossed his face and he grasped her arm. "You do remember!"

"What?" Libby shook off the moment of comfort and faced John.

"Seville Square. You recognized it."

The park was little more than a vacant lot, with plush green grass and a couple of black wrought-iron benches. No elaborate white gazebo or cement sidewalks had yet been built. But the Episcopal church, which had become a museum in 1993, was on the far right side. Solid and reassuring somehow, it looked just the same as it had the last time she'd seen it.

"Libby?"

"I'm sorry," she said, taking a deep breath and forcing her mind back to their task. "Which way?"

They turned right and found the boarding house easily. A huge white clapboard structure, it boasted a crude, hand-painted sign reading *Burnett Boarding*.

"Shall we?"

Taking Libby's elbow, John led the way up the three steps to the door and knocked.

He pressed the round button next to the door, and they heard a buzzer sound behind the door. After several minutes, footsteps could be heard.

"Yes'm?" the middle-aged woman said, by way of a greeting. A dusty rag hung over one slightly bent shoulder, and her gray hair stuck out in wiry wisps.

John introduced them both, then told the woman why they'd come.

"Yes'm, I get sailors regular. Don't have any right now, but I hear a few vessels have come in today."

"We're interested in some sailors who were originally employed on the *Elise Marie*. They came in today on the *Wild Card*, and we were hoping some of them might have come here for a room." He read their names off the paper Beck had given them.

"They might, but not tonight most likely."

"Why not?"

She quirked a gray brow and grinned, showing badly chipped and yellowed teeth. "Well now, you're a man. If'n you'd been out to sea for months, what would you do first thing after settin' foot on dry land?"

Libby flushed and John frowned, obviously disturbed by the woman's bawdy remark.

But the proprietress of the boardinghouse only cackled dryly. "Yep, they're most likely out gettin' foxed now. They'll buy 'em some company for tonight and come looking for a decent bed sometime tomorrow, after they sober up. That is, if they don't get another ship out first."

"Well, thank you," they said, turning to go.

At the street, John turned back. "Wait here," he said. He jogged back up the walk and caught the woman before she closed the door. He said something, she nodded, and Libby saw him hand her a coin from his pocket.

She waited for him to return to her side. This time, she took his elbow as they walked back toward the park on Alcaniz Street.

"Do you want to go back to the hotel?"

She paused, glancing around. Suddenly, she wanted to see more of the town. It might be her only chance, and it was the chance of a lifetime.

"Can we walk around some more?"

He nodded, and they started across the expanse of grass. As they reached the other side, Libby heard a bell clang and jerked around.

"A trolley!"

"Pensacola's newest attraction," he boasted, not understanding her surprise, but seeming pleased by it. "Would you like to ride?"

She smiled up at him and bit the corner of her lip. "I'd love to," she breathed, jolted anew by the astonishing events she found herself taking part in.

A trolley, in Pensacola! She hadn't even known there'd been one here, and yet here it was before her eyes. A bright, cherry-red wooden structure with sparkling windows and gleaming brass trim. The pole atop the roof connected to low-hanging wires running the length of the street as far as she could see.

"Come on," John said, grinning at her enthusiasm. He took her hand and they glanced both ways quickly before darting across the road.

The conductor accepted their penny fares and waited for them to be seated. Libby touched the wicker seats, ran her finger over the oak supports, and opened the window, all with the exuberance of a child. John eyed her surreptitiously from the corner of his eye, but didn't comment.

She saw the conductor open the box over his seat and turn the cylinder so it read *East Hill*.

"The trolley's become quite popular with the affluent residents of the hill," John whispered, leaning in toward Libby so close that she could smell the sunshine on the heavy fabric of his clothing. His warmth engulfed her as they pressed together on the narrow seat.

"Oh?" She looked over the other passengers on the trolley and noticed the elaborately garbed women and men settling in for the ride.

"Yes, they can afford the fare, so they take the trolley in the evenings to catch a breeze."

The sun was setting as the box-like trolley chugged ahead. Libby settled against the comfortably cushioned back of her seat and let the faint current of air sweep over her. She could certainly understand why the folks of this bygone century would need whatever small measure of relief they could find as summer approached. Florida could be oppressively hot, even with modern air-conditioning and the light clothing prevalent in her time.

They rode on in silence until a passenger, a businessman two seats ahead of them, pulled the cord to inform the conductor that he wanted to get off.

The trolley jerked to a stop, and the man collected a leather satchel and stepped down. Libby followed him with her eyes as he started across the walkway to a low iron fence.

She gasped, and the strangled sound died in her throat. The house the man was approaching looked familiar. Libby whipped sideways in her seat, trying to keep the man in sight as the trolley lurched forward.

A pretty young woman came to the door to greet him, a small child on her hip. Libby saw the man kiss the woman's cheek and take the baby from her arms before closing the door.

She swallowed hard, realizing where she was. The Historical District! The man's home had recently been renovated in Libby's time under the careful scrutiny of the Historic Society. She'd gone there once, for a meeting with the prominent attorney who'd bought it for use as an office complex.

Next door, another house was under construction, and she watched the workers gathering their rudimentary tools as they prepared to end their workday. This house was being built for someone. Another prominent family would soon inhabit it. Laughter and tears would ring through the rooms for generations to come.

And then, in a hundred years or so, some wealthy accountant would purchase it for a tax write-off.

"Libby, is anything wrong?"

Facing the front once more, Libby could only shake her head.

"Are you ready to go back?"

"Yes, I think I am," she said, deciding it might not be a good idea to see too much of the past. Somehow, she didn't think she'd ever look at downtown Pensacola in the same detached light again. That is, assuming she ever saw it at all.

They reached the end of the line, and the conductor jumped down to disconnect the long pole from the overhead wire and walk it around to the other end of the trolley. He reconnected it and climbed aboard, situating his seat in what had been the back of the conveyance.

The other passengers filed off the trolley, each one flipping the back of the double-sided seats to face the opposite direction.

Libby and John stood and repositioned their seats so they were now headed back the way they'd come. Again, the conductor opened the box and rolled the cylinder, this time making the lighted sign read *Palafox Street*.

Chapter Sixteen

Libby and John returned to the hotel that night tired and disheartened. Silently, they walked through the lobby, rode up in the elevator, and crossed the polished wood floor of the hall to the door of Libby's room.

"Don't be too disappointed," John said, finally breaking the silence. "Maybe someone will hear something from the sailors off the *Elise Marie*. We left word at a dozen places where we could be reached at the post. Everyone seemed eager to help, and they all promised to let us know if anything turned up."

Libby forced a thin smile. "Thank you for offering a reward for information. I'm sure that accounted for some of the eagerness to help."

John flushed and shook his head. "It was nothing."

He took Libby's hand in both of his and pretended to study the perfect half-moons of her fingernails. Her eyes took in the top of his head as he continued to look down. The soft swirl of a cowlick crested the crown of his skull, somehow making him seem younger and more vulnerable. She had to fight the urge she felt to trace the boyish feature with her fingertip.

Would he look up at her if she did? Would she see a softer, more approachable mien than he usually wore? Or would the pain and bitterness etched permanently into the lines of his face still be there?

Libby longed to open her door and draw him silently into her room. She wondered briefly what his reaction would be to such a brazen move. She let her mind imagine the beauty of a night spent in his arms, and her blood heated. Nervously, she cleared her throat.

"Thank you again for coming with me, for all your help."

He looked up, met her gaze, and smiled. "I just hope it does some good."

"I'm sure it will." She saw his gaze drop to her lips, and the resulting sensation spiraled through her. Her fingers tightened on his. They'd shared the day together, but more than that they'd shared concern and disappointment. It had drawn them closer.

He leaned forward and she met him halfway. Their lips touched, pressed, and feathered. He drew back, a question in his eyes. She closed her eyes and parted her lips. He took them with his, the kiss full of the passion and need that had bound them since their first meeting.

Libby rose to deepen the kiss, and he clasped his hands around her waist to pull her more fully against his body. Her hands fluttered about, looking for a place to rest, then settled on his shoulders. She opened her mouth to his questing tongue, kneading the muscles of his arms with trembling fingers.

When they finally parted, both were winded, as though they'd run a great distance. His eyes drooped sexily. Libby had never seen a more perfect man, and her pulse sped up even more.

But behind the desire and longing, she saw the flicker of vulnerability she'd wondered about just moments ago. The little boy, orphaned and alone, still resided inside the hardened man before her.

She had to remind herself yet again that she could not stay in this time with him. She would return home the first chance she got. And he'd be left behind, confused and possibly hurt.

He'd confessed on the docks that he wanted her physically. And she was honest enough with herself to admit she'd not be adverse to a relationship with him. But she also knew, with a cold certainty she couldn't ignore, that it would be impossible. They had no future together, and John didn't need someone in his life whose presence was only temporary.

He'd been deeply affected by the loss of his family, and when he decided to open his heart and his life to someone, it would be forever. Libby couldn't offer forever. The time she had left would never be enough for all the things she longed to share with him.

Pressing a chaste kiss on his cheek, she decided not to start something they couldn't finish. "Good night," she whispered.

He didn't pause, didn't seem upset by her sudden withdrawal. He took the long, thin key she'd removed from her reticule and opened her door.

"Good night, Libby."

He let her into the room, waited while she lit a lamp, and then said good night once more. Libby watched him go, her heart aching.

After removing her clothing, she used the water basin to take a sponge bath and slipped beneath the crisp hotel sheets.

They had to return to the post in the morning; John needed to get back. And they still had very little information about Thomas Kane. All they could do was go home and hope for a break.

Libby prayed it would come before Langdon lifted the ban. She wasn't sure she could leave not knowing Caro's fate. The more she thought about it, the more she realized how hard it would be for her to go back at all. Especially without ever having known John's love. Would she forever wonder what might have been? Would she return to her time and find all the men somehow lacking now that she'd met him? Was she destined to seek out the man who could take the place of a ghost?

"Well, I'm sorry you didn't learn anything in Pensacola, Libby, but you were right. I've never seen John look so good."

Caro puttered around the kitchen in her robe, having just risen from a nap. Pilar had welcomed Libby back and departed for home. Her haste left Libby with the notion that things had improved between the Boudreaxs. John hadn't come in, but had gone straight to the post.

Now Libby tried to look sufficiently disappointed so Caro wouldn't suspect that the story of looking for her family had been a ruse. But she couldn't quite carry it off.

John did look good, and she knew she'd had a hand in it by getting him away from the post—and Geronimo—for a time. And nothing, not even their failed mission, could lessen her triumph there.

"Yes, he does, doesn't he?"

Caroline saw the excitement dancing in Libby's bright eyes. She grinned widely, studying the younger girl, then laughed out loud.

"Well, I'll be. You're in love with the Captain."

Libby ducked her head, suddenly shy. What could she say? The truth flashed on her face like a neon sign. She'd never felt this way about anybody before, and she had no experience trying to hide the emotions.

"I'm just tickled pink," Caro said, dropping the striped dishcloth she'd been holding and taking Libby's hands in hers. "Oh, I just know you two are going to be so good for each other."

Libby flinched, realizing she'd given Caro the wrong idea. She couldn't let the housekeeper think there would ever be anything between her and John.

"I know you want to find out what you can about your past, and of course John just wants to forget his, but you'll work it out. Why, already—"

"No, Caro," she cut in, trying to stop the woman before she had their wedding planned and a name picked out for their firstborn. "You don't understand. I love John, I won't deny it. But I'm leaving in a few weeks, and where I'm going John can't go."

"Can't go? What do you mean?" Her face lit up and she hurried on. "If it's his post here that's worryin' you, don't let it. He's been thinkin' of leavin' the Army for some time, Libby—I don't know if he told you that. If you've got family somewhere you got to get home to, I just know

251

he'll want to go with you. I've seen the change you've made in him, Libby. How could anyone miss it? And, I have to tell you, it warms my heart to finally see somethin' besides loneliness and despair in his eyes."

"Oh, Caro, I don't want to hurt John. I've seen the change in him, too, and I wish things could be different between us. But they can't."

The tears came then, as she'd known they would. For days she'd tried to tell herself it wouldn't be this hard. But she'd only lied to herself. It would break her heart to leave John.

"Hush, child," Caro soothed. "You're confused because of the memory loss. . . ."

"No." Libby lifted her head and met Caro's enthusiastic gaze with new determination. She cared for this woman and, no matter what the consequences, she couldn't lie to her any longer.

"I don't have amnesia, Caro. I never did. I know where I'm from, and I know I have to go back there when the time comes. All this," she said, waving at the room but indicating her life there, "has just been temporary. I never expected I'd find people here I'd come to care for as much as I've come to care for you and John. I thought I'd just bide my time until I could get back to Fort Pickens and leave." Another rush of tears filled her eyes. "I never dreamed I'd fall in love."

"Why, Libby? Why would you pretend you

couldn't remember anythin'?"

Libby read the hurt and confusion on Caro's face, and shame gripped her. "I'm sorry, Caro. But I couldn't tell anyone the truth." She still couldn't. Who would believe her?

"I see."

Now the lined face held disappointment. Libby cursed to herself. Had she only made things worse? Caro felt betrayed. She'd confided her deepest secrets and feelings to Libby, but as much as she longed to, Libby knew she didn't dare reciprocate. All she could do was try and make her friend understand.

"Caro, please try to understand," Libby pleaded, her lips trembling. She fought for control, but she couldn't bear the overwhelming grief she already felt. "I didn't mean to hurt anyone."

Caroline quickly took Libby's hands and pulled her into a fierce hug. "Shhh, it's all right. You don't have to tell me anythin'. I know about keepin' things inside, Libby. Just know I'm here if you want to talk. If you can't tell me what's troublin' you—well, that's all right, too. I never meant to pry."

No, Libby thought. Caro would never pry. She hugged the housekeeper with more affection than she'd known she could feel. Libby had never had a great relationship with her mother. Oh, she loved her mother and was loved in return. But they'd never been as close as she and Caro were at that moment.

"If you say you can't stay, then that's that. I'm sure you know best. But, Libby," Caro said, pulling back to look at her. "There isn't any reason you and John can't enjoy the time you have."

"But, Caro . . ." Libby started.

Caroline held up her hand, motioning Libby to be silent. "Nope, you don't have to tell me another thing. You say you love the Captain, and I say that's all that matters. If you're married, betrothed, or whatever, that's none of my business."

Libby quickly shook her head, eager to tell Caroline it was nothing like that. But Caroline only silenced her once again.

"You've been good for John, and I know he'll only get better with you lovin' him. I know there's folks who'd be shocked by what I'm about to say, but I've lived a long time and I've learned that life is too short to worry about what other people think. If it feels right in here," she said, clasping a hand to her chest, "I say you have to grab what happiness you can."

Libby scrubbed the tears from her face and sat back in her chair. "You don't mean . . ."

"Yes, I do. I told you about my past. You know how much I loved Thomas, even though I knew he would never marry me. But I'll tell you right now, I never regretted one minute of the time we had together. And if I had to do it all again, I wouldn't hesitate. Sometimes all you get in this life are brief moments of happiness. And that's better than no happiness at all, I can tell you. If it isn't meant for you and John to spend a lifetime together, then so be it. But you've got to make the most of what time you have while you can."

"Are you suggesting an affair? But Caro, he'll only get hurt when I leave."

"At least he'll be feeling somethin', which is more than he's done in years. There are good and bad emotions, Libby. I'm not denying that. But livin' without any feelings a'tall ain't really livin', is it?"

Libby scooted out of her chair and gripped the back of it in her hands. Her heart was pounding so hard that she could hear it in her ears. She scanned the kitchen briefly before letting her eyes go back to Caro. A tumble of perplexing emotions assailed her.

"If I told him the truth—if he understood that I can't stay," she ventured, swimming through the tide of confusion. "Then it would be all right. If it was what we both wanted, then we could, couldn't we?"

Caro grinned. "I don't see why not. You're both adults. You ought to know your own minds."

"Yes. Oh, yes, I do. I know I love John. And even if he doesn't love me, I know he cares."

She thought of his arousing admission on the

docks of Pensacola Bay, and the heat of longing sizzled inside her once again. He wanted her as much as she wanted him. And Caro was right—there was no reason they shouldn't give in to their feelings. As long as she was honest with him, he wouldn't get hurt.

She looked at Caro and wondered how the woman had developed such a progressive attitude for her times. Not that Libby believed in casual sex. She never had and she never would engage in a superficial fling. But she loved John Faulk. Deeply and passionately. And she could never feel ashamed of that. Still, that didn't mean John would agree.

"It's easy for you to say something like that, Caro. And it's easy for me to justify how I feel, but there's something we haven't considered. What will John have to say about it? He's so incredibly honorable. Won't he feel obligated?"

Caro shrugged absently, but her eyes continued to watch Libby closely. "You'll never know if you don't give it a try. Besides," she added with a knowing grin, "you'd be surprised how little honor means to a man when he's caught in the throes of passion."

Yes, Libby reminded herself, some things never changed. And this wasn't the first time she'd found similarities in the opposing centuries. Caro was right. She and John should make the most of the time they had together. And it was up to her to make the first move.

Chapter Seventeen

He didn't know how much longer he could take it.

John shoved the papers on his desk aside and swept his hat off the rack. Damn the Apache. Damn the Army. He'd had enough. Earlier he'd almost presented Langdon with his resignation. Now he wished he had.

A fierce urge gripped him and all he wanted was to be home, with Libby and Caro. They brought peace to his tumultuous world. And he craved peace in his life more than anything right now. He was sick unto death of the fighting, the manipulating, the betrayals.

He'd walked to work that morning, and now he cursed his lack of a horse. He wanted to be home immediately.

Brisk strides ate up the ground between the post and the row of officers' houses. He passed several soldiers, but they all read the expression in his dark eyes and gave him a wide berth.

As his house came into view, he paused. It wouldn't do to go barging in foul-tempered. Libby read his moods uncannily. It had troubled him at first, this invisible link connecting the two of them. But no longer. He accepted it, used it himself to gauge her thoughts. And what he read on her beautiful face still amazed him.

What would become of them? His desire for her surpassed any emotion he'd ever felt. He longed to know every detail of her life. He loved her.

Yes, God help him, he loved her. And even if he hadn't known the feeling often in his life, he recognized it now.

But what surprised him even more than his own feelings were the ones he'd seen in her eyes when she looked at him. Unless he was sadly mistaken, she felt the same about him. It had taken a mighty resolve not to accept what she seemed to be offering lately. Only his uncertain future kept him from sweeping her into his arms and into his life for good.

How had it happened in so short a time? He didn't know. But if he had to say when he lost his heart, he'd freely admit it had been the moment she fell into his arms at Fort Pickens. Even then, he'd felt it. The sound of his heart coming to life again had reverberated in his ears.

And, unlike the times when he'd fought attachment, he'd welcomed the sweet pain of longing. Libby made him feel again—and what a feeling!

His steps were lighter as he closed the distance to the house. A ghost of a smile manifested itself on his lips. It felt strange at first, smiling, laughing, but he'd quickly gotten used to doing them again. With Libby's help. Always, Libby.

The back door was open to snare a breeze should one deem to come their way, and he stopped in a patch of shade from the porch and watched silently. Libby bustled around the kitchen, stirring, wiping, pouring. As usual she reminded John of a small whirlwind; she seemed to be everywhere at once. He shook his head, a grin tugging the corners of his mouth.

The tail of her skirt tucked into her waistband, her feet bare, she stepped quickly across the flour-dusted floor. A streak of something sticky and dark slashed across her forehead, and the spiked tips of her curled bangs lodged there. A flush colored her cheeks, and drops of perspiration dotted the exposed skin of her chest. He'd never seen anyone look lovelier. He stepped lightly onto the porch, the sound of his boots muted by her clanking and muttering.

"What smells so good?" he asked, chuckling when she whipped around so fast that a small metal bowl flew out of her hands and struck him in the shin.

"Oh, John," she cried, her hands going to her face, her dress, and back up to her hair. "What are you doing here?"

He chuckled again and stepped into the kitchen. Now that he had a closer look, it resembled the aftermath of a tornado.

"I live here."

A bright red flush covered her cheeks, and she whipped a strand of gloriously wild black hair out of her eyes impatiently.

"I meant, what are you doing home so early? I didn't expect you until later."

A small frown threatened to chase away his grin, but he fought back the remembered frustration. He didn't intend to let his problems seep into the bright, cheerful kitchen.

"I decided to take the rest of the day off."

"Oh."

It wasn't the reaction he would have imagined, but he decided not to let her somewhat cool reception bother him.

"So what are you cooking?"

"Dinner."

He grinned. "Yes, well, I can see that. I meant, what is it?"

"Oh, um—shrimp. Shrimp Creole with rice and new potatoes."

"Smells delicious. Caro find a new recipe? I don't think we've had this before."

"It's my recipe. Caro's gone to visit with Pilar since Captain Boudreax has all-night duty at Pickens again. We're—I mean, it's just going to be me and you."

John swallowed hard. Alone? He hadn't bargained on that. Was it a good idea, the way he felt tonight?

"Well, I'll get cleaned up and be back in a jiffy to lend you a hand."

"That's all right," she said choppily, shoving aside all the splattered utensils. She brushed her hands down her sides. "Everything's almost done."

She rushed to the doorway. "Just let me put on something else and I'll fix you a drink in the parlor."

She shot out the door and disappeared up the stairs before a reply could even form on his tongue. What on earth had gotten into her? She acted as if she had a bee in her bustle. Except of course, Libby never wore a bustle, or petticoats either, he'd bet. No, he always felt lucky to find her garbed in a modest dress and somehow suspected that to be no small concession on her part.

He went to his room and changed his shirt for a clean one, sponging the perspiration from his chest and arms. He removed his sidearm and sword and dusted off his boots. Shaking the queue loose at the back of his head, he ran a comb through his hair and opted to leave it unbound.

Sensing Libby's embarrassment at her untidy appearance, he purposely lingered longer than necessary in his room to give her time to freshen herself.

When he entered the parlor a half hour later, Libby stood with a glass of whiskey in her hand, as promised. She looked lovely in a pale yellow gown sprigged with tiny flowers and cinched in at her waist with a wide yellow ribbon. Her hair hid beneath the fragile-looking piece of embroidery he'd seen her wear in Pensacola. A hesitant smile played at her lips.

"You look very pretty," he said.

Her smile blossomed.

"You look very handsome," she replied, her eyes telling him that her words were more than courtesy.

She took a step forward, the drink held out to him, and tripped on the hem of the dress. The whiskey spilled from the glass, the glass fell to the floor, and Libby stumbled forward.

John's arms reached for her and he broke her fall with his chest. Her breasts pressed intimately against him, and he tightened his hold for a long, aching moment, relishing the feel of her body next to his.

262

"Oh, sh—" She managed to bite off the last of the curse, but John fought a bout of mirth at her reaction.

When he couldn't stand it any longer, he laughed and set her on her feet. Her glassy eyes froze the laughter in his throat. "What is it, Libby?" Was she going to cry? Lord, he'd never seen her cry, not even when she'd been taken forcefully from the island and made to face Colonel Langdon.

"Nothing," she said, turning away and bending to pick up the glass. It had landed on the braided rug intact, but the whiskey stained the floor.

John reached down and, clasping her around the waist, swept her back up to her feet.

"I have to clean this mess up."

"No, leave it. Talk to me, Libby. You're about to cry."

"No, I'm not. I'm just irritated with myself. You'd think I'd be used to these skirts by now."

Again her words lent truth to his suspicions. She knew every detail of her past. But where could she have come from that she hadn't worn long skirts? It made no sense.

"I need to check dinner."

"Libby." His call stopped her at the parlor door. She turned to face him, her eyes full of disappointment.

Already missing the feel of her in his arms, and not wanting to lose the closeness, he simply held out his hands. She looked uncertain, wary, but after only a second she flew into his embrace.

"I wanted everything to be perfect. But you got here early and I looked a mess. Then I spilled the drink," she babbled into his shirt.

"Perfect? For what?" He tipped her chin up but refused to release his hold on her.

She tried to lower her head, but he held her gaze. "Tell me."

"I wanted to make this night special, because . . ."

A rocket of awareness went off in him. He noticed the scent she wore. He felt the ridges of her corset beneath his fingers. Caro had told him that Libby refused to wear the thing before. Suddenly he knew what it all meant. And panic gripped him.

But so did desire, and his passion had been held in check too long. He breathed her name on a sigh and lowered his mouth. Finally. He'd longed to kiss her like this ever since he'd first set eyes on her. Their brief encounter that night in the kitchen had only fueled his need.

Parting her lips, he supped from their sweetness. God, he couldn't get enough. He pressed her body closer. She molded her form against his. He groaned; she answered with a soft murmur of encouragement.

His hands ached to touch her skin, and he brought them up to cup her face, her neck.

Boldly, her own fingers trailed up his forearm and she led his questing hand to the curve of her breast. John's ears pounded with the beat of his heart. He cupped her breast, formed it, reshaped it. His fingers slipped into the neckline of her dress. Flesh warmed flesh. She cried out and bent to give him access.

"Libby, Libby. God, we can't do this." His lips trailed her neck and throat. His trousers were so tight that he feared his buttons would soon give way with audible pops.

"Yes, John, we can," she told him, her own hands caressing his back wildly. She skimmed every inch, as though to imprint him on her palms.

"I want you so badly . . ."

"I want you as much," she confessed, not at all shyly.

His arousal grew. He could almost hear the thread holding his fasteners groan.

He drew back, a coldness seeping into the space where she'd been. He wanted her warmth against him, but he knew he couldn't have her. Not now, maybe not ever.

"I can't, Libby." With a supreme effort, he released her completely and stepped back. She swayed toward him, and he almost lost his resolve.

"My life is so uncertain. I can't say the words I long to say to you."

She tipped her head and wet her lips nervously with her tongue. The action nearly sent him over the edge.

"I don't need words. And I don't want to waste what little time we have together with regrets."

Could he? Misery assailed him. He wanted desperately to cling to her. To keep her with him forever. But what did he have to offer her? He'd already decided he couldn't stay with the Army. He had no prospects, no home outside of this one he'd be forced to give up with his commission. He had nothing. And if you took into consideration his emotional state, he had less than nothing.

She bravely took the initiative when his lips refused to speak the words that would end their loving.

"I don't care about the future, John. I'll have to go soon, and I couldn't stand leaving you without ever knowing your love."

"Oh, Libby, I love you. I do." He pulled her back into his embrace and held her so tightly that he feared he might crush her. "But I could never make love to you and then let you go. And it wouldn't be fair to ask you to stay with me when I don't even know where I'll be or how I'll be living. God help me, I would ruin you for just one night in your arms."

She drew back and met his eyes. Hers shone with the inner fire he'd ignited and even now longed to stoke.

"Oh, John, is that what's stopping you? You're worried about my reputation?"

"That, and your future prospects. You'll meet someone else, Libby. And I can't let you give to me what rightfully belongs to the man you'd marry."

She gazed into his eyes with new understanding. "I no longer have what you're concerned with taking," she admitted, slightly embarrassed.

He read her discomfort and narrowed his eyes. "You've been married?" He couldn't hide his shock. Why had the thought never occurred to him? She wouldn't speak about her past; even Doctor Stein had speculated about an abusive husband.

"Are you still?"

"No, it isn't like that. I've never been married. I—" She stopped abruptly, her eyes wide with guilt.

Anger replaced his initial surprise. She must have seen his look of shock. Regret crossed her face.

"Let me explain," she said, quickly stepping toward him. He backed away.

"Who, Libby?"

"It doesn't matter," she hedged. "It was a long time ago."

"Did he force you?"

"No."

He felt her word like a blow to his gut. "Coerce

you?" She shook her head, those gorgeous green eyes filled with apprehension. "Seduce you?"

"No. Please understand. . . ."

"You had an affair with a man, Libby? You went to him willingly, as you were about to do with me, now?"

"It wasn't like it is with you, John. I thought I loved him, but I was young. He wasn't interested in anything long-term, and I agreed."

"Just as you did with me, right here, a moment ago."

"No," she cried, clutching his arm. "I didn't love him.

"My God, Libby. That makes it worse." He shook off her stiff fingers.

"You don't understand how it is where I come from. Things are different."

"Where is it you come from, Libby? Tell me where this place is where the women don't dress in modest clothing and where intimacies are entered into without commitment."

Her lips opened, but no sound came forth. Anguish filled her eyes and she bit off a sob. He wished he could forget what she'd told him, but he knew he never would. His anger and feelings of loss made him push harder.

"I think it's time you gave me some answers. I know you don't have any memory loss. You probably never did. What were you really doing on the island that day? Plying your trade as I first thought? How big a fool have I been,

Libby? Is your whole reason for being here a lie? Did you think you could do better here on the post than with the Indians and soldiers at Pickens? Was I going to be your first customer? Or a patsy? Did you imagine me falling in love with you and taking you away from all that? I suppose a Captain seemed like quite a catch."

A cry of pain escaped her white lips, and she clutched her stomach as though he'd struck her. But he wondered if he'd scored a direct hit. *A place where women don't wear modest clothing and intimacies are entered into without commitment.* A whorehouse. The answer hit him like a bolt of lightning, and he felt the bile rise in his throat. Was that it? Was Libby running, not from an abusive husband or father, but from a life of prostitution?

The curse she hadn't uttered earlier now broke from him. He shook his head, trying to deny what he feared was the only explanation.

He turned and strode from the room. Climbing the stairs three at a time, he struggled to put as much distance between them as he could. But he heard her behind him, following with frantic steps.

"John," she cried, bursting into his room without knocking. "Let me explain."

"No, I don't want to hear it. God help me, I loved you. Don't ask me to hear all the details."

"But it isn't what you think. I swear."

John closed his ears to her pleas. Reacting

269

from some inner pool of self-protection, he grasped a portmanteau from under the bed.

"What are you doing?" she asked, her voice trembling.

He bit back the urge to go to her and comfort her. His fists clenched at his sides. With sharp movements he began to toss his clothing into the bag.

"I'm leaving. I'll find somewhere else to stay until Langdon lifts the ban. Christopher Boudreax can take you back to the island when the time comes. Then you can go back to wherever it is you came from."

"John, please."

He knew she was crying now, really sobbing. It hurt him to see her strength dissipate beneath his anger, but his own pain went too deep for him to feel any sympathy now.

She blocked the doorway and he hesitated. Tears flowed over her face and dropped onto her bodice, the wetness spreading like a rippling pool. He touched her cheek, the only gesture he felt able to make, and brushed past her. With no idea where he was going or what he planned to do, he walked out of the house without looking back.

Chapter Eighteen

Libby stared at her swollen face and red-rimmed eyes in the mirror and grimaced. She had to stop crying. She looked horrible. Caro had taken one look at her and reverted to her mother-hen role. Libby couldn't keep punishing herself for the falling-out with John, but she couldn't let Caro wear herself out in her concern for Libby either.

"Pull yourself together, girl," she told the grieving face in the mirror. "It's not the end of the world. Shake it off."

How many times in her life had she come home crying over someone's taunts, or some bully's jabs, and her brother, Gene, would say that to her? *Shake it off, Lib. They're not worth it.*

But Libby knew it wouldn't be that easy this time. Because John *was* worth it. He'd jumped to the wrong conclusions, and she should be furious with him for that. But she knew his conclusions came from her lies and half-truths. And his own limited world.

How could she have been so stupid as to blurt out that she wasn't a virgin? Why hadn't she considered what an admission like that would mean to a man like John? A man from a whole different era?

Because, she consoled herself for the hundredth time, you're not from his world. You couldn't have guessed how he'd react. You don't think the way he does and you never will—if you needed further proof that you don't belong here.

"That's for sure," Libby grumbled, splashing cool water on her bloodshot eyes. She hadn't slept well for two days, since John stormed out, and it showed. Dark circles ringed her red-rimmed green eyes.

"I look like I'm decorated for Christmas."

Behind her Caro laughed. "Well, I hadn't noticed it before, but now that you mention it they do sorta look festive."

Libby glanced back at the housekeeper and forced a tight smile. "Thanks a lot."

"I got another skirt for you. Sue just brought it from the laundry all pressed and hemmed."

Libby folded the damp washcloth and set it

down beside the basin, frowning at her reflection one last time. With a shake of her head, she turned to face Caroline. "You really shouldn't have bothered, Caro. I have more than enough to wear now."

"But you need something especially pretty for when Captain Boudreax takes you to the island. You can't wear what you came in."

A question had continued to plague Libby, and now she summoned the courage to ask Caroline something she'd wondered about for some time.

"Caro," she said, facing the older woman. "Weren't you curious about my odd clothes when John brought me here that day? You never said a word to indicate that you found me odd. Didn't you want to know what I was doing on the island dressed that way?"

"Sure, I was curious. But you know me. I try to mind my own business and not make snap judgments about folks. You looked pretty shaken up and seemed lost and confused. I figured you'd get around to telling me in your own time if you remembered anything you wanted to talk about. And if you didn't, I wouldn't ask."

"Did I thank you for that?" Libby whispered, suddenly feeling deeply obliged to this woman who'd made a frightening trip less traumatic.

"Sure, lots of times."

Libby saw the embarrassment on Caro's face and reached for the skirt. It was a beautiful blue-

and-white pinstriped linen. With the white, tailored shirtwaist she had she'd look like a real Gibson girl. And since the look portrayed by Charles Gibson had not yet been discovered, she might even start a trend of her own.

"It's lovely," she said, caressing the fine cloth. Caro had lots of clothes fashionable several years earlier, but she wore only dark skirts and plain white blouses around the house. Libby thought it was a shame and made up her mind right then to remedy the situation. It was long past due and, she told herself, it would get her mind off John's disappearance.

"What are you wearing?" she asked, feigning a casual interest.

"Me?" The housekeeper looked taken aback. "I won't be goin'."

"Nonsense. Langdon said he's going to allow the Indians to do their Corn Dance, which everyone suspects is really a war dance, and people are flocking in droves to get passes. Pilar told me she's going and looking forward to it even if it is frightening thinking about the Apache going on the warpath."

"Pshaw. War dance. What nonsense. If you ask me, they're all scarin' themselves silly over nothin'. The Apache wouldn't dare try a raid now, no matter what the editor of the *Pensacola Commercial* says. I suspect he's drummin' up business for his yellow newspaper."

Libby laughed, thankful at least that she still

could. Maybe she would survive this heartache after all. "I suspect you're right. But there's nothing wrong with a little ambiance to add to the excitement. You don't want to miss it."

Caro shrugged. "I haven't thought much about it." She glanced at Libby out the corner of her eye and grinned. "But maybe I'll go after all."

"That's the ticket," Libby said, putting her broken heart on hold. She struggled to look merry. "Now, let's go see about an outfit for you."

As she crossed the parade ground that evening, the moon shone brightly. The stars twinkled overhead, and Libby considered making a wish on one.

Can you wish for love? she wondered. If she thought it would do any good, she'd stay here all night until she'd made her plea to each celestial body. With a wry grin, she trudged on, her feet finally getting used to the long, cumbersome skirt.

She surveyed the shadowy silhouettes made by the Army post buildings and thought of John again. It seemed she thought more and more of him the longer he stayed gone. It had been two days, and they'd had no word from him. No one seemed to know where he'd gone or when he'd return.

She'd gotten accustomed to the ache in her

chest, feeling it there now like an old acquaintance. Would the pain ever subside? She'd been hurt before, but never like this. This chasm between her and John was so permanent, so final. He was going to let her leave without a word. And she knew that when she left Barrancas this time, John would be lost to her forever.

She twisted the length of purple ribbon in her hands. Sue, the head laundress, had eagerly offered it to Libby when she'd heard it would be used to make over a dress for Caroline to wear to the Corn Dance. The dress was a bit outdated, but with a few touches, Caro would look as stylish as the most elite women of Pensacola.

Libby was just thankful to have something to do. She couldn't stand the waiting otherwise.

Her skirts brushed the rails of the fence bordering the parade ground and she turned abruptly, a thought plaguing her mind. It would take only a minute to stroll casually by John's office and see if there was any sign of him there. She wanted to at least say good-bye.

Caro told her he'd never have stayed the night in the small office, but would have gone to the barracks instead. Libby suspected that he would have slept standing up to avoid any mention of her.

His office stood apart from the other row of buildings, as though added later when the influx of officers had demanded expansion. A rough-hewn, shed-like building, it had only one window. She stopped, stunned, as she realized that the tiny pane was lit from inside.

A wave of relief nearly knocked her over. Had he been there the whole time? Anger swept over the relief like fire through oil. How could he worry her so? Damn his stubborn pride anyway. She had a good mind to tell him a thing or two.

Good sense prevailed, however, and she thought it might be wise to see if he were alone before she burst in on him. She eased up to the window and pressed her back against the uneven planks alongside it. Tipping her head, she chanced a quick glance. What? Who?

She leaned closer. Someone was in the office all right, but it wasn't John. She knelt down and saw that the window had been opened a crack. No doubt the room would be airless without that small concession.

She turned her ear to the opening, listening, and peered through the glass. All she could see were the backs of two uniformed men. They leaned against John's desk, heads close. Neither of them was blond. She turned her ear to the window and listened.

"I told you to stop worrying. I heard him tell Langdon two days ago he wouldn't be back before Thursday. We're safer meetin' here then in the open."

"We'd be even safer if you hadn't lit that

lamp," a terse voice answered.

"That window"—he motioned toward Libby and she sucked in her breath, fearing discovery—"faces the bay. Who's going to see a little light?"

"I'd still feel better if you put it out."

A muffled curse followed, and the light was extinguished. Libby took her lead from the men's furtive actions and slunk lower into the shadows of the wall. She didn't know what they were up to, but she decided it would be a good idea to find out. She listened.

"Langdon's decision to allow the Indians their celebration couldn't have come at a better time. Me and Mick have worked out the details. He's going to be here any minute and then I'll let him explain. But suffice it to say, that damned Geronimo won't be playing up to the tourists around here for too much longer. I reckon his funeral will be the last show those Apache put on."

Libby shoved her hand in her mouth to keep back her cry of alarm. What was she going to do now? These men were plotting something. An assassination attempt? An accident? She didn't know, and she couldn't wait around to find out. This Mick, whoever he was, would be here any minute and there was no way he'd miss seeing her. And his accomplice was right. No one could see this side of the building from the post grounds. If they caught her snooping . . .

Lunging from the ground, she stumbled and staggered over her skirt hem until she could gather the fabric in her fists. Sprinting across the darkened ground toward a small clump of trees, she stopped behind one fair-sized pine and looked to see if she'd been spotted. No one lurked on the moon-washed horizon, so she steadied her breathing and tried to control her racing heart.

Had she made noise? Had they heard her? Sweat broke out on her lip and neck, but she didn't hear the sound of footsteps following, and slowly she began to relax.

What should she do? She had to tell someone what she'd heard. But who? Caro, Pilar, Captain Boudreax?

She couldn't tell Captain Boudreax. For all she knew, he might be one of the men involved. She couldn't tell Pilar for the same reason. That left Caro. But what could the housekeeper do? They wouldn't know whom to trust with the information, and Libby had no faces to identify the assassins and only one name. Mick. That could be a nickname, a partial name. It wasn't much help.

Dammit, where could John be? She needed him now, more than ever.

Another thought struck her and she gasped. Could John be involved? He hated Geronimo, with good reason. And even if he didn't know about the plot, would he stop it? Or would he be grateful to the soldiers for doing what he longed to do? No, she'd never believe that. John had honor. She trusted him to do the right thing. She had to.

After several frantic moments, she managed to collect her thoughts. Oh, why hadn't she stayed close enough to get a look at the man as he arrived? She should have tried to find cover where she could watch and listen. But even as she chastised herself, she knew she'd done the only sensible thing. Only bimbos in bad horror movies took chances like that. She couldn't risk getting caught. If she disappeared, as quickly and mysteriously as she'd appeared, who would think twice? John? Her heart had to admit the improbability of that thought.

No, she'd done the right thing. Now she had to get home with the information. Then she could decide what to do about what she'd heard.

Libby decided that she wouldn't mention the previous night's adventure to Caro. The woman's heart wasn't strong enough yet to chance any excitement. She forced herself to behave normally even though her insides quivered like jelly. When John returned, she'd give him the information; until then there was nothing she could do.

"Perfect," Libby said, touching her fingertips to her lips. "Absolutely perfect."

It had taken a strong will to get Caro to agree

to it, but Libby knew that all her efforts had been worthwhile when she watched the housekeeper swirl in a circle. They'd argued and fussed ever since the previous afternoon, but Libby had gotten her way. Caro was dressed to the nines in a stunning yellow and lavender outing dress with a beaded bodice. A lavender sash circled her waist, its ends trailing over the overskirt they'd fashioned so she could wear a bustle.

Her hair was swept up into a chignon, with one lone curl left to dance around her right shoulder. A large cabriolet bonnet of purple satin dipped low over one carefully arched eyebrow.

My God, Libby thought. She must have been dazzling in her youth. No wonder she'd broken hearts when she left Pensacola without a trace. Biting her lip, she studied the effect. If Thomas Kane could only see Caroline now.

Caro ruined the effect by blowing a stray wisp of hair out of her eyes noisily. Together they laughed, but Libby thought her friend was secretly pleased with her appearance.

The sound of the front door closing stiffened her spine. With a nervous glance, she whirled toward the parlor door, waiting for the face she knew she'd see.

"Settle down," she heard Caro whisper behind her. But it was too late. Her heart jolted, then raced. A ragged breath lodged painfully in her chest. Her legs trembled beneath her and she wished she were seated, fearful that she'd disgrace herself by collapsing.

John stepped through the opening. His gaze locked immediately on her. A sad, tired expression dulled the cinnamon brown she'd grown so fond of, turning his eyes the color of mud.

"Libby," he said with a nod. Without another word, he turned to Caro. "Why, Caro, the way you're dressed I'd think you knew ahead of time we were having company."

"Company," Libby heard the housekeeper mutter. Company? she thought. Lord, how would she ever get through the evening with another person on hand to witness her misery?

"Yes," John said, stepping back to the doorway and motioning someone forward. He grinned brilliantly, and his joy was like a knife to Libby's already wounded heart.

"I believe you know each other," he added unnecessarily as the man came into the room. The look on Caro's face and on the stranger's spoke volumes on how well they'd known each other.

The man was tall, with a husky build and a warm smile. His hair was light brown and thinning, his eyes golden brown. A bulky knit shirt covered a chest wide with muscles, and he wore rough homespun trousers.

"Thomas," Caro whispered, the color draining from her face so fast that Libby feared she'd have another heart attack. She rushed forward, but the man was quicker. He took Caro's elbow and led her to the sofa. They sat down, knees touching, and their whispered voices reached Libby. She stood, frozen, for a long moment until the pair fell together in a fierce embrace.

Caro's soft crying tugged at Libby's heart as John motioned her from the parlor, leaving the two alone together. He stared at her a long moment, then turned without a word and headed for the kitchen.

Libby had never been so happy, or so miserable, in her life.

Chapter Nineteen

"How did you find him?"

John faced the stove, busily stoking the fire. He dropped a piece of wood into the black belly and shoved the heavy door closed. Picking up the graniteware coffee pot, he went to the pump and filled it with water. When he started to dump coffee into the pot, Libby stepped forward and took it from him.

"Let me do that," she said.

He leaned against the table and ran his hands tiredly over his face.

"I had a message in my office the other day when I got there. From one of the sailors off the *Elise Marie*. He'd heard about my offer of a reward from the barkeep at the tavern. I left to go meet him. I didn't know how long it would take, so I told Langdon I'd be back Thursday. I figured if I hadn't found out something by then, I'd forget the whole thing."

He looked haggard and drawn to Libby, and she longed to throw herself into his arms and press happy kisses all over his handsome face. She wanted to tell him the truth—tell him everything—and start over. Instead, she stood silently as he continued.

"The sailor turned out to be the lead we'd hoped for. He'd sailed with Thomas for almost two years. He said that on their last voyage Thomas learned of his brother's death. When they made port, he told the Captain he had to go to Mobile, where his brother had lived. After that they'd heard rumors. The brother wasn't wealthy, but he'd done all right. With no heirs except Thomas, they figured their buddy had come into some money, maybe property.

"From there it was a simple matter of going to Mobile, looking up the obituary, and following the trail to Thomas Kane. I told him my name, why I wanted to find him, and about Caro's condition. He left me in the dust all the way back here."

Libby smiled, collected a tray, and placed four cups on it. She poured the brewed coffee into a decorative ceramic pot and added napkins and a few of the chocolate cookies she'd baked the night she'd made John dinner.

"Thank you," she said, awkwardly.

"I didn't do it for you," he said, not harshly. "I want Caro to be happy, too."

A huge lump of bitter regret choked off Libby's reply. She shouldn't let his words hurt her. But they did. Had she imagined they'd fall into each other's arms and everything would be all right? Maybe so, she admitted ruefully. She could see it wouldn't be that way.

"Shall we join them now?" he said.

She read the flicker of anxious tension in his eyes. He didn't want to be alone with her. It might have been funny, if it hadn't broken her heart a little more. She swallowed the thickness tightening her throat.

"I have to talk to you first," she said, knowing she had to tell him about the plot against Geronimo as soon as possible.

"I don't think . . ."

A coldness settled over him and she felt the chill. Lord, he could barely stand to be in the same room with her.

"It's important. And urgent."

He refused to meet her eyes. His arrogant stance hadn't softened; in fact, it seemed more rigid than ever. His shadowed jaw hardened.

"Whatever it is, I think . . ."

This time raised voices coming from the parlor cut off his words. They both turned to look in that direction.

"That's Caro," Libby said unnecessarily.

An answering bellow rattled the windows. "And Thomas."

Together they sped toward the couple, skidding to a stop in the doorway of the room where they'd left the two in an embrace minutes earlier.

"I said get out," Caro shouted, snatching the beautiful bonnet off her head and throwing it to the floor. Thomas trampled it on his way to the fireplace, but neither seemed to notice the damage. Caro's pins had fallen away with the hat and her hair fell to one side crookedly.

"Dammit, I came all the way from Mobile to see you. I'm not leaving."

The housekeeper noticed Libby and John in the doorway. "Throw him out, Captain," she ordered like a drill sergeant.

If she hadn't been so flabbergasted, Libby would have laughed at John's startled expression. He looked like a little boy who'd been called on in class and didn't know the answer. Her problems, and even Geronimo's, faded temporarily beneath this new crisis.

"Now, Caro," he soothed, stepping gingerly into the room. "What's happened?"

Libby didn't know what to do or say. She reached out and gave John an encouraging push. He shot her a helpless look. Apparently he didn't relish being the referee any more than she did.

"You!" Caro whirled on the two of them

287

suddenly and John stumbled back, accidentally treading on Libby's toe. She yelped and he jumped.

"Sorry," he mumbled, his attention already returning to the housekeeper as she bore down on him.

"This is your doin', isn't it? You told him I'd gotten feeble and needed someone to take care of me, didn't you?"

The housekeeper bore down on them, and Libby ducked behind John's massive shoulders. "I should've known you were cookin' something up. But I never thought I'd be betrayed in my own home."

"Now, Caro . . ." John said, starting toward the angry woman with more courage than Libby would have credited a lesser man with.

"We didn't tell him any such thing. Thomas can tell you . . ."

"Oh, that one's already made himself perfectly clear," she said. "He wants to marry me, take me to his brother's fancy house, and have folks wait on me 'til I die of boredom."

"I never said that," the sailor corrected quickly. He strode forward and met Caro's angry gaze head on.

"I said I wanted to marry you. And now that I have the house in Mobile and my brother's estate, we can both retire."

"Retire! Nobody is puttin' me out to pasture, you dad-blamed cussed fool."

"Caroline." John's sharp word cut the air like a command.

The housekeeper lowered her voice, but her eyes still held fire. "You never wanted to marry me before. You're only here now because he told you I'd been sick. Well, as you can see, I'm fine. I don't need your pity."

"Pity? You don't know me very well if you think I'd marry someone out of pity." The stern face softened, the whiskey eyes saddened. "I always wanted to marry you, Caro. I just didn't see any way. I knew how much you hated my voyages, but I didn't have any other skills. Sailing was my livelihood."

"You loved it," she accused.

He bent his head then looked back up at her. "Yes, I loved it. But I loved you, too. Do you know what hell I went through when I came back and you were gone? Not a trace of you remained, not a whisper of where you'd gone. I thought I'd go crazy remembering the times we'd had together. Wanting more."

Libby touched John's arm and they crept silently out of the room and back to the kitchen. If possible, John seemed even more disturbed now than the first time they'd been alone together. A bleakness filled his eyes, and two white lines bracketed his frowning mouth.

"I don't think they want coffee right now," Libby said lamely.

John glanced up as though she'd drawn him

from some deep, disturbing thought.

"I'd better check in with Langdon. Let him know I'm back."

"Wait," she cried, when he turned toward the back door.

He stopped, but didn't face her.

"I've got to talk to you."

"Later," he snapped, jerking the door open and disappearing into the afternoon sunshine before she could form a reply.

The post chaplain sweated in the heat of the early June sun. Although the bride and groom stood cool beneath the shadows of a moss-draped oak, the minister's position offered no shade.

John longed to tug at the high collar of his dress uniform, but resisted the urge. Across from him he watched a small bead of sweat appear on Libby's upper lip. She dabbed it with her finger, her eyes never leaving the happy couple in front of her. Something tightened inside John and he looked away. Why couldn't he get her out of his mind?

Why couldn't she forget him? Libby wondered, feeling the stifling heat raise the mercury in the thermometer another degree. Caro and Thomas looked wonderful. Happiness glowed from their eyes as they faced each other and spoke their vows. But a yearning loneliness filled Libby, and even her joy at Caro's good fortune couldn't lessen the aching emptiness inside her.

John cursed himself. Why had he spoken to her so harshly? He didn't even believe half the things he'd said to her. He knew for certain now she hadn't tried to use him. Libby didn't have a deceitful bone in her body, and if she'd omitted telling him of her past, she must have had a damn good reason. And he'd bet his life she'd never been a prostitute. He'd been with enough of them to recognize the hard, cold, lifeless quality they all had, as though the tender part of them had died long ago.

Libby's eyes were full of life and love. When she looked at him, he felt renewed. Her zeal poured out, encompassing him and making all things seem possible.

Or it had. Before he'd squashed it beneath his bitter rejection. Again he cursed himself.

Damn this heat. Libby felt sweat trickle down her back beneath the hated corset. She itched under the tight lacings, and her skin heated unbearably.

Even as she listened to the words that bound Thomas and Caro together in marriage, she fought her irritation. How much longer? Standing in the open yard had seemed like such a romantic idea when she'd suggested it to Caro. Now she longed for the cool interior of the house. Only for her friend's sake did she push the notion aside.

Marti Jones

"You may kiss your bride," the chaplain said, taking a handkerchief from his back pocket to swab his face.

Thomas did so, with vigor. Behind her Libby heard the cheers of Pilar and Christopher and several other guests. She pushed her own troubled thoughts aside and clapped loudly, forcing a wide smile.

"Congratulations," echoed all around the newly married couple.

John stepped forward and took the opportunity to offer his former housekeeper a chaste kiss. "Best wishes," he told them both.

Libby hugged Caro. "Thank you," the older woman whispered, tears shining in her eyes.

Libby could only nod. She released the bride and stepped back. After Pilar had offered her personal congratulations, she came to stand by Libby.

"Shall we go in and make sure everything's ready?"

Libby couldn't draw her gaze from John's imposing figure. He looked so handsome in his uniform, his sword and sidearm gleaming in the sun, the gold stripe down his leg accenting the length from hip to ankle. His shoulders strained the fabric of his coat and made his waist and hips look incredibly narrow by comparison. His long hair, neatly tamed by the blue ribbon, shone like ripe wheat.

"Libby?"

Forcing herself to look away, Libby faced Pilar. "Yes, let's go inside. Everyone will be eager for a cool drink after this heat."

They went into the dining room. Libby poured glasses of punch as Pilar took the covers off several cold salads. Before they'd finished, the guests began to wander in.

For the next two hours Libby served and smiled and tried to hide her true feelings. She'd miss Caro, but the housekeeper would be better off in Mobile with Thomas. The joy she felt for her friend couldn't be greater.

But beneath the happiness her heart ached. Every painful breath reminded her how things stood between her and John. And time was running out.

He hadn't returned from the post until long after she'd fallen asleep the night before. He hadn't even been aware of the wedding plans she and Caro had made until they'd sent word to him that Thomas wanted him for his best man.

John had sent a message back, accepting. Libby and Pilar had thrown the ceremony together while Caro and Thomas got reacquainted. At the appointed time, John had materialized, pressed and dressed.

They hadn't discussed Geronimo, or even what would happen later when Thomas took his new wife home with him. But the knowledge that tonight they'd be alone in the house

293

had contributed to Libby's nervousness. Heat suffused her from inside as well as out until she thought she'd burst into flames.

"Are you all right?" Pilar asked, coming to relieve Libby at the punch table.

"It's getting hotter in here," she explained, hoping Pilar believed the explanation. "I think I'll go upstairs and take off this corset. It's cutting into my sides."

Pilar nodded in understanding, and Libby briskly cut through the crowd in the dining room. She swept up the stairs and into her room, pushing the door only partially closed behind her.

She unfastened the buttons on her blouse with record speed and tugged the damp garment off. With frantic fingers she unlaced the corset strings and shoved it down over her hips, smoothing her skirt back into place around her freed waist.

"Libby?" John knocked softly and the door swung open. He froze, taking in her damp chest above the neckline of her chemise. The thin underwear clung to her breasts and outlined them for his view.

"I'm sorry, I saw you come up. You looked flushed. I thought . . ."

"It's all right," she said, picking her blouse up and holding it to her heaving chest. "I'm fine."

He nodded, his motions jerky and stiff.

"Good. Well, I'd better get back. Thomas and Caro are about to leave."

"I'll be right down," she told him. He started to leave, and she called out, "John?"

He turned back. Their eyes met and she saw the familiar desire mixed with painful denial.

"I really have to talk to you. Tonight."

His jaw tightened. Was he thinking about the coming night alone together? Was he wondering what it would bring?

"Fine," he said. He pulled his gaze free of hers and left the room.

Libby donned the wilted blouse and made her way back to the parlor. The guests were saying their farewells to the newlyweds. She joined in, shouting happy wishes and hurried good-byes as Thomas hustled Caro out the door to the waiting carriage. Someone had tied streamers of white crepe to the back of the conveyance along with several old shoes.

The couple waved and laughed as the carriage pulled out of the yard and onto the road leading away from the post.

All that remained to be done was the cleanup. Libby saw Christopher squeeze Pilar's hand and then release her reluctantly. Pilar smiled brightly and nodded at something he said.

So, they'd patched things up between them. Libby was glad. It seemed everyone had found happiness. And she knew she'd had a hand in bringing it about. That thought should have made her glad, but she only felt the sadness deepen within her. Why hadn't she been able to find a way to solve her own problems?

"I won't be staying for dinner."

John's words shouldn't have come as a surprise, but they did. "Why not?" Libby asked, fighting disappointment and a touch of anger. "I know it's only leftovers from this afternoon, but . . ."

"I'll be staying at the barracks until the day of the Corn Dance."

"What?" Aghast, she could only stare at him. She hadn't expected this complication. They'd never have a chance to settle anything between them if he avoided her.

"I think, under the circumstances, it would be best."

Libby studied his unyielding demeanor. His face was void of expression, his jaw grimly set. Wounded, she crossed her arms and looked away. Gathering the tiny shreds of anger, she wove them into a blanket to douse her hurt and confusion.

"Fine, hide. See if I care. You've been running since the day we met. I don't know why I thought you'd face what's between us. For that matter, you've probably been running for years. Well," she said, narrowing her eyes and staring hard into his shocked face. "There's one thing you can't run from. Somebody on your post is planning to assassinate Geronimo. Next week, at the Corn Dance."

He stiffened as though she'd struck him. Libby saw the shock and horror twist his face. His strange eyes lit with inner fire.

"What the hell are you talking about?" White-knuckled fists pressed into his sides. He rose to his full, daunting height.

Libby swallowed her apprehension and faced him, her own body rigid with righteous indignation. "I went to your office the other night looking for you."

His eyes softened briefly, but then he drew a mantle of hardness over them.

"Two men were already there, talking. A third was on his way, so I couldn't stay long enough to hear more or they'd have discovered me."

"Are you telling me these—men used my office to meet? And that you felt you were in some kind of danger from them?"

His tone reeked of incredulity. Under the circumstances, Libby couldn't blame him. It did seem incredible, even to her, and she'd heard and seen it firsthand.

"Well, you tell me, Captain. If you were plotting to assassinate a public figure like Geronimo what would you do with someone you found snooping around?"

"You heard them say this? About the assas-

297

sination? You couldn't be mistaken?"

"I heard them say they were meeting in your office because they knew you were gone. And then they said Geronimo's funeral would be the last show the Apache put on. I'm not mistaken—I was listening at the window the whole time."

"Christ, Libby," he exclaimed, slamming his palms down on the table in front of him. She jumped. "What the hell did you think you were doing? If this is true, you could have been killed."

"If it's true? Do you think I'm making this up?" She bristled, her fingernails digging tiny furrows in her palms.

"Of course not. Why would you?" He scrutinized her closely, gauging her reaction.

"Why, indeed," she snapped, offended by the implication underlying his words. Suddenly she just wanted him to go, leave her alone, before she broke down and let him know how badly he'd hurt her. "Look, I've told you what I know. Now I want to know what you're going to do about it."

"Do? What do you expect me to do?"

She gasped. "I expect you to stop them."

"What makes you think I could, even if I wanted to?"

She swallowed a dose of pure fear. Trying to get a hold on her careening emotions, she shook her head. "I know you, John. You could never let them murder that man."

"Let them? Dammit, Libby, what do you think I've been trying to do myself for the last sixteen years?"

Chapter Twenty

Libby's mouth fell open. A harsh breath caught in her throat. All she could do was stare, speechless, for a long moment.

John's fierce countenance smoothed out at her reaction, and he plowed his fingers through his hair, dislodging the ribbon, which fell to the kitchen floor.

"You can't mean that," she finally stammered.

"No? What makes you so sure?"

"Because I know you."

"You don't know anything about me. Nothing at all."

"I know you're not cruel and heartless."

"I'm that and more. And do you know why?"

"I think I know why you think you are. But you're not any of those things."

"Oh? Let me tell you something about my life, and you might find you feel differently. When I was ten years old, Cochise, the Apache chief, and his band of renegade braves paid a visit to my family's farm. I watched as they butchered my parents in our yard. My sister, just thirteen at the time, was taken captive. I got off lucky, if you can call it that. They took me to the trading post in Sulphur Springs and swapped me for whiskey and supplies. I was a green kid in short pants, but I swore that day I'd hunt the Apache down and make them pay."

What could she say? When Libby looked into John's eyes, she imagined him as a boy, living the horror, never able to close those deep brown eyes without seeing the faces of his parents and sister.

He saw the pity, and disgust quickly replaced the pain on his face. "My luck held. There was a man at the trading post that day, a retired Colonel. He took me home with him. A little later, the war broke out and he reenlisted. I stayed there, with his wife, until he returned. It took four years. When he finally came home, he'd lost a leg. So for another six years I put off my quest for vengeance. But it was never far from my mind.

"When I turned twenty, the Colonel called in a few favors and got me an appointment to the Military Academy. He said if I wanted

Marti Jones

to fight Indians, that would be the best way to do it. In seventy-five, I graduated and volunteered for the Sixth Cavalry. I did field duty in New Mexico and Arizona, saw the elephant in the Victorio Campaign, and rode with Crook's expedition in Sonora in eighty-three. And I was there when Geronimo and the remaining renegades surrendered to Miles."

He stared at her hard then, but Libby refused to look away. She'd wanted to know; now she knew. He'd seen so much, witnessed so many painful things. But still she couldn't believe that his heart was cold. She'd felt the heat within him when they kissed. Somewhere, beneath the hurt, a loving soul lurked.

"You tell me," he challenged. "I've waited for this day for twenty-six years. Why should I do a damn thing to stop it now?"

Libby shook her head even before his last word had trailed off. "No, you're not a cold-blooded killer. I won't believe that. That's the hurt little boy inside you talking. You've spent your life trying to bring your parents' killers to justice, and maybe the reality of their punishment didn't live up to your ideal of how it would be. But you're still a man of honor."

"You're wrong. I told you before, you don't know the real me. Not the hard, black shell that's inside. That's all I am anymore. I've hated for so long I don't know how to do anything else."

"You're lying," she whispered, stepping closer, tears finally coming to her eyes. He'd fought a good battle, but he wouldn't win this time. Because she'd cracked that shell and seen the sunlight shine through. When he held her, loved her, there was no hate in him. She touched her fingers softly against his chest and pressed closer.

John looked at her as if he were memorizing every feature. He didn't move to touch her, but he didn't pull away.

"When you held me, kissed me, a warm, loving, gentle man fought to get out. Kiss me now, John. And set him free. Set yourself free."

His hands came up slowly, hesitantly, to grip her arms. His head lowered. Those wonderful, expressive eyes drooped, their lids closing lazily. Hot breath, scented with whiskey, fanned her face. Aching to feel what she'd missed so desperately, Libby leaned into him.

Suddenly she felt his body stiffen. The hands holding her tightened painfully, and he shoved her away. A look of such bitter resentment filled his face that she staggered back.

"No, damn you," he ground out. "No, you're wrong." He spun around and slammed through the back door. It flew back, hit the wall, and banged closed behind him.

He was gone.

Libby smelled something burning. Looking down into the pan, she cursed. Grabbing a dishcloth off the peg over the dry sink, she removed the scorched skillet of eggs from the stovetop.

Why had she thought cooking would get her mind off her troubles? All she'd managed to do was ruin another pan. Not to mention that she could have burned the house down and not even noticed.

Pressing her fingers to her throbbing temple, she wondered where John had gone. Would he come back? What could she say to him even if he did?

She couldn't understand how he felt. No one could unless they'd lived through what he had. In her time, people realized how badly the Indians had been treated. They felt pity and shame at the horrors the natives had been put through.

But for the first time Libby realized that there were a lot of victims of the westward expansion. And some of them were orphaned little boys.

She might have told him the plight the Indians would face. The trials and tears yet to come. She knew a little about the reservations and camps the Indians were sent to. But would it change his heart?

Was it possible for a man to give up a quest he'd burned with for so long? He wasn't a conqueror or a developer. It hadn't been his decision to take Indian land. The government had given his parents that right, then turned them loose at the mercy of the territorial Apache. John didn't want that land now to raise cattle or farm. He only wanted retribution. And he needed to lay to rest a memory he carried like a scar on his soul.

And Libby knew absolutely nothing about the kind of pain that went that deep.

She pried the clump of black eggs out of the skillet and dumped them into the trash. She put the pan in the sink and wiped her hands on the dishcloth.

When it was all said and done, she couldn't really help. Not when it mattered the most. She'd been a fool to think she could. Nothing in her life had qualified her to deal with a situation like John's. Her twentieth-century ideas and beliefs didn't even fit in his world. And neither did she.

Four days remained until the Corn Dance. Christopher would take her back to the island at that time. Hopefully she'd return home.

But what would happen to John? How was she ever going to go back to her life not knowing what his life held? How was she ever going to forget him?

She wouldn't.

She knew that, if nothing else. No matter where she went, no matter *when*, he would always be a part of her.

"Libby."

305

Startled, she whirled. As though she'd conjured him up, John stood in the dining room doorway. Lord, he looked so handsome in the blue uniform. She'd carry that picture of him in her mind forever, bold and daring with his silver epaulets shining, his sword and sidearm polished and gleaming. And the funny, cocked hat tipped rakishly on his head.

He reached up and swept the hat off, twisting it in his hand.

"I came back to get some things. I didn't mean to bother you."

"You don't have to go, John. This is your home."

He shrugged. He'd never thought of the house as his home; she knew that now. She realized that he hadn't even referred to the place the Colonel took him when he was a boy that way. A new anguish twisted inside her. He had no place to call home. No family.

"John," she said, reaching out to him. "What are you going to do?"

He studied the toes of his boots for a long minute, avoiding her eyes, then shook his head. "Don't ask me that. I can't answer it."

"I'm a good listener, if you want to talk."

Again, the negative shake of his head. "No, there's nothing to discuss any more."

Did he still believe the things he'd accused her of when they'd fought? Was that why he refused to let her help him? Or did he realize, even if she refused to admit it, that there was no help for him?

"I won't be long."

He turned and left the room, his polished boots echoing on the stairs. She heard the door of his bedroom open and close.

Now what would she do? She had to tell someone about the plot against Geronimo, but she didn't know whom to trust—except for Pilar, whom she didn't feel able to confide in on this matter. She was alone.

Fighting back the tears, she scrubbed the mess from the skillet and dried it, setting it next to the bowls and plates she and Pilar had washed after the party. Assorted dishes littered the top of the table, waiting to be put away or returned to their owners.

She picked up a tray of crystal punch glasses which had come from the walnut sideboard in the dining room. At least she could see that things were put back where they belonged. It gave her something useful to do while she considered her next move, and the next housekeeper would appreciate it if John didn't.

"Libby." John swung around the doorframe, a stack of freshly pressed shirts in his arms. He collided with Libby, knocking one side of the tray from her hands. Glasses fell around them, the crystal shattering in a resounding crash that seemed to go on forever before finally dying down to a pitiful tinkle.

Both stared, mouths agape, at the mess. Shirts hung askew from his arms where he'd reached for the glasses in a futile effort to save a few. And suddenly, fiercely, Libby was angry.

"Dammit!" she shouted, throwing the empty tray to the floor. "That does it!"

John held up his hands, the shirts fluttering like flags of surrender. Hands on hips, she faced him.

"I've had it with you," she cried. "Nothing I try to do for you ever works out. You won't talk to me, you won't let me help you, and because of some damned misunderstanding you won't even admit you care for me. Well, fine. I love you, John Faulk, you stubborn jackass. And it's your loss if you don't want that love. I personally think you need a friend right now, but if you're determined to suffer alone, go right ahead."

She shoved past him, vowing that she wouldn't offer him another thing. Not even to clean up the mess he'd made.

His hand snaked out, snagged her arm, and yanked her back into his arms. The shirts fell to the floor atop the crystal.

For a long moment they stood silently staring into each other eyes. Then he smiled.

"So you love me, do you? After all the things I said to you? After the way I acted? Even now that you've seen the blackness of my soul?"

His hard arms held her close, her arms pinned at her sides. She tipped her head back and glared at him, but he only arched a golden eyebrow in question.

Libby hadn't meant to make that admission. Not sure what his words meant, or that secretive smile, she refused to repeat her confession.

"You don't deserve me," she chided, fighting the hot wave of awareness his nearness caused. "You're stubborn and muleheaded. I made a mistake once, I'll admit that. But you made a bigger one. Because you're throwing away the chance at something wonderful."

"Am I?" The smile disappeared. He rubbed her back tenderly, his fingers rippling over every curve and plane. "Show me how wonderful."

She snorted and looked away so he couldn't see the fire leap to life in her eyes. "It's too late."

"Where's your spirit of adventure, Libby? Where's the pluck and mettle you've berated me with since I brought you here? Where's the woman who stormed into my life like a tornado?"

"That woman has a past you can't accept and expectations you can't live up to," she taunted.

He shook his head, a hint of a smile coming to the full lips. "No. I don't give a damn what's happened in your past. I realized that almost immediately, but I couldn't take back the harsh words I'd said. You made me feel things I've never known existed. Things I thought I didn't want to feel, ever. I came alive around you, and I admit it scared the hell out of me. So I ran. But I'm through running now. Touch me, Libby. Make me live again, the way you did before."

Their eyes met and held. His were wild and passionate, hers wary and hesitant. The air electrified around them. Blue-white currents of desire hummed along her skin everywhere his body touched hers.

"No." She offered the feeble protest.

He laughed and pulled her tighter, molding her body into the shape of his. "Yes, oh, yes. Libby, love me."

His mouth claimed hers roughly, seeking, demanding. She couldn't breathe, couldn't think. All her senses fled except her sense of touch. Her flesh burned where it met his; her mouth came alive beneath his lips.

He bent over her, gathered her up, and set her atop the table. His arm swept out and cleared the rough surface. Plates, bowls, and silverware fell to the floor. Libby cried out, but he swallowed the sound as he reclaimed her lips.

Her breath was coming in harsh, uneven pants when he finally ended the kiss. She gasped, and he swooped down once more, plundering her mouth forcefully with his tongue until her legs grew weak and her arms trembled.

Greedily, she reached out and tugged at the buttons of his jacket, pushing them through the holes. The heavy cloth fell away at her touch, and she spread her hands over the surface of his hard chest. She felt his nipples bead beneath her sensitized fingertips and heat centered in her belly. Her thighs parted and he slid between them, grinding his arousal against her dampness.

With a sharp pull, he parted the front of her blouse and buried his face in the fullness of her breasts. His hand swept over one small globe, pushing down her chemise to expose her skin to his hungry mouth. He kissed first one, then the other, bringing them both to a tight peak.

Libby groaned and fell back against the table-top. John followed her down, his body pressed full against hers, his arms cradling her back.

Fumbling between them, she released the buttons of his trousers. He sprang free, already full and wet.

"Yes, yes," he moaned, working the hem of her skirt up around her hips. She led him to the part in her drawers and he entered her.

He threw back his head and cried out as he buried himself in her heat. He shuddered and went still, and she felt his hands softly clasply and unclasping on her buttocks. When he'd gained control, he moved.

311

Libby's body tightened around him and sweat broke out along her brow. She rubbed her face against his chest and saw the perspiration trickle over his nipple, down to his flat belly and into the concave of his navel. She leaned forward and followed the path with her tongue until their joined bodies prevented her from bending any farther.

A low animal groan rose from deep within his chest, and she reveled in the power she felt in his arms. He withdrew almost to the point of exit, and then slowly resheathed himself.

Again he withdrew, and again he entered her fully. Libby writhed beneath him. Her legs wrapped his, her ankles locked together. He laved her breasts, caressed her buttocks, and pressed deeper.

Their bodies sang in exquisite harmony. They soared higher, toward the peak of satisfaction. And then they melted together in a downpour of explosive pleasure.

Sweat fused their skin, and their breaths rushed out at a lightened tempo. He slumped in her arms, and the fire turned to embers. Libby welcomed his weight, relishing the sound of their mingled heartbeats pounding in her ears. She never wanted to move. Never wanted the moment to end. She pressed her lips to his neck and felt his body spasm in response.

"Uuummmmnngh."

The weak exclamation filtered through the

wild tangle of her hair and she smiled softly.

"Me too," she sighed.

When they could both move again, John swept her into his arms and carried her to his room, where he slowly, reverently, removed the rest of her clothing. He shucked his boots and skimmed out of his crumpled trousers and together they crawled, exhausted, beneath the sheets.

Libby snuggled against his side and let her cheek rest on his chest. John made contented sounds in his throat as his arms collected her closer.

"You said my past didn't matter to you," she reminded him, between nibbled kisses. "Did you mean that?"

"I never meant anything more," he vowed, tucking her head beneath his chin.

"Good," she sighed. "Because I've decided to tell you where I'm really from."

"It's not important," he said. "All that matters is that you're here now."

"Oh, I think you'll be interested in this story," she said, a husky chuckle escaping her kiss-swollen lips.

"No matter what you tell me, I'll never feel any differently about you than I do now."

"That's nice," she whispered, turning to look up into his sweet cinnamon eyes. "Because what I'm about to tell you is a wild story."

"Uumm." He bent to kiss her mouth and gently nip her lower lip. "The wilder the better."

"I'm glad you feel that way, John. Because this is a tale of two worlds."

Chapter Twenty-One

"Your world—and mine."

Sensing her desire to share this part of herself, John pushed up in the bed. He settled against the carved oak headboard and tugged her petite form over his. His body tightened in response to the feel of her on top of him, but he ignored the reaction. Libby finally meant to have her say and he wouldn't deny her.

She stared up into his face and said bravely, "I'm not from your world, John."

His eyes darted left, then right, then back to settle on her impish face. "You're not?"

She shook her head, her curls bobbing in an enticing dance around her cheeks.

"You might have noticed that I talk differently, I dressed differently, and I had a few—progressive ideas."

Watching Libby's nervous grin struggle into place, he sat up straighter. Whatever she was about to say, she was finding it difficult. Having gotten used to her outspoken ways and bold personality, John experienced a flash of apprehension.

"Go ahead," he encouraged, rubbing her back soothingly. "I've already told you nothing can change my feelings for you now."

She chuckled then, a shaky little laugh. "Oh, John, don't be so sure."

Something in her voice sent cold apprehension over him. He'd meant what he'd said. Nothing she told him now would change the way he felt about her. He loved her, no matter what. He'd realized that almost as soon as he'd left the house after their argument. But he knew her past could affect their future.

"I'm—I'm not . . ."

"Go ahead, Libby," he said, coaxing her through her difficult admission. "Just say it. I promise you I'll understand whatever it is you tell me."

"How can you understand it, when I don't understand it myself?" She bit her lip, then blew a heavy sigh and straightened. "I'm not from your time, John," she blurted before her courage could desert her. "I wasn't even born until nineteen-hundred and sixty."

At first he thought she'd said eighteen-hundred and sixty. He couldn't understand why that should have been hard to admit. Then he realized he'd misunderstood. He sat up in bed, dislodging her.

Libby wrapped the sheet around her to cover her nakedness, but he didn't bother with such niceties.

"What did you say?"

Her eyes followed his movements. He could tell she was waiting to see whether or not he believed her. Certain the stunned disbelief he felt must show on his face, he didn't bother to hide it. Instead, he concentrated on keeping the more damning thoughts from being revealed.

Had she lost her mind? Was she lying? What possible reason could she have for concocting such a tale?

"It's true, John." She knelt on the mattress, her hair wild, her face still flushed from their lovemaking. "I was born in nineteen-hundred and sixty, graduated from high school in nineteen-hundred and seventy-eight, finished college in nineteen-hundred and eighty-two. Never married, but you know that. I worked for other people for several years and finally opened my own business two years ago. I went to Fort Pickens the day you found me because a friend of mine called me. He's a park ranger. Fort Pickens, in my time, is a part of the National Park Service. It's a tourist attraction, John."

John's body stiffened in shock. He almost

317

sprang from the bed, desperate to put some space between them.

She'd gone berserk. It was the only answer. Not wanting to startle her, he slid slowly to the edge of the bed, surreptitiously looking for his pants in case he needed to don them in a hurry.

Maybe he should go for the doctor. No, Stein couldn't treat her for delusions; he'd said so himself. He wasn't a fancy city head doctor. Libby needed someone who understood the workings of the mind. He'd get her the help she needed. He'd make sure she got over whatever ailed her.

"I'm not crazy, John," she said.

He jumped guiltily. "I didn't say—"

"You look horrified. It's not hard to figure out what you must be thinking. I know it sounds crazy. Why do you think I couldn't tell you before? But I haven't lost my mind."

Libby could see he wasn't convinced. Anxiety and uncertainty lined his face. One leg hung off the mattress as though he thought he might need to make a quick getaway. She needed something to convince him. She searched her mind and finally thought of something.

"Look," she said, turning sideways on the mattress. "See this?" She pointed to her upper arm. "That's a smallpox vaccination."

He nodded. "Yes, I know. They've been doing them for years. I've had one myself, although mine didn't leave a scar."

"Oh." Disappointment replaced the animation on her face. "I didn't realize that. Well, let me see."

She pulled back one side of the sheet and exposed a thin pink scar along her right side. "How about this? I had my appendix out five years ago, hardly even left a scar."

"Doctor Stein has operated for stomach fever a time or two."

Libby sank back, nearly defeated. What could she say? What could she do to make John believe her?

"I've got it," she cried. "I heard Caroline say the president of the United States is Grover Cleveland, right?"

He nodded.

"Well, the next president will be Benjamin Harrison." She jerked her head in a satisfied nod.

"That's very interesting," he said, his voice rife with false enthusiasm. "But since *I* have no idea who the next president will be, how does that help?"

"Oh, damn, I didn't think of that."

She sank back to the mattress, her mouth twisted in thought. John inched farther away, and she knew she had to act fast. She was losing him. The look on his face told her he was concerned and dismayed by her outburst. If she didn't come up with something quick, he might very well have her locked away in some asylum before she could click her heels three times and go home.

"Oh, I know," she cried, jumping to her feet. He scrambled back, startled by her excited shout and fast movements. "I'm such an idiot. Why didn't I think of this right off? It's perfect. You know I didn't have time to learn much from the Indians at Fort Pickens before your men turned me over to you."

He nodded again, but curiosity now replaced the apprehension. She could tell he was waiting to see what she'd come up with next.

"Well, I know that one of Geronimo's wives is named Ga-ah. She arrived with the women and children right before the ban."

"Pilar could have told you that."

"Yes," she admitted. "But does Pilar know she'll die in September of 1887? Or that she'll be buried right here at Barrancas?"

"How could you . . ."

"And that the Indian Perico and one of his wives will have a baby in March of 1888?" She was on a roll now. She'd listened to the tour speech John Ferrell recited enough to know it by heart. She repeated it all now.

"In May of 1888 the Indians will be moved without advance warning to Mobile, Alabama. From there they'll be taken to Mount Vernon."

John's eyes widened and he stood slowly, watching her closely. She knew she had his attention now and she rushed on.

"Three Indians will die at Mount Vernon and be buried in the Mobile National Cemetery. Chappo, Fun, and Ah—" The name escaped her and she snapped her fingers.

"Ahnandia?"

"Yes, that's it."

Her enthusiasm wound down and she glanced up to see if anything she'd said had had an effect on him. The look of amazement in his eyes couldn't be missed.

"Do you believe me now?" she asked, hesitant in case he still thought her deranged.

He shook his head, as though to clear it. He seemed to realize he was naked and picked up his trousers from the floor and slid them on. With only two buttons fastened, he stopped and met her eager gaze.

"The move to Mount Vernon won't be completely without warning. I suspected something was up when Stein told me Langdon had ordered physicals for all the prisoners. The Colonel told me he'd received a letter from the President asking his thoughts on the Indians' situation. Langdon is eager to be rid of them. He told me he suggested a move to the President in a letter he posted the day we spoke. Only he and I know what he proposed."

"That they be sent to Mount Vernon?"

"Yes. He also told me Stein had diagnosed

Ga-ah with Bright's disease and he didn't expect her to live long enough to make the move."

They stared at each other for a long moment, neither speaking. Libby knew he was struggling with the impossibilities she'd presented him with. He couldn't fully accept that she was from the future, but he couldn't figure out how she knew all she did either.

"What else do you know?" he finally asked.

Libby wasn't sure if he suspected her of spying or if he thought she'd gotten lucky on a few points and made the rest up.

"I know you've decided to stop the assassination attempt."

He blinked and narrowed his eyes. "What makes you say that?"

"Because I haven't told anyone but you what I overheard. And I know for a fact there was never a recorded attempt on Geronimo's life while he was held captive at Fort Pickens. In fact, Geronimo will go on to national popularity and even visit Washington. He'll live until February 1909, when he'll die of natural causes at Fort Sill."

He didn't answer. Turning, he went to the window and stared out at the crystal waters of the gulf. Libby longed to go to him and lay her hands on his burdened shoulders. Her heart ached for him, but she knew his strength would help him through.

"Yes, I plan to stop the plot to kill Geronimo," he said.

His forehead fell against the glass pane with a thump. "I wanted to ignore what you told me, pretend I didn't know or care about it. But I couldn't. I realized a long time ago that the Apache only fought to protect what they considered theirs. But I couldn't let go of my quest. Every time I thought about what the Indians had suffered, I felt as if I were betraying my family. I wanted justice, but the things we've done in the name of justice were no more just than the Apache's ways."

"They're going to suffer a lot more before it's over with," Libby told him.

He nodded and swept the loosened hair from his face. "I know." He turned to face her, and she couldn't stop herself from going to him. He took her in his arms and she snuggled close.

"Thanks to you, I think I can finally put my pain and anger aside. But there are those who never will. And they resent the fame and attention the Indians have been receiving."

"It doesn't get better for a long time," she warned him.

He clutched her tight. His long hair fell over her shoulders, and she absorbed the feel of his body through the thin sheet.

"I'm tired, Libby," he said. "Tired of the fighting, the killing. Tired of the hate and bitterness."

Libby buried her face in his chest. She couldn't bear to see his misery without breaking down herself.

"It isn't all bad," she told him. He pulled back and gazed into her eyes. "Some wonderful things are going to happen in the next hundred years."

He looked overwhelmed by all she'd told him, but he forced a smile.

"I still can't believe you're . . ."

"From the future?" She saw him wince and she laughed. "I'm still not convinced this isn't some kind of dream myself. I keep pinching myself to make sure it's really happening."

"How is it possible? How could something like this have happened?"

She shook her head. "I don't know. Geronimo said something about the oak tree being magic. I'm not sure I believe that, but then I didn't believe in time travel before I came here."

"Yes," John said. "I remember something now. When we first brought the Indians to Pickens, they were supposed to clear the grounds around the Fort. Geronimo said they couldn't cut down the oak on the tip of the island because it had special qualities or something. He mumbled a lot about their god and the tree's power."

"He tried to tell me when he found me that morning, but I'm afraid I didn't understand a lot of what he said. All I knew was that I woke up that day in nineteen-ninety-three and ended up here."

"Nineteen-ninety-three," he whispered. "My God, I still can't comprehend any of this."

"Don't feel bad. I've been living it and I still don't understand it."

"It isn't that I don't want to believe you, Libby. I'm trying, really I am. But the thought that time travel is possible simply doesn't make sense."

"No, it doesn't. Not even for someone with a progressive mind like me. I was terrified, and all I wanted to do was get back to that tree and get home. But I decided somewhere along the way that I'd think of it as an adventure. I couldn't do anything until I could return to the island, so I made up my mind to make the most of the situation until I could go home."

"Home." He pulled back and met her gaze. His eyes filled with trepidation. "If you leave, I'll never see you again. Hell, if all this is true, I'll be long dead before you're even born."

"Don't," she cried, clasping him tightly around the waist. "Don't talk about your dying. I don't want to think about it."

"Dammit, Libby, we have to think about it. I love you. I can't lose you now. What are we going to do?"

"There's nothing we can do. I have to go back, John. I don't belong here, you know that. I'd never fit in. I'm always making mistakes, like that day on the parade ground. I'm used to being independent, having my career. I like cars and blow-dryers and microwaves."

"What?"

"Modern inventions, John. I'm used to living with a lot of them. I don't know how to survive in this time. If it weren't for you and Caro, I don't know how I'd have made it this long."

"I'll help you. It'll be all right."

Libby's heart was breaking. What could she say to make him understand?

"I have family, friends. They must be out of their minds worrying about me," she said. "What will they think if I just disappeear?"

"What will I do if you leave me now?"

He sounded so lost, so forlorn. Libby wanted to tell him they'd be together always, but she couldn't. She'd always known she'd have to go back. She didn't belong in this time, and she never would.

"I don't know," she said, hugging him close again. "I just don't know."

He held her and the sheet fell to the floor. His hands stroked her, rekindling the banked embers of passion. He swept her up and laid her gently on the bed, loving her with tender longing.

Their coupling was sweet, slow, with under-currents of sadness and desperation. They both knew their time together was nearly at an end.

Chapter Twenty-Two

"Stop, stop, no more," John laughed, covering her body with his and silencing her with a loving kiss. "I can understand the automobile and maybe even the airplane, but moon exploration? You're asking my primitive mind to stretch too far."

Libby chuckled, pressing feather kisses along his neck and chest. The sheets around her were rumpled from their lovemaking, and she burrowed deeper into the folds. John pressed closer and she closed her eyes, reveling in the feel of his body against her. She savored his weight and warmth, the brush of his hair-roughened skin against her soft flesh, trying to implant the sensations on her mind forever—knowing, once she returned to her own time, that they'd have to last that long.

"All right," she said, murmuring against his throat. "I think you've heard enough about the twentieth century for now."

"I agree. Besides," he said, rolling to his side and carrying her with him. He kissed her lips once more, lingeringly. "I have to get to work."

They'd loved and talked most of the night, barely sleeping at all. Now Libby groaned and snuggled into John's shoulder. "I don't want you to go."

"I don't want to go," he told her, running his hand over her waist to her thigh. He cupped her leg and drew it up over his. "I'd be happy to stay here with you forever. But I can't. I have to talk with Langdon about what you overheard. I have to see if I can find this Mick and learn who he's working with."

Libby nodded. She knew what had to be done. But her heart only understood one thing. John loved her, she loved him, and they'd finally found happiness. With the days quickly dwindling, she didn't want to waste a single moment of their time together. Her heart ached, but she would have a lifetime to grieve. Until then, she'd savor these moments and be happy.

"Kiss me good-bye and then go back to sleep. I want to think all day of you lying in this bed, beautiful and disheveled."

She kissed him, but she knew she'd never be able to sleep once he'd gone. The bed would never feel the same without him in it.

She watched him wash, the water trickling over muscles she'd felt quiver with desire. She smelled his shaving soap, admired the long, sure strokes of the ominous-looking razor. He drew his clothes on slowly, and she felt her hunger for him grow. She envied the clothes against the skin she longed to touch. Her hands ached to draw him back to her, but she didn't. The sooner he spoke with Langdon, the sooner he'd be able to get back.

He buckled his sidearm and sword into place and adjusted them low on his hips. Bending down, he cupped the back of her neck and planted his mouth possessively over hers. Libby returned his kiss hungrily, conveying all the emotions she felt at that moment.

"I'll be home as soon as possible," he said, his eyes heavy-lidded with passion.

"It won't be soon enough," she told him, her own husky tones expressing the need she felt, the pain she fought to hide.

He stroked her cheek. She leaned into his touch. Then he was gone and she sank back against the quickly cooling sheets. She hugged the pillow to her face and breathed his scent. For the rest of her life she'd remember how it felt to wake next to him, touch him, love him. Every day of her life she'd miss all the things she'd learned to appreciate in one morning.

329

*   *   *

Libby heated water and bathed in the hip-tub in the kitchen. She washed her hair and finger-combed her curls. One of John's shirts made nice lounging attire, the lacings down the front exposing a good slice of cleavage. She made a dinner of chicken and cold potato salad, poured herself a glass of wine, and waited. She and John might not have much time together, but she'd see that what they had would be special.

She sat on the parlor sofa, her long tanned legs stretched out along the plush brocade cushion, and reclined against the carved arm. Darkness had settled over the house an hour earlier, and she lit only one lamp in the foyer. In the parlor, she'd distributed taper candles. She lit the wicks, enjoying the way the wax smelled and the way the small, flickering flames cast the room in romantic hues and shadows.

Her efforts weren't wasted. John came in calling her name, and she answered in a throaty voice. His eyes widened in surprise, his grin spreading as he stepped to the parlor door.

"What is this?" he asked. His voice sounded strangled, and he reached up and unfastened the top button of his coat as though it were suddenly too tight.

"This is just one of the advantages of the twentieth century. The women aren't shy and retiring. We go after what we want, speak our minds." She ran the bottom of one foot up the side of her other leg in her best sexy pose. "We pursue our desires."

"Oh," he choked out.

"So, how do you feel about these modern ideas?" She realized she might have shocked him, might even have turned him off with her obvious seduction. A tiny butterfly of apprehension fluttered in her middle. But his smile turned devilish, and he took a step toward her.

"Damned lucky is how I'm feeling right at this moment. And," he added, with a rueful glance at his tightening trousers, "ready for whatever you have in mind. Definitely ready."

Libby chuckled and set her glass aside. She rose to her feet and sidled up to him. "Well, now, sir," she drawled. "Hold that thought"—she glanced down his length—"until after dinner."

With one swift movement, John scooped her into his arms and juggled her against his chest, settling her high in his embrace. "No, ma'am," he said. "Dinner is just going to have to wait."

He carried her up the stairs, kicked the door to his bedroom open, and deposited her on his bed. He kissed her hard and then drew back to remove his clothes. In less than a minute, he'd stripped off his weapons, boots, and uniform. He joined her on the bed.

"Never in my life have I spent a day like today," he told her. "I couldn't wait to come home to you. All my life I've been alone. Today, my impatience to be with you nearly drove me mad."

"I missed you, too," she said, kissing his throat and letting her fingers play over his tightened nipples. "I thought the day would never end."

His hands busied themselves on her flesh, touching, caressing, memorizing. She knew she'd never get enough of the feel of him, not in a thousand lifetimes.

"I love you," she murmured, rolling beneath him and taking his welcome weight. "Love me."

"Forever."

Libby didn't know how many hours passed before her stomach rumbled and John's attention was diverted from their loving.

"I'll be right back," he said, planting a hard kiss on her mouth.

He strode from the room, bold in his nudity. She watched his buttocks flex and harden with each step, his firm thighs pumping. She sank back against the sagging mattress and moaned. Lord, he was magnificent. Damn, she was lucky. God, she was miserable.

How was she ever going to leave him? Could she do it? The real question was, could she stay? Already Libby knew the answer. She couldn't. As much as she loved John, she missed her world. And without John she'd be alone here. If anything happened to him, she wouldn't know how to function. She didn't know what skills she'd need to survive. And she wasn't used to being so dependent on someone else. She needed her work, her ability to make a living on her own. She'd fought too hard to make it; she wouldn't know how to give it all up and just be a wife.

Not that he'd asked her, she realized suddenly. John had mentioned her staying, but he hadn't said in what capacity he wanted her.

"How about a picnic?" he said, breaking her musings as he strolled through the door, tray in hand.

Cold fried chicken and lukewarm salad accompanied a fresh bottle of wine, glasses, and napkins.

"Sounds good to me." She scooted over in the bed and made room for him. He set the tray on the bedside table and frowned down at her.

"I think we sprang the straps under that mattress. You look kind of droopy there."

"I hope you're referring to the bed and not to me personally," she teased as he went to the footboard.

"You look beautiful and well-loved," he told her, twisting the knobs and tightening the straps. "And now you can sleep tight."

"What?" The phrase caught her off guard, and for a moment she could almost imagine him as a modern man, living in her world. He'd

look right at home in a Brooks Brothers suit—
or jeans and cowboy boots.

"I said you can sleep tight, now that the straps
have been wound."

She chuckled. "Is that where that expression
came from? I always wondered."

"I don't know what you are talking about,"
he said, plopping down beside her, "but I'm
more concerned with feeding my complaining
stomach."

"Oh, that's such a typical male remark."

"Well, I'm just a typical hungry man," he
said, biting into a chicken leg.

Libby laughed and accepted the piece he
handed her. They ate the salad from the bowl
and drank half the bottle of wine before their
hunger subsided.

Putting the tray aside, he pulled her between
his bent legs, his chest to her back, and rested
her head against his neck.

"How did it go with Langdon?"

He sighed loudly and pressed his mouth to
her hair.

"About the way I expected. He wanted to
know if your information could be trusted, if
you could be trusted."

Libby wanted to feel affronted, but couldn't.
Under the unusual circumstances, she didn't
blame the Colonel.

"I assured him you could. I even told him you
had opened up to me a little and that I thought

you were just running from a troubled home life. I hope you don't mind, but I didn't want him to forbid you to go along to the island when the time came."

"Thank you," she said, feeling the cold shadow of loss cast a chill over the bed. She hadn't wanted to think about leaving until the time came, but the reality seemed to always be right there, on the surface, waiting to jump out at her.

"Anyway, we searched the post records and found two candidates for the Mick character. One was a Private we'd signed on in San Antonio. He'd always struck me as being a bit too bloodthirsty, so we decided to pay him a visit. The minute we began questioning him about being in my office, he tried to run. He's in the guardhouse now, but he refuses to talk. Langdon's filed formal charges and he'll be tried."

"What about his accomplices?"

"Not much to go on there, I'm afraid. We questioned every man in his division, and one name came up more than once. It's only speculation, but I'll be watching him until the night of the dance."

"Do you mean you think they'll still try the assassination attempt? Even with their accomplice in custody?"

"I thought of that. Langdon wanted the men arrested, all of them. So we spread the word that Mick had been caught drinking on duty. That will explain his being in the guardhouse without alerting the others that their plan has been discovered. Langdon's holding Mick with strict orders that he's not to talk to anyone, so he shouldn't be able to get word to them that we're on to the plot."

"What do you want me to do? I didn't see their faces, or much of them at all for that matter, but I could try and identify them. Maybe their voices . . ."

"No," he said, his arms tightening around her middle. "I'll handle it. I don't want you involved any more than you already are."

"But, John," she complained, trying to turn in his arms.

He held her firmly in place. "No buts, Libby. Let me handle it. I don't want you in danger."

"Don't go chauvinistic on me," she threatened, half teasing, running her hands along his thighs seductively.

"Don't tell me men in your time let their women dabble in peril. I can't believe my species has changed that much in a hundred years."

"Oh, ho, you'd be surprised. Women in my time are cops, private investigators, even prison guards."

John shook his head, his lips gently caressing the top of her head. "Not my woman," he told her. "I couldn't let you do something that might put you in harm's way."

"Just living in my time is dangerous enough," she said, wondering if she were crazy to refuse his offer to let her stay here with him forever.

"In what way?"

"Crime, mostly. Rape, murder, burglary. It's all been on the rise for some time. No one seems to know where it will end."

"Then stay with me. Let me protect you."

The offer tempted her more than she'd have thought possible. But in her modern heart, she knew it would never work. Ignoring the sharp stab of regret, she answered glibly, "Sure, all I have to worry about here are Indians, plague, and archaic medicine."

"I could take care of you here. I'd always protect you."

She turned to face him, kneeling between his outstretched legs. "Then come with me. I'll let you be my knight in shining armor."

His face lined with sadness. "I can't. You say you know nothing of my world. I know even less of yours. I couldn't drive one of your automobiles or fly an airplane."

Libby chuckled. "Not everyone can pilot an airplane. I can't. But you could learn to drive."

"You talk of the mistakes you would make here—what would I do the first time someone asked me about the former presidents, or well-known inventions? And how would I earn a living? I sincerely doubt there is much demand for an old-fashioned cavalry officer and former Indian fighter."

Libby sank atop his chest and sighed. "Oh, John, there must be some way. There must be a time somewhere we can both live in together."

"There is," he said, rolling her over and gazing into her pain-filled eyes. "Right here, in this house, this room, this bed. There are no differences here. There is only me and you. And our love, which is timeless."

Chapter Twenty-Three

Timeless did not mean forever, Libby realized as she rolled up her leggings and T-shirt and stuffed them into the oversized reticule John had given her.

Their time together was at an end, and Libby felt as though she were dying inside. She dressed in the bright, cheerful, pinstriped skirt, the snowy-white shirtwaist, and a straw bonnet with a matching blue ribbon. She took pains with her unruly hair, pinning it into a ball beneath the bonnet's crown. But there was nothing she could do about the forlorn droop of her mouth or the constant dampness in her eyes.

"Ready, love?" John asked, coming up behind her and wrapping his arms around her middle.

She closed her eyes and leaned against his chest, letting his body form to hers. Reveling in his warmth, she tried to gather strength from his nearness.

"No," she admitted. "I don't think I'll ever be ready to leave you."

"You can always change your mind and stay."

She blinked back the tears and met his gaze in the cheval mirror. "You could always change your mind and go," she challenged.

He held her so tightly that she fought for breath. But she didn't mind. She longed for his touch, craved it every moment. Their days together had been magic, but now it had to end. Too soon she'd have to walk away from it forever, and she wanted to collect memories like seashells for the lonely months ahead. She turned in his arms and held him close for a long moment.

"You look lovely," he told her.

Libby smiled at the abrupt change of subject. They'd promised not to talk about their parting. They'd vowed to live each moment to the fullest and let go with courage and love when the time came. She found her courage deserting her, though, and her love was quickly turning into something clinging and weepy. She longed to melt into his arms and give up her world for another minute in his embrace. She stepped back and smiled.

"Thank you," was all she could force past her emotion-clogged throat.

"Shall we go?"

She nodded, pressed her fingertips to his cheek, and swallowed back tears.

The wharf at Barrancas teemed with people of all shapes, sizes, and social standings. The worn wooden structure threatened to collapse under the strain, but the eager occupants seemed not to notice or care. They laughed and joked, the women twirling lacy parasols, the men smoking cigars or pipes. Across the water Libby could see a huge ferry approaching.

"Will that hold all of these people?" she asked John, her anxiety plain on her face.

"Yes, don't worry. Besides, this is only one ferry, one trip. There are three ferries running today, making excursions as fast as they can cross over, drop their passengers, and get back."

"How many in all?"

"My office has signed over five hundred passes, and that doesn't include the men of the press and the folks out there in the bay on their private boats."

"How on earth are we going to keep an eye on one man in that crush?"

"Not we, Libby. Me. I told you before, I want you safely out of the way before Langdon and I move in on our suspect, or suspects."

341

Marti Jones

"No way, John." She held her hand to the top of her hat and tipped her face up. The sun shone off the golden lengths of blond hair he'd combed and secured earlier. But the severe style couldn't banish the image she carried of him in her mind. She pictured him with his hair flowing, his eyes glazed with passion. That's how she'd always remember him, looking down at her as he gave her the very heart and soul of himself.

She swallowed the desire that had her knees trembling weakly and shook her head. "I won't leave until I know you're safe. No"—she stopped the argument she saw coming—"I can't go until I know everything is settled and you're all right."

"I told you, I won't put you in danger."

"I'll stay out of the way and let you and Langdon handle everything. I promise." The whistle blew and the ferry chugged up to the wharf, bumping the wooden pilings and scattering the last of the seagulls. People milled around, the steady flow dragging Libby and John toward the water's edge.

"Come on." He took her arm, and together they walked slowly to the ramp and waited as the crowd pressed onto the ferry.

When it came their turn to board, Libby hung back. Beneath them she could see the rippling water lapping at the shore. Clumps of brown seaweed bobbed in the current, its tangled tentacles reaching out to the other creatures swimming nearby. She looked away, trepidation tightening her throat.

"It's all right," John soothed, leading her up the incline to the deck of the ferry. "I'm right here. There's nothing to be afraid of."

"I'm not afraid," she lied. "I just don't like crossing the bay this way."

"Yes, I remember," he teased. "But I'm afraid it would take too long to build you a bridge like the one you described to me. You're stuck with this for now."

His smile reassured her, and she found herself returning it.

"Yeah, well, I hope this is the last time I have to do this," she said, not thinking.

Suddenly her words struck them both. Their smiles died simultaneously. They froze, staring at each other as the ferry filled and the ramp was lifted. If she succeeded in going home, it *would* be the last time she crossed the waters of the bay in such a way. But it would also be the last time she'd cross with John, his arm comfortingly around her shoulders.

Each moment took on a sharpness, a richness of emotion. Libby thought, *This is the last time I'll see him shade his eyes from the sun that way* or *this is the last time he'll adjust my bonnet so my nose doesn't burn.*

John must have felt the same because she caught him glancing at her, his eyes dark with longing. A bittersweet smile played at his lips, and she wondered if he were remembering their last wonderful days together—the bath they'd shared, the meals they'd missed, the snacks they'd eaten in bed to make up for it.

A horn sounded, breaking the spell, and Libby glanced across the water. The *Willie C* blew its horn once more, and she watched the excursion boat pass, people crammed into every inch of available space. The flatboat it towed was also loaded down with passengers.

The ferry bumped the dock, announcing their arrival at the island. An excited rumble swept the crowd. Already Libby could see large groups of tourists gathered in clumps around the perimeter of the fort.

Her eyes searched out the old oak tree, and she felt her heart flutter. Would it work? And would she be able to climb into those branches when the time came? She swung her gaze abruptly away, not ready to face that difficult question yet.

She saw Geronimo holding a gaggle of giggling women captive by selling them buttons off his shirt. John had told her that the crafty old Indian sewed more on each night in order to make money off the visitors. A heavyset woman in a pink ruffled dress tucked her handkerchief in the medicine man's pocket and then covered her mouth shyly when he tipped her a bow.

Libby looked to John, expecting to see the hard, tense lines of bitterness. The faint tinge of understanding she saw surprised her.

"I guess it's hard to imagine them as murderers when you see them in this setting," he acknowledged.

Libby nodded. "Yes, without television and live video to bring the brutal truth to life, they can't really understand."

She'd explained press coverage in the modern world to John, and he pressed her hand in understanding. She realized that tonight would be some sort of test for John. Had he finally put it all behind him for good? She could see the certainty in his eyes as he closely watched the Indians, and she knew he had.

"Shall we take a stroll and locate our suspects?" he said, taking her hand in his.

She smiled at his easy acquiescence. So he'd decided to let her stay with him, or maybe he was no more eager to go to the tree than she was. She didn't know. All that mattered was that she'd be with him until the intrigue was over. Then she'd leave, heartbroken but assured he would be safe.

They circled the parade grounds, skirting the edges of the crowd. Men, women, and children occupied the steep hillside and filled the path leading to the ramparts on the east side. The declining sides of the glacis made convenient seats for the spectators. The picture they made looked very much as Libby imagined a Roman amphitheater would look like when filled.

The Indians had set up several areas of interest, selling everything from beaded trinkets to woven blankets. Quite a little business, Libby thought, wishing she could manage to take some of the wares home with her. What a souvenir!

But she and John had discussed it, and they both felt she shouldn't try to take anything from this world with her when she went to the tree. They'd decided she should duplicate the circumstances of her arrival here as closely as she could.

That was why she'd brought along the leggings and T-shirt. When the time came, she would change back into her own clothes, leaving behind the garments Caroline had given her.

"Libby."

Libby and Faulk turned, seeing Pilar and Christopher waving from a relatively flat spot on the glacis. She had spread a blanket for them to sit on and an open picnic basket sat beside the blanket. Libby waved back and Pilar motioned them up.

"Now what?" Libby said.

They stepped closer, and Faulk offered a rare smile to the couple. "We thought we'd stroll around a bit. Libby wants to see if she remembers anything."

Immediately their faces bore sympathetic frowns, and they nodded in understanding.

"Oh, you go on ahead. We'll save you a spot," Pilar said softly.

"Thank you," John said. "But that isn't necessary. I don't know how long we'll be."

Pilar nodded once more. "Let me know if you need anything, Libby."

Libby smiled and felt the lump in her chest tighten. She really would miss Pilar.

The sun sank lower as evening approached, and long shadows crawled across the ground. Everyone knew the dance was scheduled for dusk, and the tension in the air grew. The excited chatter of the crowd swelled into a deafening din. Libby's head ached, her ears ringing with the sound until she longed to escape from the crush and find a quiet spot.

All the while John strolled along, his walk casual but his eyes alert to every move.

"There he is," John whispered through tight lips. "Name's Davis." His expression never changed, but Libby felt his body stiffen.

She followed his gaze and saw the Private wending his way through the crowd. Beady, shifting eyes seemed to take in the position of every Indian present. His uniform hung on his thin frame, and he walked with a limp.

"I don't know," she said, frowning to see better. "I only saw the two in your office for a minute, and they had their backs to me. Neither moved away from the desk, so I don't know if he's one of them."

"I'm certain he is. Several of the men connected his name to our friend in the guardhouse. I've been watching him closely and he acts wrought up," John told her. "If only . . ."

His words trailed off, and Libby looked from his narrowed eyes to the Private. The man sidled up to a small tripod holding a coffeepot over a cook fire. Another soldier stood by the fire, drinking from a tin cup. The Private picked up a cup from the ground and poured coffee from the pot. He raised the cup to his lips, but he did not sip from it. Instead, Libby saw his mouth move behind the cup.

"That's it," John said.

The other man never met Davis's eyes, instead turning to the side away from the Private, but Libby saw his whispered reply.

John muttered a curse. "I didn't suspect Lawson. How did those two ever join ranks?"

"You think he's the other man?" she asked, trying to get a closer look at the man. "Darn, I wish I'd seen them better. I just can't tell from this angle. They could be the ones, I suppose."

"They'd better be," John said. "Or that old Indian might just die while we're on a wild-goose chase. Langdon didn't trust anyone else, since we had no idea who the third man might be, so it'll be just him and me."

The men parted company, and John and Libby followed the one named Davis.

"Maybe we should split up. I could watch Lawson and you could stay close to Davis," she suggested as they watched the other man scamper off across the fort.

"Not a chance," John said, grasping her hand and holding it firmly in place on his arm. "I don't even like the idea of your being involved. There's no way you're going off alone to follow a possible assassin. Langdon'll take care of it now."

Libby thought it was a mistake to let Lawson disappear, but she had to agree with John. What could she do, even if he did try something? She had no weapon.

Just then Langdon appeared across the grounds. John motioned toward the retreating figure of Lawson, and the Colonel nodded, hustling toward the man.

The sound of drums took Libby by surprise and she jumped.

John pressed her hand. "They've started," he said.

"Yes."

She heard the soulful sounds of the drums and saw the pile of scrap lumber in the center ignite. Three warriors came out of the casements, skirting the cannons mounted there, wearing the traditional knee-dresses of the Apache. The fire cast eerie shadows on the walls around them, and the Apache women began to wail, the ghostly sounds echoing off the brick enclosures.

Captivated, she stood staring as the chanting billowed over the crowd. Geronimo and Chief Naiche beat switches against a dried hide while another warrior played a camp kettle covered with a stretched hide like a drum. All the while the three costumed warriors danced, ribbons dangling from their arms. They wails of the women seemed to signal them when to change direction. Each man wore a horned headpiece and carried what looked like a sword in one hand and a crossed piece of wood in the other.

The muscles of John's arm tensed beneath her hand, and Libby turned her attention back to him. She didn't know how much time had passed. Mesmerized by the ritual, she found that the sun had fully set. There was a full moon, but the still-fierce fire threw large areas of the fort into shadowed darkness.

"What is it?"

"Let's go," he said.

They shifted their way through the captivated audience. Libby saw Davis winding his way toward the tower bastion. The casements along that side of the fort formed a long, tunneled corridor. She watched the man disappear into the shadows.

"Where is he going?"

350

"Come on," John urged, grabbing her arm and tugging her along. They entered the open arches and scanned the cannons and pyramids of cannonballs set up there.

"According to the rundown Geronimo gave Langdon, he and the warriors should be about finished with their part of the dance."

They looked back toward the parade grounds and saw the warriors end their performance. A roar of applause erupted, and suddenly the crowd seemed bigger and more forceful. A breathless, claustrophobic sensation swept over Libby. The air thickened, and she struggled for breath.

Rumor had it that the Indians would continue the dance until morning, but Libby didn't see how they'd ever be able to go on. Already the sweat caused by the heat and their frantic movements was washing away the paint they'd carefully applied to their bodies.

Then a young Indian girl began a graceful, soothing dance, and Libby's nerves settled back into place.

"There," John hissed, pointing to a dark figure darting along the casement walls. As he passed one open archway, Libby saw that it was Lawson. Another shadowy silhouette joined his, and they disappeared down the corridor.

Libby and John walked swiftly but silently several yards behind them. They followed through the tower bastion to the cannon

Marti Jones

emplacements. They skirted the heavy iron weapons and passed the powder storage room on the northwest corner.

"This is it."

She heard John's whisper and turned toward the main entrance of the Fort. Geronimo and Chief Naiche were standing in front of the sallyport. The massive wooden doors stood open to admit the spectators.

"Stay here."

"No, John," Libby called out softly, but he had already vanished into the dim interior of the fort's main quarters. She clenched her fists and muffled an expletive. Glancing around, she knew she couldn't just hide in the corner and await the outcome of the confrontation.

She dropped the reticule, slipped around the cool wall, and tiptoed across the brick floor. On the other side of the entrance, she pressed close against the archway and peered around it.

Darting shapes scurried this way and that. She eased into the first room and recognized it as the place where she'd been held when she first arrived. It was dark and empty now, and she wasted no time crossing to the other doorway.

This room led to another and another; then she came out in front of the northernmost gunpowder storage room. The door had been padlocked, so she bypassed the room. Next she came to the mine chambers. Empty in her time, they now contained barrels of black powder. She knew from the tours she'd taken that they could hold up to three thousand pounds. Enough to blow this whole side of the fort sky high if ignited.

She tiptoed past those as well.

The open windows on the back side of the gunpowder storage room opened into this corridor of the fort, and she peered into them as she went by, but only blackness stared out at her. The small openings weren't big enough for a man to crawl through anyway.

Where had John gone? she wondered. The shapes she'd been following seemed to have vanished suddenly, and Libby glanced around, uncertain which way to go. The officers' quarters behind her had been empty, the corridor ahead of her seemed the same. She stood, pondering her options for a moment. Just then she heard something. A boot on stone? She couldn't be sure.

Stepping back, she tried to scan the darkness, but what little moonlight filtered in through the openings at the end of the hall barely reached her position in the middle.

She tried to draw a mental picture of the fort. She'd been in it so often that she ought to be able to traverse it blindfolded.

But there were changes, minute and substantial, in the older fort. Things that were here now would not be here in her time. Likewise, she'd noted missing pieces that wouldn't come until later in the fort's long history.

Thinking she'd lost John and the assassins, she turned to go back the way she'd come. A hand shot out of the darkness behind the nearest archway, and Libby cried out. But it was too late. Her bonnet had fallen off somewhere along the way and someone, Davis or his accomplice, now had her by the hair. He yanked her into the narrow casement alongside the mine chamber.

Libby immediately realized her mistake. This area of the fort had been converted to a storage room in the late 1800's, complete with steps leading down to a heavy door. She'd passed the casement unnoticed in the dark because she had forgotten its previous existence.

The pressure on her scalp increased, and she fell toward her captor. Hot shards of pain raced through her head. Burning fear competed with the physical agony.

"What the hell are you doin' here?" a coarse voice asked in her ear. Malodorous breath assailed her and she cringed away, but the man kept his grip, forcing her to lean closer to him.

"I—I'm lost. I wandered away from the crowd. I was just looking for the way back."

"Liar," he growled. "I saw you with the Captain earlier. Everybody knows you've been his woman since you came here. Where is he? What's he up to?"

"Nothing," Libby said, reaching up to ease the pressure his clenched fist kept on her hair. He slapped her hand away.

"You'd better tell me, or I'll be doin' more than tugging your curls."

He gave another vicious yank to prove his point, and stars exploded before her eyes. She cried out again and struggled to free herself, but her efforts only increased her discomfort.

"All right, all right," she said. "I'll tell you. But please, let me go. You're hurting me."

Obviously confident in his superior strength and intelligence, he did as she asked. Libby spun around, delivered a quick, brutal knee to his groin, then clasped her hands together and brought them up under his chin with all the force she could muster. He doubled over and then sailed back, his head snapping against the brick wall. Dazed, he slid down the archway and settled in a limp puddle on the floor.

"You've got a thing or two to learn about liberated women, buster," she told him hotly, mentally dusting her hands in satisfaction.

She stepped back and froze. The cold circular barrel of a gun pressed into her back through the fabric of her shirtwaist.

Chapter Twenty-Four

"Well, well, look what we have here."

Libby didn't need to turn to know who held the weapon. She should have known Private Lawson would be lurking nearby. She wanted to stomp her foot in frustration and aggravation at herself. How could she have let her guard down, not once but twice?

An ominous click sounded in the cavernous darkness, and she felt the gun barrel waver.

"Looks like a damned traitor to me," a lovingly familiar voice said.

Libby wilted with relief as John's words flowed over her. She glanced back over her shoulder and saw him reach out to take Lawson's gun from his trembling fingers. She realized that John's gun was trained on the would-be assassin's back. Lawson seemed to realize his fate. He sagged with defeat.

"Good work, Libby," John said dryly, eyeing her across the private's shoulder. "But I thought I told you to stay put."

She was saved a reply as Davis shifted and moaned. "I think he's coming to," she said, stepping away from the two captives. John reached out his free arm, and she stepped to his side.

"Langdon," he called out loudly.

The shuffling of feet announced the Colonel's arrival along with that of the two Indians Davis and Lawson had been following. Geronimo held a rope, and together he and Naiche bound the Privates' hands and then anchored them together, back to back.

"Excellent," Langdon said. "Nice of you to lend a hand, little lady," he added to Libby.

She smiled, not even offended by the sexist term. After all, she thought, when in Rome . . .

"My pleasure, sir."

Several officers arrived, Christopher Boudreax among them. They dragged the prisoners to their feet and led them away. Christopher stopped, turned back, and met Libby's gaze. He smiled, too.

"Thank you, ma'am. For everything."

Libby knew that he and Pilar had reconciled, and she'd seen the love in his eyes for his wife the day of Caro's wedding. She returned the smile and nodded.

357

He followed the others through the darkened corridor. The sound of his boots died, and Libby found herself in the fort with only John and Colonel Langdon.

"I'll be offering your name for a commendation, Captain," Colonel Langdon said, holding his right hand out to John. "You handled a most regrettable situation in a professional and precise manner. The President will be pleased."

"Thank you, sir," John said, shaking hands with the man. "But that isn't necessary. I was only doing my job, after all."

"Nonsense. I know how you felt about Geronimo and his men. Things could have turned out very differently today. You're a good soldier. I wish you'd reconsider your resignation."

Libby gasped. John had resigned? When? Why hadn't he told her?

"I appreciate the compliment, Colonel, but my mind is made up. My job here is finished."

"There will be more situations in the future. I could use a good man beside me. Everything isn't settled with the Apache yet."

"I know. But my part is complete. I can't go on fighting them, and I can't be a part of their extinction. You know as well as I do that they were sent here because the President didn't think they could survive. Everyone expected them to die off one by one. It was the only way to do away with them without massacring the whole bunch. At one time I thought I didn't care. I find I do now, and so my position conflicts with my beliefs."

"I understand. Go to Washington, John. Tell the President how it really is here. Do what you can to make things right. That's all anyone can ask."

They shook hands again, and Langdon turned to Libby. "John tells me you're leaving?"

Libby nodded and fought a twinge of alarm. Would he let her go, just like that?

She saw him nod to John and then he smiled. "Good-bye, Miss Pfifer. You have added pleasure to an otherwise unpleasant assignment. I know John will help you any way he can. I wish you every blessing."

Libby hugged the old Colonel and blinked back tears. "Thank you for your kindness and understanding, sir. I'll remember you fondly."

She thought she heard him clear his throat awkwardly, but he covered it with a cough and disappeared down the dark corridor.

"Ready?" John said, taking her shoulders and drawing her close.

Libby bit back a ragged breath. She felt more tears sting the backs of her eyes, and her throat tightened painfully.

"I don't want to go," she admitted, her voice breaking.

"Hush," he whispered, holding her close. "You know that isn't true. You miss your home, your family and friends. You know they must be wild with worry."

"Why did you resign?" she asked, wanting to know and longing to prolong their time together. John leaned back against the wall and sighed.

"I had to. You heard what I told Langdon. The government thinks that if they confine the Indians to unfamiliar territory, they'll never survive. They want them eliminated. I lost my taste for revenge some time back, and family loyalty can only reach so far. I can't exterminate a whole race just because of the losses I suffered. Something has to be done."

"What do you plan to do?"

"Christopher and I discussed it, and we've decided to go to Washington and petition the President to allow the Indians to return west. They won't be allowed back in Arizona or New Mexico, but maybe Oklahoma or Wyoming. Somewhere they can settle. Survive."

Libby knew where the Apache would end up. She'd heard stories of the reservation in Oklahoma. Now she wondered if John and Christopher would be instrumental in bringing about that event.

"Or maybe I'll just wash my hands of the whole thing and go back to Arizona. I haven't seen my adoptive folks in a long time, and they're getting older. I might find I like ranching better now than I did when I was a kid. Of course, there's still my family's farm. I own it. I never was much of a farmer, though, so maybe not."

She clung to him and let his old hurts seep slowly away. She felt that he was filing his life into neat little pockets of time. John before the Apache attack, John after, John now. She felt the battle within him as he considered the future. A future without her.

"I'm ready now," she said. She was only causing him more pain by delaying the inevitable. "We'd better go."

He took her hand, kissed it, and led her through the darkened fort. They came out in the entrance chamber, and she fumbled around the corner for her reticule.

"I need to change."

"In here," he said, motioning toward the first officers' quarters. She slipped inside, and he stood watch by the door as she quickly stripped off the antiquated clothing and donned her leggings and T-shirt. She'd worn her own underwear beneath the dress so she wouldn't have to deal with a corset or petticoats.

"All set," she told him, touching his shoulder. He turned and grinned down at her attire.

"I think I could get used to seeing your body outlined in those tight trousers. Turn around."

She chuckled and did as he asked. She laughed at the wolf-whistle he gave.

"Yes, sir, I sure wouldn't mind that aspect of your time at all."

"Come on, you rogue." She took his arm and started forward, but he didn't move. Turning back, she saw that his smile had disappeared.

"All jokes aside, Libby, I'm going to miss you like hell."

She choked back a sob and forced a shaky laugh. "Me, too, Captain. Me, too."

He clasped her to him so tightly that she dropped the clothing she'd held. They clung together for a long time. Neither wanted to end the moment; neither wanted to begin the end.

His mouth found hers and she welcomed his kiss. His hands caressed every inch of her body as though he could brand the feel onto his fingertips. Hers did the same.

They kissed.

They wept.

They touched.

They ached.

Finally Libby pulled away, the taste of John's mouth mingled with the saltiness of her tears.

As they walked out the doors of the fort, neither spoke. They'd said all that needed to be said with their hearts.

Holding hands, they walked across the prickly, stubbly ground toward the end of the island. And Old Patriot.

Halfway to the tree, Libby realized that she'd left Caroline's dress lying on the brick floor of the fort, where it had fallen. She almost stopped, grasping any excuse to go back. But she didn't. Instead, she felt it only right somehow. She had nothing on her person now that didn't belong in the twentieth century.

As if with a surgeon's scalpel, she'd cleanly cut away all the outer trappings of her time here. No one would know to look at her what she'd been through. No one would ever see the permanent reminders she'd carry in her heart the rest of her life. With a strange certainty, she knew she'd go home tonight. She felt it.

She'd come full circle, back to the beginning. To the end. For her, the adventure was almost over. But she knew that without John, the future was bleak.

"Wait." She jerked to a stop, her legs paralyzed.

John gazed up at the gathering clouds in the sky.

"No, Libby. No more waiting. It's time."

She looked up at him, but he refused to meet her gaze. She knew he felt the same wrenching pain she did, but he would not let her back down now. She'd told him she needed to go home, and he would make sure she got there no matter how much it hurt him.

She walked on.

The dark, blurred shape at the edge of the island transformed itself into the familiar trunk and branches of the oak tree as they drew closer.

She studied the bright green leaves, the healthy bark, in the moonlight. What a shame that such an unhappy fate awaited it.

Again she wondered if it had survived. She felt certain it had. She wished she'd been there to see the stages of its healing. If her plan worked, she'd be there to see it thrive once more. And she alone would know its secret.

Chapter Twenty-Five

Making a cup with his hands, John hoisted Libby into the tree. He watched her shimmy up the trunk and settle her bottom into a small wedge where the trunk forked. He resisted the urge to grab her dangling foot and haul her back to the ground.

Was she crazy? Was he? If this was insanity, then they both must be mad. Because she truly believed the wild story she'd told him about being from the future, and he believed her.

"Anything yet?" he asked, longing to touch her, hold her, anything to keep his fingers in contact with her until the end.

"Nothing," she called down.

A fierce mixture of relief and impatience engulfed him. He wished she'd stay forever.

At the same time he wished this night were already over. Fierce pain filled him. Pain such as he hadn't felt since a brisk morning twenty-six years ago.

But losing Libby now was worse than losing his family had been. A child could never understand the agony John felt tighten his chest. He understood only too well that he was losing Libby now as surely as if she were dying.

He paced restlessly beneath the tree and wished something would happen. Anything at all to break the unbearable tension coiling his nerves into tight, useless fists.

The moon went behind a puffy cloud, and the blackness engulfed him. His heart gave an odd lurch, and his mouth went dry.

"Libby?" he called, terrified she wouldn't answer.

"Still here," she said, her reply accompanied by a small shower of leaves as she shifted position.

"Are you sure that's where you were when it happened the first time?" he asked, again pacing back and forth beneath her.

"Well, the tree was bigger then, fuller. I can't be certain, but, yes, I'm pretty sure," she said.

"Maybe you should tell me again exactly what happened. Maybe we aren't doing something right."

He heard another rustle and her foot dropped down, barely missing his nose. He resisted the temptation to the reach out and stroke it.

"I climbed up to examine the tree, my foot slipped, and I fell. When I opened my eyes on the ground, everything had changed."

"Were you unconscious?"

"I don't think so. I remember slipping and falling, hitting the ground, sitting up. I don't think I was ever knocked out."

"You don't suppose you'll have to recreate the moment exactly?"

He heard a sound, half chuckle, half groan.

"I hope not. I'm afraid I'm too much of a coward to throw myself out of a tree purposely."

He thought Libby was the bravest person he knew. Grown men would have lost their minds if they'd been forced to endure the things Libby had.

"I was thinking," she said, shifting again. "Maybe the whole phenomenon is on a timetable or something. You know, like every ten years, or when the moon is in the seventh house."

"What?"

"Sorry, that's just an old expression."

"Old?"

She laughed. "You've got a point."

He had no idea what might have caused Libby to be brought to his time, and he suspected that she was just throwing out ideas, so he didn't answer.

In the distance he could see the glow of the bonfire from inside the Fort lighting the night sky. A few white clouds drifted by overhead, occasionally blocking the light from the full moon, but otherwise the sky was clear.

"You don't have to stay with me," she said.

He thought he heard a catch in her voice. He felt certain there would be one in his when he answered. "I'm not leaving you."

She sighed and gave a shaky laugh. "Good, I was hoping you'd say that."

He paced toward the outer branches of the tree and back. When his feet stopped moving, he could hear the sound of the Indians' drums and imagine the noise of the crowd.

"Sort of anticlimactic, isn't it?" she teased.

He grinned. "I have a feeling it will get more exciting as soon as the action starts."

"You don't think I'm stuck here, do you?"

He heard the tremor in her voice and hated the thought that she feared being trapped here, in his time.

"You said you got here without even trying. There's no reason to think you won't be able to go back."

"Yeah, I guess," she whispered.

They fell silent again. John didn't want to get too far from the tree, but his nerves refused to let him remain still for more then a few seconds.

"One o'clock and all is well," Libby called

out a few minutes later, startling and amusing him.

"Any other news, town crier?"

"Nothing."

This time her voice held a definite note of uncertainty. He considered climbing the tree and sitting with her, holding her. But he leaned against the rough trunk until the impulse passed. No purpose would be served by torturing them both that way.

He closed his eyes and listened to the sound of the water lapping against the shore. Boats bobbed nearby, empty of their owners.

He strained his ears, and his eyes narrowed. Maybe all of them weren't quite as empty as he'd thought. He took a quiet step toward the bay and heard a muffled giggle and an answering warning.

Ah, a pair of amorous lovers had obviously chosen to take advantage of the festivities to slip away unnoticed. He walked closer to the shore and tried to make out the name on the boat just to give himself something to do. A wry smile tipped his lips.

"I feel . . ."

Libby's words trailed off. John whipped around and raced toward the tree. Had she sounded different? Could it have happened while his back was turned?

"Libby?" His boots slipped on the dry, dead

369

leaves beneath the tree, and he struggled to remain on his feet.

"Yeah?"

He released his pent-up breath and sagged with relief. "What happened?"

"Nothing. But I think a knot is digging into my back. I feel like I'm being run through."

John furrowed his fingers through his hair, snagged the strands loose from the ribbon and cursed. His heart settled back in place, and his legs trembled with gladness. He'd thought she was gone forever.

"Do you want to come down for a while?"

"No, I better not. Maybe it's too soon. I'll wait a little longer."

"Guess what I just discovered?" he said, hoping to lighten both their moods with light chatter and cheerful news.

"What?"

Yes, the strain sounded clearly in her voice now. He scrubbed his hand over his chin and forced himself to sound lighthearted.

"The Boudreaxs have slipped off to have a romantic rendezvous in Christopher's boat. You really worked a miracle there."

A heavy sigh drifted down to him.

"That's nice. I'm happy for them."

He heard the unspoken thoughts she refused to put into words. Caro and Thomas were happy. Christopher and Pilar were happy. Why hadn't she been able to make things right for them, too? He'd asked himself the same question a hundred times. Maybe . . .

He sank to the ground and rested his back against the oak. Time passed slowly, and his muscles and joints ached. His legs cramped and he stretched, then fell back to recline on the grass. He watched the stars and thought of all the times he'd seen their brilliance outshone by the gleam of laughter in Libby's eyes. The black velvet overhead couldn't compete with the silky blue-black locks of her hair. The full moon couldn't match the light of her smile.

Would he ever get over the loss? He knew he never would. But neither could he ask her to give up her world for him. He'd wait here with her forever if he had to. He'd do anything in his power to make her happy.

"John, how long has it been?"

He'd begun to think she'd dozed off up there. He sat up and tried to peer at his pocket watch. He waited until a cloud passed from in front of the moon, then called out, "About two hours."

"Is it after three?"

"Yes, twenty past."

"I got the call to come out here about this time of the morning that day. I figure it took me maybe thirty minutes to get here. Another twenty until I fell."

"About four o'clock?"

"Yeah, it must have been."

"That's less than an hour from now."

"Yes."

Her voice shook, and he longed to comfort her. Instead, he clenched his fists against the unfairness of it all and remained where he was.

The dance must have ended shortly after that. He watched people making their way toward the docks. Boats filled, and ferries arrived to transport the tourists back to the mainland. He stayed beneath the branches of the oak; hope mixed with despair in his heart.

The last ferry blew its whistle, and he glanced up into the leafy shelter.

"That was the last load," he told Libby.

"What time is it?"

He pulled out the watch, snapped it open, and felt a quick burst of optimism.

"Four-thirty."

"I don't understand. I know it wasn't this late when I fell. Something should have happened by now."

"Libby . . ."

"I know what you're about to say, John, but I felt certain I'd get back. I can't explain it—it was just a feeling I had when I saw the tree earlier. Something told me I wasn't meant to stay here. I don't understand," she repeated weakly.

He could hear the strain and confusion in her voice. No longer able to stand her despondency, he grabbed the lowest branch and swung himself into the tree. She gasped when he first appeared, but then she scooted over and made room for him on her perch.

John pulled her against his chest, and she slumped into his embrace. They sat, holding each other, for a long time. His foot, dangling over the limb, fell asleep, and he shook it to bring the circulation back.

Finally she looked up at him, her eyes bright. "It isn't going to happen, is it?"

"It's nearly five o'clock. Soon it will be daylight."

Libby glanced around. The night was still dark, showing no sign of morning, but she knew he was right. Within an hour, the sun would rise over the walls of the fort and she'd still be here. Suddenly she wondered if her presence here was meant to be. Maybe she didn't belong in the twentieth century after all. Maybe her place was with John.

"It isn't going to happen," she told him firmly.

John pressed a kiss against her forehead. "I'm sorry, darling. I love you and I want to spend my life with you, but I would have let you go willingly to make you happy."

"I know," she whispered. "But the truth is, I'm not as disappointed as I would have thought."

"Do you think—I mean, could you be happy—"

"With you? Yes, I think I could. If you think you could put up with a wife who's a little odd. I might embarrass you at times with my lack of knowledge and outspokenness."

"Shh, don't be silly. I'd be proud to have you by my side. Proud to introduce you to my world as my wife."

"I love you, John."

"I love you, too. Shall we go to the Fort and have a cup of coffee before we take the skiff home?"

Libby groaned and stretched her cramped legs to bring them back to life. "Coffee sounds wonderful. Home," she said, her voice husky with emotion, "sounds even better."

John jumped to the ground and held out his hands for her. She slipped from the tree, and he caught her against his chest. All the desire and longing he'd fought for hours rose to the surface, and he bent his head and kissed her.

Libby stood on tiptoe, leaning into his body, deepening their embrace. John cupped her head and held her mouth in place beneath his. His kiss was a promise, a vow, an apology. Because, God help him, he was glad she hadn't left him. He knew she'd miss her home, her family. And if the plan had worked, she'd have gone. Her ready acceptance of his proposal stemmed from her knowledge that she had no other choice. But he didn't care. He would take her on any terms.

They parted, but he refused to release his hold on her. "I'll make you happy," he swore, feeling guilty at his own joy. If he were allowed to share her life, he would try and make her regrets few.

She pressed a kiss on his mouth and ran her hands over his chest as though assuring herself that he was real and solid. A sad, sweet smile turned up one corner of her mouth.

"Let's go," she said, glancing back once to look at the oak.

He kept his arm around her shoulders as they strolled back to the fort. The Indians sat around on the cannons and the ground, smoking long, thin pipes and talking.

John spotted a small group of soldiers huddled around the cook fire and led Libby toward them.

Halfway to the men, Libby saw Geronimo and Naiche leaning against a tent pole. She lifted her hand and gave the old Indian a wave. The stark distress on his face confused her, and she stopped.

"John, what—"

He followed her troubled gaze and saw Geronimo hurrying toward them. He knew the old Indian meant her no harm, but his arm tightened all the same.

"No, no," the Indian said, gesturing wildly. He rattled off a string of Apache words, and Libby turned toward John.

"I'm not that good at interpretation," he admitted. "But I think he said something about you being enchanted and a moon cloud."

Naiche came up beside the medicine man and his eyes went from the old Indian to Libby. He muttered something and turned to point in the direction of the tree.

"Usen said you would be here. That's why he wasn't surprised to see you in the fort earlier." John listened to Geronimo's anxious chatter and then held up his hand to stop the flow of words he couldn't keep up with.

"But you're supposed to go away."

Libby glanced from John to Geronimo. She shook her head.

"I tried to leave, it didn't work. Tell him, John."

But before John could translate, Geronimo spoke in broken English.

"Must go back," he said, pushing her shoulder lightly. He pointed toward the end of the island. When Libby didn't move, he shoved her harder.

John held his hand up to warn the Indian not to touch her again, but Libby brushed it aside.

"Usen say you go back. Make good magic for our people. You stay, no good comes."

"I told you, I tried to go back. It didn't work. I've decided to stay here. John and I are going to be married." She motioned toward herself, then John, then made a sign of clasping their hands.

Geronimo's agitation grew. He tried to break

376

their hold on each other. John stiffened, and several soldiers seemed to finally notice the confrontation. Two separated themselves from the others and started toward Libby's group.

Sensing trouble brewing, she tried to calm the old Indian. But he began to speak rapidly again.

"The arrow," John said, shaking his head. "What arrow?"

Geronimo pointed to the sky. Sure enough, Libby saw the cloud overhead. It looked just like an arrow, its puffiness extended at both ends, one pointing out, the other in.

Sensing that he now had their attention, Geronimo slowed his words.

"Arrow pierces moon," he said, making hand signals to match his words. "Magic comes." He stretched his arms wide and encircled Libby's shoulders. "Usen takes you to do good for Apache."

"When the arrow pierces the moon," John repeated, "Libby will go back where she came from?"

Geronimo smiled and shoved Libby again. "Go, go."

"No," she cried, looking frantically toward John. "I'm not going. I want to stay with you now. You said you wanted me to stay." She turned to Geronimo. "I love him," she said, pointing to John. "I want to stay with him."

"No stay," he shouted. "Go!"

"No!" She shook her head fiercely. "I won't."

The soldier nearest them broke into a trot. Libby knew they must appear to be arguing. She didn't want to cause Geronimo trouble, but she couldn't do what he asked. She'd been prepared to leave John. She'd told herself it was the only thing she could do. But when she hadn't gone back, she'd been relieved, thrilled. She knew now that she didn't want to be without him. Ever.

She met his widened eyes and saw the shock of realization fill them. She saw the pain return, the resignation.

"No," she told him, clutching his shirtfront. "I can't leave you now. I won't."

The concerned soldier slid to a stop a few feet away, but she hardly spared him a glance. Her eyes pleaded with John.

"Say something," she finally demanded, unable to bear his stunned silence. "Tell him I'm not going back."

John's eyes darted from Libby's frantic face to Geronimo's stern countenance. She could see the indecision. She squeezed his arm, her fingernails digging half circles into his flesh in her anguish.

Suddenly she saw the determination cross his face. He looked up. The tip of the arrow inched toward the moon. Love-filled eyes turned to her, and he shook his head slowly, heartbreakingly.

"Go," Geronimo said, his voice firm but calm now.

Libby started to object, but her arm was grabbed and she felt John clasp her about the waist. He started to run, half-dragging her across the parade ground.

"No," she yelled, digging her heels into the dirt. But he tightened his hold and forced her along, stumbling and tripping, hauling her toward her destiny.

Chapter Twenty-Six

"Stop," Libby yelled, yanking her hand back. "No."

John started forward again, and Libby's arm screamed in pain. She feared he'd pull it from its socket if she didn't go along.

"I don't want to go," she argued uselessly.

John stopped, swept her into his arms, and charged toward the tree. He wasn't listening, but she knew she had to try and talk to him.

"Please stop," she cried.

"You've got to go, Libby. You heard what Geronimo said. You belong in another time."

She bucked and writhed until she slid from his embrace. "I belong here with you. I know that now."

Again he clasped her hand and raced for the

tree. She slid through the brambles and crushed shells, her boots raising dust.

The oak loomed before her, and she renewed her struggles. But John's strength won out.

He clasped her around the waist, lifted her high in the air, and with one fierce thrust tossed her over the lowest branch of the tree. Her stomach connected with the limb, and she felt the air whoosh from her lungs. The bark bit into her skin though the thin T-shirt. She tried to slide back, but he pressed her firmly in place.

"Let me go," she shouted.

"I am," he told her, his voice harsh with sadness.

"Then let me stay."

"I can't."

"Dammit, John—"

"Libby, you must go. For God's sake, think what you're saying. If you had time to consider, you'd know I'm doing the only thing I can."

She twisted and reached for his fingers, trying to pry them from her waist. But John held firm. She kicked and heard his grunt of surprise when her heel connected with his jaw.

A shadow passed in front of the moon, and Libby knew the cloud was in position. She fought wildly. All around her, the tree's arm-like limbs cast lengthening silhouettes on the ground.

She felt the pull then, as though her blood

were rushing against her flesh. She tried to kick out, but her legs felt leaden. The force grew in magnitude until Libby collapsed, limp, around the limb. Her bones pressed into the wood. She tried to speak, to call out, but even her throat was paralyzed.

Suddenly an electric blue light flashed. The whole area was alight with a ghostly glow. The white-hot glare stung her corneas.

And then it was gone. The force released her so quickly that her momentum propelled her forward, and she tumbled head first over the branch. She landed, facedown, on the ground, with a resounding thud. Once more the breath rushed from her body. Pain spiraled through her.

Her senses returned slowly. She saw the blades of grass twitching beside her nose, felt the warm breeze ruffle her hair. Lifting her head, she smelled the scent of fresh-cut wood.

When she could focus, she pushed to her knees. The pinkish rays of morning lit the area, but blackness filled her soul.

She could see the pier off to the side, the white-and-blue wooden buildings in front of her. The gift shop, the museum, the restrooms. They were all there. Just the way she remembered.

Desolation swept over her, and she covered her face with her hands, feeling the dampness on her cheeks. She'd come home, but home wasn't here for her any longer. She'd regained her world only to lose the only reason she had for living.

Stumbling to her feet, she wiped the tears from her lashes. John wouldn't want her to fall apart. He'd done the only thing he could do. Now she had to pick up the pieces and go on. She couldn't let his sacrifice be in vain.

Ignoring the small aches in her body and the larger one in her heart, she took a step forward. Just then, she heard a rustle behind her. She froze.

Another whisper of movement was accompanied by a cascade of falling leaves. Feeling the flutter of a thousand butterflies take flight in her stomach, she turned and looked up.

"Whoooeee," John shouted, his head poking through the heavy-laden branches.

He flipped over the limb and dropped to the ground. The ribbon had fallen from his hair, and the long strands flew back and settled on his shoulders.

Libby staggered back, her hand clasped to her lips to stifle her outcry. Her head shook back and forth vigorously, her brain denying what her dazed eyes saw.

"How? How?" she choked out, when finally her power of speech returned.

John grinned, brushed himself off, and shrugged. "I don't know. I felt the pull taking you away. My hands were holding your waist. I told myself to let go. But I couldn't. Deciding to keep you with me no matter the consequences, I tugged, but you were fixed to that branch and wouldn't budge. My mind was made up. If your place was in the future, so was mine. So I held on. And here I am."

A sob broke through Libby's trembling lips. Blinded by her tears, she toppled into his arms. He caught her easily and clutched her to his chest.

His mouth came down on hers with a hunger that matched her own. She reveled in the feel of his body beneath her hands. Making fists with her hands, she pounded him lightly on his chest, assuring herself that he was real.

He pulled back and laughed. Then he grasped her in his arms and swung her around, her feet several inches off the ground.

"Oh, Libby, I love you."

"John, you crazy fool. What have you done?"

He chuckled, and they sank to the ground together.

"The only thing I could," he said, his hands holding hers so tightly it hurt.

Libby's laughter floated up to greet the morning. She tossed her head and planted a kiss on his frowning mouth.

"What is it? What's the matter?" Her smile faded.

"Nothing. Everything's perfect. But I'm afraid

I didn't have time to make any definite plans. I have to figure out what I'm going to do here."

"You're going to marry me and live happily ever after."

He touched her cheek, and his eyes lingered on her face for a long, tender moment. "Yes, I am. But I won't let you take care of me. I need money, a means of support."

"Don't worry about that," she told him saucily, knowing it would hurt his pride if she offered charity. "You're in full uniform. Your sword and pistol alone would bring enough money for you to live on for a long time."

"These?" he said, eyeing the mentioned articles.

"Yes, not to mention a hundred-year-old Cavalry uniform in mint condition."

He looked relieved briefly, then the frown lines returned. "I need to work, Libby. I need to do something."

This time Libby had no quick answers. She couldn't think of a thing except to offer him a job in her business, and she suspected that he'd reject the gesture soundly.

He pursed his lips and then his eyes lit with excitement.

"You said the Apache were still struggling in your time?"

"That's right."

"Well then, I can still do what I planned. Only

I'll be doing it in another time. I want to help them somehow."

Libby stared at him in amazement. Her eyes widened with wonder.

"What is it?" he asked.

"I just had a thought, John. What if I was sent back in time for this very reason?"

"I don't understand."

She scampered to her knees and met his baffled gaze. "What if," she said, "I was sent back in time to find you and bring you here so you could help the Apache. Geronimo said I had to go back, that it meant good for his people. Maybe that's because you were meant to come back with me."

He studied her, a tumble of emotions crossing his face. A bewildered expression settled in his eyes. He shook his head, nodded, then frowned. Finally he took her hands and lifted them to his lips. A smug smile played at the corners.

"And maybe," he said, his mouth moving against her knuckles. "You were sent to me because the gods knew I needed you. They looked down and said, there's an empty hull of a man who needs a fiery, spirited woman to love him and make him live again. And so they kidnapped you from your time and dropped you in mine."

"Well," she drawled slowly, "I guess that's possible, too."

They laughed and hugged, and his mouth found hers again. This time they lingered over the kiss, both absorbing all the glorious feelings they'd thought lost.

John laid her in the grass and covered her body with his. Her head fell back. His mouth nipped at her throat. She ran eager hands over the sharp contours of his back and chest. He let his lips trail over her neck to her shoulder. Their passion threatened to consume them.

The sound of an engine brought Libby out of the fog of desire, and she pushed John aside.

He frowned down at her, his eyes glazed with need. Then his ears caught the sound, and she saw him stiffen in alarm. His head whipped around, and he spotted the Jeep as it pulled to a stop on the paved road several yards away.

"What in the name of Sam's cat is that contraption?"

Libby laughed at his expression and laid her hand on his arm. "That is an automobile. And that," she added, pointing to the figure climbing from the Jeep, "is a ranger."

"I can see I have a job ahead of me just learning what people here take for granted."

His tone held more than a hint of apprehension, and Libby sympathized with his position. After all, hadn't she felt the same when she found herself without the usual amenities?

"It's all right. I have a wonderful set of encyclopedias. You'll catch up in no time."

Marti Jones

He didn't look as confident as she sounded, but he stood and pulled her to her feet all the same, prepared to meet the first challenge head-on.

John Ferrell jogged up to them and stopped. His red hair stood out from his head like a rooster's cone and his freckles were dark blotches on his pale face.

He snapped the radio from his belt and spoke into it. "I found her—yeah, she appears to be fine. I'll let you know. Over."

He let his gaze travel all the way down her body and back up to her face. His glance darted to John for a moment but quickly returned to Libby.

"Where have you been?" he asked. He took another look at the Captain, and this time his eyes caught the clothing, hair, and accessories. He mimicked Libby's beached fish routine for a moment, then dragged his eyes back to her.

"Who the hell is this?" he whispered, jerking his head to the side.

"John Ferrell, this is Captain John Faulk. Captain, this is the senior park ranger of Fort Pickens, John Ferrell."

The men eyed each other warily, and Libby couldn't help laughing again.

"For the time being, I think we should just call you the Captain and you the ranger. It'll keep down confusion."

"Don't bet on it," John, the ranger, said. He

388

frowned at her and then turned to the Captain. "Where did you get that getup? I haven't heard of any reenactments in the area."

Libby's humor broke loose and she doubled over. "Where have I heard that?" she asked no one in particular.

The Captain looked down at his clothes once more and shrugged helplessly. The ranger seemed to let the matter go for the moment as he said, "We sure could use you when we do tours. Damned if you don't look like the real thing."

This time the Captain's smile came quickly. "Is that right?" he asked.

Libby wanted to reach out and hug her friend, but she hesitated. Something wasn't right. Something . . .

"We've been combing this island for nearly two hours, Libby. My God, you don't know what I went through when I came back and you were gone without a trace. I've been sick thinking something had happened to you."

Libby's jaw fell open and she stared at the ranger, dumbfounded. She looked back over her shoulder and took her first good look at Old Patriot. The oak was just as she'd left it, its trunk recently scarred, its dislodged bark still clinging in places.

She snapped her mouth shut and looked back at John Farris. "Do you mean I've only been gone a few hours?" she cried. "That's incredible!"

"Why? How long did you think you'd been gone?"

Libby laughed out loud. This time she did hug him. She threw her arms around his neck and squeezed hard. He reached out instinctively and let his hands rest on her waist, and she saw Faulk's hand drop to his sword.

She stepped back and smothered her giggles. "Oh, John, I wish I could tell you," she said. "I really do."

He looked from her to the Captain, clearly puzzled. Libby cleared her throat.

"So are you going to be able to save the old tree?" her friend asked, apparently deciding to let the more bizarre questions wait until a later time.

Libby's laughter died down, and she scrutinized the damaged oak. For a moment a hint of her old insecurities tried to rise to the surface. But then she met the Captain's gaze and grinned widely.

"You bet," she told them both. She'd done something no one else had done. She'd traveled through time. She'd reunited old lovers, saved a marriage and a legend, and found a love as timeless as the ages. Taking care of one lone tree should be a snap.

"You bet your life I am."

She stared at Old Patriot as the sun climbed over the aging, crumbling walls of the majestic fort. Beams of light danced across the clear, cloudless sky and encircled the outstretched branches. She squinted and peered intently toward the glistening leaves.

Above the highest peak of the tree, in a blinding gleam of light, she thought she saw a face. The face of an old Indian. He smiled and disappeared, and Libby rubbed her eyes, wondering if the apparition had really been there at all.

She felt John's arm encircle her shoulder, and she looked up into his face. The cinnamon eyes lit with wonderment. He nodded and she smiled.

"Hey, did you guys see that?" John Ferrell asked, shielding his eyes as he gazed over the tree toward the horizon.

Author's Note

Fort Pickens National Park is a wonderful place to visit if you should find yourself around the panhandle of Florida. You will see the casements, the officers' quarters, and the missing corner section just the way it is described in Libby's story. You will even see where Geronimo and his band lived for 18 months.

What you will not see is Old Patriot. The oak tree as described in these pages exists only in this author's imagination. And, as Libby told John, there is no mention of an assassination attempt during the months of Geronimo's incarceration. However, the story of his life and capture is no less fascinating without it. It is a vital part of American history, and I strongly recommend it to any and all lovers of the past.